Owned

A BDSM Erotic Romance
The Owned Series: A BDSM Exploration

by NICKY IRELAND

Title Verso

First Published - November 2023
Imprint: Independently published

www.linktr.ee/nickyireland

ISBN: 9798866937653

Copyright © Nicky Ireland 2023

This book is a work of fiction and, except in the case of historical fact any resemblance to actual persons, living or dead, is purely coincidental.

All rights reserved. No part of this publication may be reproduced, stored in or introduced into a retrieval system, or transmitted, in any form, or by any means (electrical, mechanical, photocopying, recording or otherwise) without the prior written permission of the Author. Any person who does any unauthorised act in relation to this publication may be liable to criminal prosecution and civil claims for damages.

A catalogue copy of this book is available from the British Library.

Visit www.linktr.ee/nickyireland
for further information.

Dedication

This novel is a heartfelt tribute, dedicated to every soul who has dared to dream—those who have yearned for a life pulsating with excitement, thriving on the thrill of the unknown, and brimming with the promise of adventure.

It is a salute to the individuals courageous enough to desire love in its most potent form—wildly passionate, intoxicatingly intense, and tantalizingly erotic. This book is for you.

I extend my profound gratitude to the readers who have considered stepping into the world I've created through my stories. Your support means the world.

Lastly, thank you to the authors who have inspired me to write, the creators of captivating tales of love and adventure that I've had the privilege to devour. To TL Swan, HD Carlton, J.T. Geissinger, Rina Kent, Penelope Douglas, Audrey Rush, Rebecca Quinn, Sadie Kincaid, Sylvia Day, Nyla K, Elsie Silver, Jescie Hall, Shantel Tessier, and BJ Alpha—you are my ride-or-dies, my muses. Through your words, you have provided me—and countless others—an escape into enthralling realms. This journey wouldn't have been possible without you.

Nicky

Trigger & Content Warnings

This novel contains explicit sexual content and is intended for mature readers of 18 years and older. It explores various sexual scenarios and power dynamics that some readers may find provocative or triggering. Please proceed with caution and prioritize your mental health and well-being.

The themes include:

- Dominant and submissive roles and power dynamics.
- Rapidly escalating chemistry between characters.
- Disciplinary actions, such as spanking.
- Anal sex scenes.
- Primal roleplay scenarios.
- Elements of BDSM.
- Bondage with a focus on Shibari Art.
- Pet roleplay scenarios.
- Consensual non-consent (CNC) situations.
- Instances of breath control play.
- Actions that may be perceived as degrading.
- Praise-centric fetishes.
- Scenes involving choking.
- Sacrilegious scenarios.
- References to drug use.
- Public sexual intimacy.
- References to body modification, such as piercings and tattoos.
- Casual mentions of speech impediments.
- Storylines revolving around sibling rivalry.
- Mentions of characters' past romantic relationships.
- References to acts of unfaithfulness.

Please note that the explicit nature of this book may not be suitable for some readers. We recommend taking into account your comfort level with these themes before deciding to read this book. Your mental health and well-being are important to us.

Disclaimer

This novel is explicitly crafted for mature readers, specifically those who are 18 years and above. It contains vividly detailed and intense sexual scenarios. Please ensure you carefully read the trigger and content warnings.

The contents of this novel are meant solely to captivate and entertain. They should not be interpreted as advice or guidelines relevant to real-world situations or BDSM dynamics. The narrative flows freely without a concrete set of rules, adding to the intrigue of the storyline.

The universe within these pages is the creation of pure fiction. Unless explicitly stated, all characters, businesses, locations, events, and occurrences are either conjured from the depths of the author's creativity or employed in an entirely fictitious context. Any similarity to real individuals, whether they are among the living or the deceased, or to actual events is an absolute coincidence.

This novel is an adventure in its own right, designed to stimulate and liberate your imagination, inviting you to delve into realms you may never have explored before. Please proceed with an open mind, but be mindful of the explicit erotic content. This book may trigger emotional responses due to its intense and descriptive sexual nature.

IMAGES
The narrative of this book is intricately woven with images, crafting a vivid tapestry for the protagonists Santiago and Nicky. Readers are invited to delve into their universe, picturing their family, friends, and the settings they inhabit, making the reading experience thoroughly engaging.

The characters and their tale have been meticulously designed to transport you on an odyssey through a romantic world spanning the vibrant cities of Barcelona, Spain, and Dublin, Ireland. The goal is for readers to lose themselves in this universe and develop a deep affection for all characters and the world they inhabit.

Owned
Spotify Playlist

Hello there, you daring explorer of love and lust!

As you prepare to dive into the rich narrative of my erotic novel, I've got an extra treat for you. A sensory garnish of sorts to make your reading experience even more...stimulating. I present to you a Spotify playlist, carefully curated to tease, tantalize and transport you right into the heart of Santiago and Nicky's story.

Scattered throughout the text, you'll notice song titles and artists. No, they're not there by accident. They're your keys to unlocking an even deeper layer of the narrative. As these songs are mentioned, hit play on your Spotify app and let the music seep into your senses.

Each song, each melody, has been meticulously paired with the scenes, the emotions, and oh yes, the passionate interludes of the story. As these characters surrender to their desires, submit to their passions, and dominate their love, the music will echo their sentiments, their heartbeats, their crescendos.

Is this a must for your reading pleasure? Well, no, but I dare you to try it. Why? Because I believe that music, just like a well-placed blindfold or a playful spank, can add an exciting dimension to your experience. This isn't just about reading an erotic BDSM novel; it's about living it, feeling it, and yes, hearing it.

So, as you prepare to embark on Santiago and Nicky's sizzling journey, keep your Spotify app at the ready. Let the music guide your path, enhance your sensations, and provide the perfect soundtrack to your wild ride.

Dive in, dear reader, and let the symphony of love, lust, and power play out in perfect harmony. Enjoy every word... and every note!

Playlist

Spotify/Owned Playlist by Nicky Ireland Author

'Lose You To Love Me' by Selena Gomez
'We Are' - Symphonic Version by Haevn
'Ride It' by Regard
'When We' by Tank
'Only Love Can Hurt Like This' by Paloma Faith
'Black is The Colour of My True Love's Hair' by Nina Simone
'Ocean Eyes' by Billie Eilish
'Dirty Thoughts' by Chloe Adams
'Blackbird' by Séamus & Caoimhe Uí Fhlatharta
'Dandelions' by Ruth B
'Gutter Heart' by Matthew And The Atlas
'Praising You' (feat. Fatboy Slim) by Rita Ora
'Joe Le Taxi' by Hanayo (Two Many DJ's Mix)
'Marianas Trench' by Cosmic Space Traveler
'Play with Fire' by Sam Tinnesz
'9 to 5' by Dolly Parton (Two Many DJ's Mix)
'I'm Waiting For The Man' by The Velvet Underground
'Giménez: La tempranica' by Gerónimo Giménez
'One Call Away' by Charlie Puth
'California Soul' (Diplo Remix) by Marlena Shaw
'Middle Of The Night' by Elley Duhé
'Fire On Fire' by Sam Smith
'Can We Kiss Forever' by Kina
'In The City' by Charli XCX and Sam Smith
'Devil Saint' by Luma
'Ascension' by Chris Palmer
'Wouldn't It Be Nice' by Kate McGill
'Tik Tik Boom' by Sage The Gemini
'Paint Me Like a French Girl' by Breakdlaw
'Just Can't Get Enough' by Black Eyed Peas
'Dressed in Black' by Sia

Santiago Maspinco

SANTIAGO (Santi)
Birthday: November 8th 1991
Star Sign: Scorpio

Sofia & Alfonso Maspinco

Jose Mascpino

Isabella Mascpino

FOLLOW ME
@SANTIAGO_MASPINCO

Nicky McKenna

NICKY
Birthday: July 6th 1993
Star Sign: Cancer

Bridget (Brid) McKenna

William (Billy) McKenna

Molly McKenna

FOLLOW ME
@NICKY_MCKENNA_

Supporting Characters

Jake O'Sullivan

Ben Kelly

Liam Murphy

John & Barbara O'Brien

Mike Norris

Arcenia Guerra

Translations

SPANISH	ENGLISH
La Esencia de Belleza	The Essence of Beauty
Cosméticos y cuidado de la piel	Cosmetics and Skincare
Tatuajes de diablos rojos	Red Devil Tattoos
Estudio de tatuajes	Tattoo Studio
Diseñadoras De Perfumes	Perfume Designers
Meditación de yoga	Yoga and Meditation
A Fuego Lento	Simmering
Restaurante y bar español	Spanish Restaurant and Bar
Amor y Fuego	Love and Fire
Mi sala de juegos	My Play Room
Barrio Gótico	Gothic Quarter
Café y pastel	Coffee and Cake
Cantante de ópera	Opera singer
Me calientas	You turn me on
Desnúdate	Get naked
Bésame	Kiss me
Te necesito	I want you / I need you
Te quiero	I love you
Mi putita	My little slut/whore
Mi chica ardiente	My fiery girl
Mi gatita	My kitty cat
Gatita	Kitty cat
Mi gatito sucio	My dirty kitty
Mi gatito obediente	My obedient kitty
Puta obediente	Obedient slut/whore
Tu eres mi puta	You are my obedient slut/whore
Puta sucia	Filthy slut/whore
Puta asquerosa	Filthy whore
Mi puta asquerosa	My filthy slut/whore
Puta hermosa	Beautiful slut/whore
Mi puta hermosa	My beautiful slut/whore
Mi putita hermosa	My beautiful little slut/whore
Mi diabla	mi diabla - my devil (female)
Mi diablo	mi diablo - my devil (male)
Mi diablita	mi diablita - my little devil
Mi amor	Mi amor - my love
Mi hermosa madre	My beautiful mother
Hola	Hello
Hola mi querido hijo	Hello my darling son
Familia	Family
Ven a jugar conmigo señor	Come play with me Sir
Rey mío	My king
Cachorra	Puppy
Mi cachorra obediente	My obedient puppy
Mi cachorra juguetón	My playful puppy
Mi chica sucia	My dirty girl
Buena putita	Good little slut
Gracias	Thank you

One door closes...

Chapter One

One door closes...

Chapter One

NICKY

Here I am, perched outside a semi-d in Crumlin, eyeballing what's about to be my new abode. My heart's doing a darn good impression of a piñata about to meet its maker. This leap of faith I've taken is doing the cha-cha on my emotions. Fear and anxiety are party crashers I didn't invite. I was pretty snug in my old life, but now, my once HD clear future looks like a foggy rear-view mirror.

In this alien driveway, it's like the sky's sprung a leak, with a waterfall crashing onto my car's roof. Selena Gomez's 'Lose you to love me' spills out of the car's stereo. The irony of these lyrics isn't lost on me.

Flying solo in the driver's seat, doubt decides to join the party. In need of a lifeline, I reach for my phone and dial him, faltering. Is it habit, or am I hoping for a U-turn on the Emotional Highway? Taking the familiar path would be the easy way out. You know, better the devil you know and all that jazz.

"Hi," says the voice on the other end of the line. A verbal dam breaks and a flood of tears washes over my face. My heart feels the weight of the loss - for him, for me, for the could-have-beens.

"I don't know if I can do this," I manage to choke out. "You've got this, Nicky. You're solid. This is the right call," he says. His voice stirs up the ghost of feelings past - things I yearn for but need to cut loose.

After a quick chat, him trying to offer some comfort despite his own emotional whirlpool, his words just don't cut it. Summoning my inner Wonder Woman, I hang up and swallow back the tears.

By Nicky Ireland

The rain outside seems to be copying my inner turmoil. Slowly but surely, determination begins to rise like a phoenix within me. Life's taken me on a - detour, but I'll recalibrate my compass. I will. I can feel the resolve brewing. With this newfound grit, I inch towards my new reality. As I step out of the car, the rain decides to turn it up a notch, and I'm rooted to the spot.

My new digs are now a symbol of the rebuilding to come – a fresh canvas eager for splashes of colour and warmth. Diving into singlehood is like jumping off a cliff, but I'm dead set on using this chance to rediscover myself. To unearth the person I've always wanted to be.

Unlocking the front door and prancing in, I find myself in a house that's laughably large for what I can afford. But hey, beggars can't be choosers, right? It's my sister's place and her previous tenants have just skedaddled. Talk about perfect timing! I get to strut my independence again. You'd think my sis would give me a family discount on rent, especially in Dublin with its sky-high prices, but nope. Not Molly. She's always been a bit self-absorbed.

Getting back on the horse as a single woman after a ten-year relationship is like trying to climb Everest. I've spent a decade pouring my heart into a man, Jake, who turned out to be more of a buddy than a lover. I craved a deep connection, and in the process, lost a bit of myself.

To spice things up, I stumbled upon Jake's little hobby - explicit sexual escapades with different guys online, sometimes wearing my expensive lingerie. Unearthing these images on his laptop was a slap in the face, resulting in a broken laptop, a cancelled wedding, and a suitcase conga line.

I was the one who packed up, not him. He owned the house we lived in, a house I loathed, in a location I detested just as much. Jake loved the place, mainly for the massive garage that could house his precious sports cars. His infatuation with those speed demons and his affinity for frilly underwear seemed to eclipse his love for me.

Sure, he had his moments of kindness, but I never felt that spark, that passion. I longed for a man who could light a fire in me, make me yearn for his touch, his mind. I wanted a man who could take the reins and let me sit back and relax.

But our relationship was the opposite. Jake was a softie, who wanted me to wear the pants. All the while he was wearing mine. I shudder at the thought. My idea of sexy wasn't having my thigh-high PVC boots rubbed up against while my partner looked at me for approval. That was the moment I knew I had to call it quits. You could say that the boot grinding was the final straw.

When the moon starts its shift, I transform my bathroom into a five-star spa - no reservations needed. I hit play on my Spotify playlist and let the sweet sound of Haevn's 'We are' wash over me. The guy's voice is so golden, it could make a leprechaun jealous. My personal hot spring embraces me, bidding adieu to the day's drama. I can almost hear my muscles sigh in relief as the warmth works its magic. The bubble bath's perfume of lavender and chamomile turns my bathroom into a summer meadow, minus the pesky bugs. Each inhale is like a mini detox, and each exhale is a one-way ticket for my worries, destination: nowhere.

An Irish welcome

Chapter Two

An Irish welcome

Chapter Two

NICKY

Living solo for the past few weeks, I'm finding myself absolutely relishing the peace and quiet. Who knew tranquility was my jam, right? But here's the catch, my wonderful sister Molly, bless her heart, insists on charging me a pretty penny for rent. Funny thing is, she owns the house free and clear. No mortgage to worry about. To her, my rent payments probably feel like finding change in the sofa cushions, but for me, it's a different story. Even with my work schedule packed to the brim, my wallet's feeling a bit light.

Speaking of work, I'm a freelance makeup artist in the commercial world, and let me tell you, I am head over heels for it. Five years in and I still get a kick out of meeting new faces, flexing my creative muscles, and tackling the unexpected challenges that pop up.

But then there's Jake. Ah, Jake. Our breakup cost me more than just a partner. You see, Jake is a big shot Creative Director at a swanky Advertising Agency in Dublin, and through him, I had landed some rather lucrative clients. But post-breakup, those clients have ghosted me. We parted on good terms, or so I thought, which makes me wonder if Jake's harboring some hard feelings.

Enough about Jake, though. Time to whip up some dinner. Now, I'm not exactly a MasterChef. My culinary skills extend to the realm of pre-packaged salads, soups, and an assortment of healthy nibbles. But hey, a girl's got to eat, right?

A knock interrupts my daydreaming, pulling me towards the front door. I swing it open, and lo and behold, my next-door neighbors stand there - an older couple I've peeped at from my window. Both are in their prime of life, their mid to late 50s. Silver-grey hair crowns their heads, adding an attractive contrast to their features. She's a petite lady, while he stands tall.

They introduce themselves as John and Barbara O'Brien. "Do come in, please! Fancy a cup of tea?" I invite, thrilled at the prospect of some social interaction. "Oh, not at all, love," Barbara comes back. "We just brought you a housewarming gift. We know you've been here a bit. Apologies for the delay, we thought we'd let you get your bearings first."

I accept the hefty gift bag from Barbara and spread out the surprises on my kitchen table. A crusty loaf of bread, a dazzling candle, a bottle of top-tier red wine, and a packet of salt spill out. The salt catches my eye, and I shoot Barbara a puzzled look.

"It's an Irish tradition, love," she enlightens me. "The candle lights your path, the bread so your home never starves, the salt to season life, and the wine to keep joy and wealth flowing."

Her words hit a soft spot, and I struggle to blink back the tears. The thoughtfulness in their gift echoes in my heart. I give Barbara a tight hug and plant a friendly peck on John's cheek.

The rest of the day unfolds in a delightful chatter, with us getting to know each other better. They regale me with neighborhood tales, and I'm laughing harder than I have in weeks. Their company not only fills my day with cheer but makes my new house feel like a real home. Their thoughtful gift and its symbolic blessing will forever remind me of this joyful first encounter with my neighbors, John and Barbara.

As the sun starts to dim, I notice how John's vibrant personality contrasts with Barbara's calm disposition. We migrate to the living room, and it seems like the ideal time to pop open the tantalizing bottle of Móinéir Irish Blackberry wine they've gifted.

John, bubbling with energy, narrates the grand story of the wine. It's a testimony of Irish craftsmanship, a salute to our rich history and culture. The wine, he says, has snatched countless awards and is a favourite among the world's top sommeliers and Michelin-starred chefs. I'm floored by the idea of such a precious gift being shared with little ole me, who would never dub herself a wine expert.

Feeling a tad guilty for indulging in such exquisite wine, I opt to complement its rich, fruity undertones (a description borrowed from John) with a medley of cheeses. I meticulously arrange a selection on a tray: creamy Brie, pungent Camembert, tangy Danish Blue, and a robust Irish Cheddar that, I'm informed, will harmonize with the wine's personality. For a burst of freshness, I scatter a bunch of plump red grapes alongside, aiming for equilibrium. Check me out. Miss fancy pants!

The night is buzzing with sparkling chatter, belly laughs, and the cozy vibe of stellar company. John and Barbara are turning out to be the gold standard for friendly neighbor's, spreading their infectious joy throughout the evening.

Even though my house's walls are paper-thin and John's knack for heavy snoring might form the soundtrack of my nights - a fact I've wisely decided to keep to myself - I'm getting quite attached to them. The warmth they bring, along with the deep sentiment behind their considerate gift, binds us together in this very moment.

Work it!

Chapter Three

Work it!

Chapter Three

NICKY

I'm on the brink of another bustling Monday as a seasoned makeup artist, ready to take the day by the horns. My client list? A colorful mix, and today's collaboration is with a regular who's gearing up for something a little out of the ordinary - a campaign for super strength tissues. Yes, you heard that right, tissues! The man of the hour, the Managing Director of the tissue company, is set for a headshot session and it's my duty to make him look his absolute best for the camera.

Being a makeup artist isn't just a pay check for me - it's a passion. No matter the personality - and trust me, this industry has its fair share of tricky ones - I pride myself on keeping things professional.

Now, let's talk about the commute. It's often the cherry on top of my day. Today, as always, I'm cruising along the breath-taking Irish coastline in my Fiat Punto. Old? Sure, but it's got character. With the windows down, the fresh sea breeze is my personal espresso shot. The pulsating rhythm of Regard's 'Ride It' adds a dancey vibe to my scenic drive around Dublin Bay. Each glimpse of the sea stokes my dream of someday living in a snug home by the water.

Right on time, I pull into the Blackrock photography studio at 7am sharp. Tucked away in a charming nook of the town, the studio is a cool blend of modern and rustic, oozing creativity and elegance. My workspace? A bright corner decked out with mirrors and a smorgasbord of makeup tools and products. It's my canvas, where I mix art and technique to whip up some serious makeup magic.

I'm basking in the joy of collaborating with one of my favourite shutterbugs, the ever-amiable family man, Paul Martin. Our bond runs deep, blossoming from

By Nicky Ireland

mutual admiration and a shared passion for our crafts. It's like we're in sync, concocting a symphony of creativity that feels more like a merry meet-up than a high-pressure photoshoot. Every day, including today, I am reminded why my job brings me so much joy.

Now, let's get one thing straight, I know that my job as a makeup artist is no rocket science. But hey, it's not a walk in the park either! It's a role that brings its own unique set of challenges, requiring a reservoir of patience, an ocean of creativity, and an unwavering commitment to professionalism. The silver lining? The commercial side of this profession pays handsomely, and for that, I'm forever grateful. A few gigs a week, and voila! I'm all set to live my life fairly comfortably and cover my bills.

Stepping into the studio, I make sure to tip my hat to everyone in the team. The ad agency folks are usually found huddled around a table loaded with coffee and pastries. In contrast, the photographer's assistant and stylists are buzzing around the place, adjusting the lights and meticulously lining up clothes and accessories.

Now, let's talk about that table. It's a feast for the eyes, filled to the brim with a smorgasbord of food - pastries, sandwiches, fruits, you name it. Ironically, our health-conscious models give these delicacies a wide berth, sticking to their green teas and salads. It's like an unspoken rule, a delicate ballet between the allure of food and the models' rock-solid discipline.

But hey, these untouched treats don't just sit there looking pretty. They feed us creatives, adding inches to our waistlines while fueling our creative minds. It's like these untouched goodies are our secret stash, our power source. The sugar kick from the pastries sparks our creativity, while the endless supply of coffee keeps us running on all cylinders. It's a delicious irony, as we relish the forbidden fruits that our model friends pass up, all in the midst of a frenzy of creativity and professionalism.

I'm introduced to the main event by Paul, the Managing Director of a zany business called Snots R Us. The name throws me for a loop, causing me to rack my brain for the inspiration behind it. Then it hits me — they're aiming for the kiddos, and what tickles their funny bone more than a little snot humor?

Running the show is Mike Norris, a guy of unexpectedly tender years, likely in his mid-20s. He's a lively blend of youthful audacity and entrepreneurial success. Mike is a human dynamo, radiating enough energy to light up a small town. His over-the-top enthusiasm hits me like a wave, draining my stamina before I've even started. I manage to plaster on a smile and offer a polite handshake, hiding my annoyance.

Mike is a real looker, his chiseled features softened by the glow of youth. His eyes are a stunning blue, matching the powerful energy he exudes. His eclectic-yet-stylish attire and his innovative business show off his creative spirit. His charm is captivating, but beneath it lies an unsettling vibe that's hard to ignore.

I gingerly guide him to the throne of my artistry, my makeup chair, promising him that this will be swift and untroubled, provided he remains as still as a statue. But alas, the memo seems to have been lost in translation. The once stately makeup chair suddenly morphs into his personal jungle gym, with him playing the intrepid acrobat.

As I brace myself for the Herculean task ahead, I spot beads of perspiration dotting his brow like morning dew on a leaf, and his nose functioning like Niagara in full swing. Picture the horror movie equivalent of a makeup artist's career, and you've got yourself this scene. My heart instantly performs a high dive into the abyss of dread.

While I'm wrestling with the deluge of sweat, his hyperactivity decides to take a joyride on a rollercoaster. And then, like a light bulb moment in a detective movie, it hits me. The constant brushing of his nose isn't a nervous tic — it's the tell-tale sign of him riding the high tide. Just another day in the life of a makeup artist navigating the murky waters of this profession's underbelly, garnished with a dash of the unexpected.

Following a feat of strength worthy of an Olympian, I somehow manage to tame

By Nicky Ireland

the waterfall of perspiration. As I'm delicately applying a veil of makeup, his hand keeps embarking on a round trip to his nose. As if it were on a frequent flyer program, his hand kept clocking up the miles.

When his hand finally touches down for a break, I'm confronted with a sight that would make even the bravest falter — a monstrous booger, waving at me from the depths of his nostril like an unwelcome guest at a party. The sight of it is akin to spotting Bigfoot in the wild: terrifying, yet oddly captivating.

As I fight the urge to dry heave, I maintain my poker face. If only we had some 'super strength tissues', I think with a silent chuckle. I calmly instruct him to close his eyes, promising it's all part of the process. Using a small makeup brush as my secret weapon, I launch a covert operation to evict the unwelcome intruder.

And let me tell you, that brush performed its duty with valor, going above and beyond in the line of duty. It bravely navigated the treacherous terrain, making contact with the booger and banishing it from the nostril.

But, as they say, not all heroes wear capes. Some meet their end in a trash can, and that's exactly where that brave little brush found its final resting place. R.I.P., my brave, bristly comrade. You served us well.

I'm zipping through the day at lightning speed, one eye blink and whoosh, there goes the morning, filled with the same old, same old. Hours? What hours? They're slipping by like sneaky little ninjas, ducking out of sight before I can even spot them. And as I'm packing up my makeup kit, each brush and palette whispering tales of endless transformations, a wave of reflection hits me.

Yeah, I've had my fair share of hurdles in this gig, times when the tough bits tried to rain on my parade. But then I realize, how lucky am I? I mean, I get to play with my passion every day, sprinkling beauty and makeovers into people's days. I'm thankful, really, for the chance to let my creative flag fly, to play around with all the colors and textures, and to hang with my peeps who get just as jazzed about this art as I do.

Hopping into my car, I take a beat to soak in the familiar vibes of my ride—the cozy whiff of leather, the engine's soft purr, the cool touch of the steering wheel under my fingertips. Outside, the world turns into a moving painting as I zoom my way home.

I guzzle down the sights that have become the bread and butter of my commute—the mini skyscrapers reaching up to high-five the sky, city streets buzzing with life, sunlight and shadows playing tag on the concrete, and the odd patch of greenery giving us a break from the grey. All these sights, so ordinary yet so soothing, knit together into this awesome journey home tapestry, the perfect wrap-up to my work day.

Salty fries

Chapter Four

Salty fries

Chapter Four

NICKY

I'm all cozy and comfy in my brand new pad, despite feeling the financial pinch of the extortionate rent I'm paying. Thank sis! Then a lightbulb moment hits me - why not use the extra rooms to ease up on the bills? So, off I go, posting an ad on Facebook Marketplace for potential roomies.

'Attention, potential roomies! I'm an Irish lass in need of two fellow adventurers to brave the ridiculous rental battlefield in a comfy 3-bedroom suburban sanctuary. Only requirements: must love fresh air (aka non-smokers) and be free from any narcotics hobbies.

Your love interests and identities? None of my business! As long as you don't mind my occasional rendition of 'Danny Boy' at 2am, we're golden!

Our fortress is nestled in a peaceful neighborhood, perfect for those who appreciate tranquility after a long day of adulting. So, if you fancy a bit of craic and are ready to share the journey (and the bills), reach out! Let's make this house a home together.'

Lo and behold, some responses trickle in and I've got a meet-up lined up for today.

By Nicky Ireland

It's a sunny Saturday morning, 10 sharp, when a knock at the front door nearly gives me a heart attack. I pull the door open and standing there is this pleasantly plump fellow, probably in his early 20s, about 5ft 7", sporting short dark hair and a belly that could rival Santa's. I can't help but grin - he seems like a friendly guy.

"Hey, I'm Ben. Here for the room," he announces. I extend my hand for a shake, "Ah, Ben! I'm Nicky. Nice to meet you. Please, come in," I blabber, leading him into the kitchen.

"So, this," I gesture around, chuckling awkwardly, "is the kitchen, obviously." Why am I so bad at meeting new people at times? "Anyway, we've got two bedrooms, a double and a single, and a shared bathroom. I have my own in my room, of course. Let's take a tour."

A quarter of an hour later, I've gleaned that Ben is a carpenter, with a specialty in vintage pianos. He's got a family farm back in Offaly, his hometown, and he's a weekend homie. Perfect!

As we meander through the labyrinthine corridors of our humble abode, the numerical dance of rent figures for the solo and duo chambers becomes the evening's hot gossip. Our dear friend Ben, with his eyes sparkling with interest, drops a proverbial grenade into our tranquil tea party - he's planning to become a part-time ghost, vanishing every weekend. "So," he begins, with the mischief of a Cheshire cat, "how about a wee discount, given that I'll be a weekend absentee?" I find myself as stunned as a deer in the headlights. "Hold your horses, Ben," I sputter, "Are you implying that I turn into a weekend landlord, subletting your room? And what's the plan - hauling your belongings to and fro like a nomad every week?" I can't resist the urge to fold my arms and raise an eyebrow, channeling my inner 'The Rock'.

He strokes his chin thoughtfully, "Hmm... I see your point. So, that's a hard pass?" I nod in agreement, "Indeed, Ben. That's a hard no. Look, if you're not head over heels for the room, there's a long queue of eager beavers ready to pounce," I bluff with the confidence of a seasoned poker player. "No, no. I'm game. Thanks. I can teleport my stuff here by tomorrow if that suits you." I emit a sigh, brimming with relief, "Fantastic! But I'll need a month's rent up front as a security deposit," I add, ushering him towards the grand exit known as the front door.

"Okay, we're all set," he proclaims, signaling the end of our meeting. Our pact is sealed, and he makes to leave. I extend my hand for the standard end-of-deal handshake, but — plot twist! He veers in for a chummy peck on the cheek. My personal space is suddenly invaded, plunging me into a world of awkwardness. Then, out of nowhere... WHAM! A stench so pungent it could qualify for a world record.

Seriously, has my plumbing system gone rogue? The embarrassment is palpable. A full-on olfactory assault takes place, led by the deadly duo of body odor and past-its-prime fast food. The assertive aroma of vinegar and salt charges at my nostrils like a bull in a China shop.

As the smell escalates, a horrifying realization dawns on me. The source, the epicenter of this olfactory Armageddon, is him! Sweet mother of pearl, I think my stomach is staging a revolt. It's as if he's marinated himself in a concoction of expired cheese, rotten eggs, and week-old tuna, then topped it off with a dash of durian for good measure. It's the kind of smell that would send skunks running for cover, and make onions weep in despair. Dear Lord, I think I'm about to lose my brekkie.

As he takes his leave, I practically slam the door behind him, slumping against it. Damn, damn, damn. The lingering stench stubbornly clings to the air, and despite his agreeable nature, I'm starting to question the wisdom of inviting him to be my housemate.

Later that day, I rationalize to myself. Could it be, I wonder, that this was a solitary incident, a brief aberration in the otherwise mundane fabric of life? Perhaps the act of dealing with pianos was his own personal gym workout - a medley of onions, garlic, and fries, all tangled up in an aromatic symphony of stench. Yes, that must be it.

By Nicky Ireland

In my mind's eye, I picture him as a Herculean figure, each piano hoisted onto his broad shoulders, carried into the sanctuary of his workshop. The sweat would be pouring off him like a waterfall, akin to a plump teenager lost in the pulsating rhythm of a high-energy rave. The hilarious image brings a chuckle to my lips, lightening the mood as the day draws to a close.

He'll respect my space. He'll keep our home clean. I have to trust my gut on this one. Or, I might just have to invest in an air freshener company.

Holy shite balls!

As the day gives way to night, I snuggle into the welcoming arms of my bed, lost in the thrilling pages of my newest erotic romance. It's my guilty pleasure, these stories, their characters so richly drawn that I feel like I've made new friends. And when their stories end, it's like saying goodbye to a dear friend, a unique kind of heartache that only my fellow book lovers will understand.

Here I am, comfortably cocooned in my sanctuary of tranquility, leisurely sipping on my Pukka Organic Night Time Berry tea. Each mouthful is akin to a lullaby, sweet and calming, pulling me deeper into the loving clutches of my downy pillow. The tranquility of the moment is so palpable, it feels like it could be cut with a knife — until such bliss is abruptly punctuated by a curious cacophony emanating from the neighboring house. It appears my neighbors, John and Barbara, are indulging in some sort of nocturnal furniture relocation.

Choosing to dismiss this interruption, I plunge back into my book, making an earnest attempt to disregard the escalating hullabaloo. However, the noise escalates, the thuds against our shared wall intensifying, causing a ripple effect throughout the stillness of my chamber. Startled, I sit up straight, baffled — what on earth could possibly be happening? I press my ear against the wall, and as the sounds become clearer, a wave of embarrassment washes over me. It seems John and Barbara are participating in a somewhat fervent romantic rendezvous. A spot of love-making if you will.

I hastily recoil from the wall, endeavoring to obliterate the chorus of sighs and gasps that ensues. Clearly, it's time to bring in the big guns — my reliable noise-cancelling headphones and a playlist packed with my favourite tunes.

As I rummage through my drawer in search of the headphones, a thunderous, deep moan reverberates from next door, followed by Barbara's piercing shriek crying out, 'Yes, Daddy!' into the quiet of the night. My eyes bulge in astonishment. It appears that John and Barbara have a penchant for a bit of role-playing.

I can't help but burst into hearty laughter, doubling over as I laugh at the absurdity of the situation. I manage to put on my headphones, and just as I hit play on Tank's 'When We', another bellow from John is followed by Barbara's ecstatic screech of 'Feck me, Daddy. Feck me hard!'. The situation is so ridiculous that I'm soon rolling on the floor, overcome with laughter. Good for them, I muse.

However, as the laughter subsides, a pang of loneliness starts to creep in. The hilarity of the moment forms a stark contrast to the solitude I find myself in. I yearn for someone to share these laughable instances with — someone to giggle with, swap stories, and find comfort in their company. With a sigh, I retreat back into the captivating world of my book, diving once more into the realm of romance and passion.

Guinness is evil!

Chapter Five

Guinness is evil!

Chapter Five

NICKY

Holy hell, is it a wild ride trying to score a second housemate! After a string of no-shows yesterday, my spirits feel a bit like a deflated balloon. But hey, there's a silver lining: Ben, my current roommate, is a pretty cool guy to live with. He's often MIA and, between you and me, that's just how I like it.

But something bizarre happens whenever Ben ventures into the kitchen. It's as if a twister has just partied hard in there, leaving a wild assortment of cutlery, plates, and bowls strewn around like confetti. It's a sight that leaves me gob smacked, especially when you consider that his culinary expertise extends to microwaving ready meals.

It's like a cutlery parade has marched through, with forks and spoons all jumbled together. Abandoned plates, still adorned with dinner remnants, and a precarious tower of bowls, each marked with the remnants of Ben's latest microwave masterpiece, are what greet me post-Ben.

But today, I'm kicking the housemate and cluttered kitchen problems into the long grass and jazzing up my Sunday afternoon by dialing up my best bud. We've been two peas in a pod since our teens, when we found common ground swooning over boy bands.

As I punch in his number, a charge of excitement zaps through me. He picks up before the first ring even ends, playfully quizzing me on my latest need. Our giggles ricochet off each other, a familiar melody in our usual banter.

"Hey, fancy grabbing a coffee?" I venture, crossing my fingers that my partner in crime, Liam, isn't all booked up. But Lady Luck is smiling down on me – he's free! And he's already offloading about his latest dating disaster. I can't help but

By Nicky Ireland

chortle. Despite being a looker with charm to boot, Liam's dating life is a magnet for misadventures.

We lock in our usual haunt for 1 pm and I feel a tidal wave of joy crash over me. No matter what curveballs life chucks my way, I know I can always lean on Liam for straight-up advice and a comforting bear hug. And sometimes, that's all I need to keep my spirits up – a good cup of joe and an even better buddy.

So here I am, nestled in our beloved haunt, a charming coffee shop on Dawson Street in the heart of Dublin, nursing a frothy cappuccino and doing my best to resist the tempting array of scones and pastries. As always, we dispense with the usual pleasantries and dive headfirst into the scandalous stories.

Reclining in my chair, I savor the rich taste of my cappuccino as Liam sets the stage for his latest escapade - apparently, a wild night that began with a fiery rendezvous and culminated in complete revulsion. Liam, a 6ft vision of tattoos, red hair, and a bushy beard, is the epitome of Irish spirit. Originally from Kilkenny, he's now a proud Dubliner, living in a gorgeous apartment just off Georges Street in the heart of the city. This fortunate lad has carved out a thriving career as an artist, a nod to his talent and perseverance.

"So, this girl...", he starts, "she was about 5ft 3", a tiny, curvy thing. Absolutely stunning. We met near The George, you know me, too lazy to venture far from my apartment, especially with the promise of some action." I chuckle, fully aware that Liam is perpetually on the prowl.

"Anyway, we grab a drink and she orders a pint of Guinness. A full pint of the black stuff! Who does that on a first date?". "A woman who enjoys a pint of Guinness, Liam. That's who." I retort, rolling my eyes playfully, curious about where this tale is going.

"Tiny thing drinks it down in one go. I swear it didn't even touch the sides. And the belch she lets out would shame a sailor." By now, I'm laughing uncontrollably at the mental image, and he's joining in.

"So... what happened after the pub?", I ask, eager for more.

"We went back to my place. Obviously." "Obviously", I echo his words. "And, you know, one thing leads to another. It's incredible. She's a firecracker and I can't get enough of her...", he drifts off, lost in thought.

"I get it, she's as insatiable as you. Then what?", I probe.

"Well, I decide to take the lead and go down on her. You know I love doing that and, trust me, she was perfect. So tight and...". I raise my hand, interrupting him "I don't need a detailed account of this poor girl's anatomy, Liam". "Alright, alright", he responds, rolling his eyes.

"So I'm in the middle of it and she's loving it. I can tell she's close to the edge. She's moaning, screaming, it's unreal...".

At this point, he starts to blush and buries his face in his hands, shaking his head.

"What?", I ask, a mix of amusement and concern crossing my face.

"So there I am, head nestled against her backside, she's filling my mouth and I'm thinking, this is nice, a cozy place to park my snout while I eat her out... ha ha... I'm a poet and I don't even know it", he chuckles at his own humor. "Stop!", I giggle, "What happened next?" I ask, impatience practically seeping out of me.

"The Guinness, Nic. That's what happens next". I look at him, my face a picture of confusion. "I don't understand, Liam".

"Guinness farts, Nic! And then, those Guinness farts became Guinness sharts". I try to hold back my disgust as I hear the tale. "Right in the middle of it all, she lets out a string of loud farts, followed by an even more embarrassing and unsanitary incident" he scrunches up his nose in disgust.

Oh holy shite... Literally! The laughter that bursts from me is like a dam that's just broken. I'm laughing so hard tears are streaming down my face.

By Nicky Ireland

As Paloma Faith's 'Only love can hurt like this' starts playing over the coffee shop speakers, I'm nearly on the floor laughing. Talk about perfect comedic timing!

"It's not freaking funny, Nic! It was disgusting. I thought I was up for anything, but scat is definitely not it".

Still trying to control my laughter, I reach out to comfort my friend, even as I'm struggling to keep a straight face. I take his hand and give it a comforting squeeze, trying my best to look sympathetic. "I'm sorry, Liam, really I am". He puts his hand on top of mine and gently rubs my knuckles. "Thanks, Nic". "I understand. You had a really crappy time", I say, breaking into hysterical laughter again.

"You're such a witch", he retorts with a chuckle, a term of endearment from him. Now he's laughing too, his face scrunching up in disgust again as he recalls the previous night's shenanigans. It makes me realize just how lucky I am to have such wonderful people in my life.

It's evident that Liam has had an experience that will scar him both mentally and physically for a long time. But he knows that with me by his side, he can find the strength to recover and laugh at the absurdity of it all.

Life is full of ups and downs, but we can always rely on each other for support – a bond made of love, trust, and endless laughter.

We sit in the coffee shop for hours, sipping on warm drinks and exchanging stories as our laughter fills the room. The bond we share is truly special - an enduring friendship that will withstand the messiest of life's moments, evidently!

As the evening unfurls its calm, I decide to spoil myself with a solo dinner date at my favourite hideaway - a cozy Irish restaurant nestled in the heartbeat of town. This place? It's a well-kept secret, my personal retreat, and let me tell you, its charm is off the charts! The homey feel, the mouth-watering dishes that always hit the spot - it's like hitting a jackpot!

Stepping inside, I'm instantly wrapped up in the scent of heart-warming home-cooked meals. The place is a beautiful blend of casual comfort and tasteful elegance. Picture polished wooden furniture, drapes with intricate embroidery, and a fireplace that's practically a lighthouse of coziness. I snag a seat by that beckoning hearth, the smell of burning peat drawing me in like a moth to a flame. I place my order and kick back.

Soon enough, the showstopper of my self-spoiling spree arrives - a piping hot bowl of traditional Irish seafood chowder. My taste buds are practically doing a happy dance as the bowl lands on my table. Fresh seafood, crusty bread - it's like a feast for the eyes and the nose. The smell of freshly baked bread mixing with the smoky fireplace scent? That's a nose concert right there!

To wash it all down, I go for a glass of Bunratty Mead. Talk about divine! This Irish gem is one of the first forms of wine humans ever made. Its roots are tangled up in Ireland's mystical lore, and I am all about that!

This magical concoction was first brewed by monks in the Middle Ages, using ripe grapes, honey, and herbs - a recipe that creates an aroma you wouldn't believe. But the best part? The legends! Apparently, newlyweds would drink this honey-infused Mead for a month ("one full moon") post-wedding. They believed it would bless them with fertility and virility - a story that tickles me pink, thus the term "honeymoon"!

My fingers trace the edges of my current literary infatuation—a potent and compelling romance novel that delves into the world of passion, dominance and submission. This exploration of desire isn't new to me; it is, in fact, a reflection of a deep-rooted fascination that has been part of my psyche for as long as I can remember.

My interest in the BDSM lifestyle has been more than a mere curiosity. I have devoted countless hours to researching and understanding the complexities and nuances of this world. Through chatrooms and forums, I've conversed with fellow submissives and dominants alike, absorbing their insights, experiences, and advice. The internet has been my portal to this intriguing lifestyle, leading me from one enlightening discourse to another, each adding a new layer to my understanding and appreciation of BDSM.

My journey has been marked by an insatiable thirst for knowledge—a drive to comprehend not just the mechanics of the lifestyle, but also the profound emotional connections it fosters. I've delved into the intricate dance of power and trust, the intoxicating allure of surrender, and the profound bond that forms when one's desires are truly seen, acknowledged, and fulfilled.

As I sit here in this tranquil restaurant, absorbed in my book and the enchanting melody of Nina Simone's 'Black is the Colour of My True Love's Hair', I can't help but yearn for a taste of the reality behind the words. I dream of finding someone with whom my deepest desires resonate—someone who understands the profound need that beckons me towards this lifestyle,

someone who shares the same rhythm of desire. With every turn of the page, every note of the song, I am reminded of this longing. This is more than just a perfect evening; it is a testament to a journey of self-discovery and the hope for a future where my fantasies become reality.

Lounging on this oh-so-comfy bench seat, the fire's heat hugging me like a cozy blanket. I'm diving headfirst into the thrilling universe my book has to offer. The chowder? Deliciously flavorful, a culinary masterpiece in a bowl! The book's enchanting tale? An absolute rollercoaster! And let's not forget the sweet tunes humming in the background - it's like the cherry on top of this perfect sundae of an evening. Could life get any better than this? I seriously doubt it. A big, goofy grin spreads across my face. In this blissful moment, life isn't just good - it's downright fantastic!

I arrive home to a text. I've just been informed by Ben, our resident genius, that the oven has thrown in the towel. How he managed to figure that out is beyond me, considering his diet consists of microwaved abominations and grease-soaked fish and chips. But, I suppose it's my duty to call my ever-so-generous (insert heavy sarcasm here) sister, Molly.

"Hey, Molly," I start, "The oven's decided to go on a vacation. Mind getting it sorted out ASAP?"

Her response comes quick, laden with her usual stinginess. "Why? You don't even use it."

I roll my eyes. "That's beside the point. It's not just me living here."

I'm fibbing, of course. The oven is as essential to Ben as a book is to a goldfish.

Molly, ever the tightwad, shoots back, "Can't your housemate fix it? Doesn't he repair stuff for a living?" I can't help but laugh. "He fixes pianos, Molly! Unless our oven's secretly a musical instrument, that's not exactly going to help."

As I'm engaged in this thrilling conversation with my skin and blister, I decide to give the oven a once-over. Lo and behold, I soon discover that it wasn't even turned on at the socket. Bravo, Ben. Another 'F' on your report card, champ.

Plenty of fish

Chapter Six

Plenty of fish

Chapter Six

NICKY

Ironing out the creases on my dress as Emiline's 'Strut' pulses through the room from my Spotify, I give myself a once-over in the mirror. Okay, not bad at all! It's been more than ten years since I last braved the dating scene. Fingers crossed I don't come off as over-eager, start a one-woman monologue, or do something totally facepalm-worthy.

A little while back, I decided to plunge into the world of online dating.

Dublin OG Seeks Dashing Twin-Flame

Hello, world! I'm a 30-year-old Dublin lass with an insatiable passion for all things arty – a colorful canvas or a monochrome photograph, I can find beauty in everything. My camera is my third eye and my paintbrush, an extension of my soul.

I'm also a self-confessed bibliophile with a penchant for what my mum would blushingly call 'cliterature.' If you catch me grinning to myself in public, chances are I've just read a saucy line in my latest book. Honesty is my policy!

I'm on a quest to find my soul mate, my twin-flame. Not just a casual fling or a fleeting summer romance, but someone who can match my emotional strength and isn't afraid to dive deep into the ocean of feelings. I promise, I'll bring the floaties!

By Nicky Ireland

My heart is as big as my wanderlust. I love to travel, seeking out sunshine and sandy beaches (I've got a bucket full of shells to prove it). But here's the plot twist - I'm also a certified pluviophile. Yes, you heard right. I love the rain as much as the beach. I know, I'm a walking contradiction wrapped in an enigma, sprinkled with a dash of irony.

If you can handle a woman who loves the sunshine on her face, the sand between her toes, the rain on her window, and the thrill of a good page-turner in her hands, then swipe right and let's write our own adventure story together. Who knows, it might just be the best 'novel' experience of our lives!

Good idea? Bad idea? Well, the jury's still out on that one.

Spot on 1pm, I'm stepping into the restaurant. Who even chooses a restaurant for a first date anymore? Certainly not me, and certainly not out of choice. But he was adamant, and me being ever so accommodating, I agreed. Maybe a bit too quickly, if I'm being honest.

This eatery is his pick, new territory for me, and not exactly my go-to spot for a meal. Suddenly, I feel like I'm in a ball gown at a picnic. A waiter ushers me to a table, and I sit down, nerves bundled up inside me like a bag of jumping beans. Spotting a dirty fork on the table, my appetite decides to take an early leave.

I flag down the waiter and hand him the offending fork after a quick explanation. Actually, I hand over all the cutlery on the table with an apologetic grin. He takes a look, and then, as if this were the most normal thing in the world, starts wiping it down with his disheveled apron. "Oh flip me, this is going to be interesting," I think. "Could you please bring some fresh cutlery? Thanks," I request, and off he goes without a word.

A tick past ten minutes after the hour and my date is already ten minutes late. He strides into the joint, spotting me. "Hey yeh, you must be Nicky. I'm Andy. Isn't this place just epic?" he blurts out, his enthusiasm perhaps a little too boisterous for my taste.

Taking a seat opposite me, I can't help but notice him do a quick once-over. I'm already planning my escape route. Don't blame me! While he's tall, say about 5ft 10". Has short brown hair morphed into dreadlocks that are tidily tucked into a man bun. A lip piercing adorns his face and his build is lean. Nerves however appear to be making him extremely fidgety and it unsettles me.

Our waiter saunters over for our drink orders. "Ladies first," he quips with a chuckle, gesturing towards me. I opt for sobriety, ordering a coke. His turn, "A blue wicked for me, mate!" Yes, he's that guy who orders an alcopop!

Drinks sorted, we delve into small talk. I learn he's a true blue Dubliner, born and bred on the north side. Coincidentally, I'm a north-sider too, though I've mostly lived in West Dublin. As he launches into a captivating yarn about his rip-roaring journey across Asia, with his younger brother in tow, my interest is well and truly stirred.

"That's amazing," I find myself exclaiming', "Go on, spill more about your travels."

His eyes light up as he dives back into his memories, "Ah, we had a great time, we did! Smokin' mountains of pot, downin' rivers of booze. 'It was bleedin' epic!" His face is all aglow, clearly chuffed with his wild shenanigans.

Suddenly, out of nowhere, he switches gears, his tone turning serious, like a record player that's suddenly been switched to a mournful tune. I'm left scratching my head at this jitterbug's sudden change of rhythm.

"Before we go any further," he starts, a bit of hesitation creeping into his voice. I respond with a cautious, "Alright...", the uncertainty in my voice mirroring the confusion in my thoughts. I'm left wondering where this tale is heading.

"Me brother and I, we had quite the adventurous spin over there," he continues, causing my patience to wear a bit thin. "Andy, cut to the chase," I interject, curious but a bit peeved.

"Well, ye see, prostitution is a common sight there," he confesses. I muster a simple, "I wasn't clued in on that, Andy," eager to steer clear of this awkward bend in the conversation.

"But we decided to dive headfirst, embrace all the experiences on offer," he continues, pausing to scratch an itch on his arm. I force a smile, responding, "Alright, sure," though my discomfort is barely concealed.

"There's a bit of a snag, though," he admits, scratching his groin with an annoyed look on his face. "I think I might've caught meself crabs." At this point, I can feel my jaw hit the floor. Is this the kind of catch we're reeling in the 2023 dating sea?!

"Alright, Andy," I manage to reply, planting me feet and collecting my thoughts. His gaze holds a glimmer of disappointment, a hint of regret. "We're not a match, you and I. But hey, thanks for being straight with me and for the craic." I grab my coat, feeling relieved we've not yet ordered, given the surprisingly slow service in this otherwise tranquil restaurant.

"Sure, no bother," he responds, surprisingly calm given the situation. As I make a swift exit, I feel a strange sensation of itching. Could it be all in my head? I shake it off, chuckling at the absurdity of the afternoon. No walk of shame for me in the morning, but a rather interesting tale to tell!

As I stride towards my car, the prospect of a quiet evening back home, curled up with a page-turner and a bottle of wine, seems more appealing than ever. And while I can't shake off the sensation of imaginary creepy crawlies, I find meself laughing at the daftness of it all.

With my foot on the pedal, I drive away from the restaurant and spontaneously decide to check out the Botanic Gardens hiding in the heart of Dublin. My trusty

Nikon camera, practically an extension of my arm, is always ready to snap the beauty of the world around me. The gardens are the perfect venue to combine an invigorating walk and some fresh air with the exhilaration of taking jaw-dropping photos.

Photography for me is more than a hobby; it's a passion that has blossomed over years. The snap of the shutter, the twist of the lens, the thrill of capturing that magical moment - it's a rush. My camera is my constant companion, not just a piece of equipment but a silent ally that helps me freeze time and memories. Sure, my memory is sharp, but the saying is spot on; a picture is worth a thousand words.

With each photo I take, I am crafting a vibrant scrapbook, a tangible collection of moments, emotions, and stories that I can revisit and relive at will. Placing these memories on paper breathes life into them, turning them into more than just thoughts in my head. It's an engaging, entertaining activity that I thoroughly love.

As I step into the Botanic Gardens, I'm swallowed by a wave of bright colors and intoxicating aromas. Blooms of all shades stretch out in front of me, their sweet scent heavy in the air. The gardens are buzzing with life, from the delicate butterflies dancing from flower to flower, to the hardworking bees humming as they go about their daily chores. Every sight and scent is a potential photograph, begging to be captured and immortalized.

I immerse myself in the gardens for the rest of the afternoon, soaking up the lush scenery and the revitalizing air. Walking among the wildlife, every step reveals a new viewpoint, a new frame for my Nikon to capture.

Every rustle of the leaves, every bird's song, every whiff of floral fragrance is a testament to the garden's vibrant life. It's an experience of pure, unfiltered joy. I'm not just a visitor here; the garden and I share a symbiotic relationship where I take away stunning photographs, and in return, I leave behind my footprints and admiration.

By Nicky Ireland

This evening, I'm relishing a solitary encounter with a bottle of Riesling. My housemate, Ben, is on a hometown adventure in Offaly, giving me the golden opportunity to soak in the splendor of being alone. Lounging on my plush bed, a fascinating book in one hand, with nothing but an oversized t-shirt for company, I'm teetering on the edge of slumber. But then, the peace is abruptly broken by the determined buzzing of my phone on the bedside table.

I grab it, and who could it be but Ben! At 2 a.m., no less. Is there no respect for the sanctity of sleep?

Ben: Hello there.

Me: What's the big idea, Ben?

Ben: Nothing much, just thought I'd say hi.

Me: You do know it's the witching hour, right? You're disturbing the spirits... and me!

Ben: Oh right, jaysus, sorry. Were you about to enter dreamland?

Me: I was at the gates, yes.

Ben: Right so.

Ben: We'll have a proper chat after the weekend.

Me: Wait a minute, what's the real scoop? You don't ping me past midnight without a good reason.

Ben: Nah, nothing to worry about, just chill.

Me: Trouble in paradise, Ben?

Ben: Why the sudden detective mode?

Me: Ben, a 2 a.m. text is like a smoke signal. It

usually means something's on fire.

Ben: Fair point.

Ben: Just pondering over a thought.

Me: Out with it, then?

Ben: Well, considering we're both single...

Me: I'm listening?

Ben: How about we become friends with benefits?

Me: Ben, are you okay? Did you hit your head?

Ben: Just a suggestion! No need for a meltdown.

Me: How kind of you, but I'll have to decline. I don't mix business with pleasure.

Ben: No bother so.

What a rollercoaster of a day! Is this real life or just a very peculiar dream?

At last, I give in to the pull of sleep, hoping that the morning sun will cleanse the peculiarities of this day. Feckin' hell, what's next?

The meeting

Chapter Seven

The meeting

Chapter Seven

NICKY

On this splendid day, I find myself venturing into the great outdoors of my humble backyard - a day so grand, it's practically hollering at me to do the laundry. A great drying day as we say. So I totter outside, loaded with a basket brimming with clothes, ready to deck out my washing line with a parade of freshly washed garments.

As I'm in the throes of hoisting a pair of knickers onto the line with a clothespin - a task so mundane, it could lull a caffeinated squirrel to sleep - my gaze, in a moment of rebellion, darts towards an unexpected spectacle. The stage? My neighbor's bedroom window. The performer? Barbara... in the absolute buff from the waist up!

Good heavens above! My cheeks ignite like a firecracker, my heart thumps a rhythm of shock as the reality of the situation dawns upon me. I've been caught, not red-handed, but red-faced in this unintentional act of peeping tom-ery. Instead of succumbing to the panic bubbling within me, I paste on the most convincing grin, as if this impromptu peep show is as normal as the chirping of the morning birds.

Babs, that absolute gem, responds with a wave that could put any royal parade to shame. There she stands, her bosom bobbing about like a pair of eager spaniels' ears caught in a gusty breeze, her arms flowing in a rhythm that would make a ballet dancer green with envy. Each undulation reveals the badges of honor from countless bingo nights. Her face splits open in a grin as wide as the Grand Canyon, radiating a joy so pure, it's practically infectious.

Oh, Barbara, love! I remain rooted in my spot, a cocktail of horror and

By Nicky Ireland

admiration brewing within me. Behold, a lady caught in what could be a mortifying situation, devoid of any hints of embarrassment, but rather, basking in the moment. As I resume my laundry duties, a chuckle breaks free, echoing through the stillness of my backyard. The audacity, the hilarity, the sheer joy of life that Barbara exudes - it's a spectacle to behold, a tale to recount, a memory to cherish. I find myself falling in love with this woman's spirit, I swear.

It's almost lunchtime and I'm taking a stroll through the scenic beauty of Trinity College, Dublin, Billie Eilish's mesmerizing 'Ocean Eyes' fills my ears via my trusty headphones, guiding me to a plush patch of grass where I plop down. Today's fatigue is real, so the golden sunshine bathing me, especially in Autumn, is a warm welcome. It's an exceptionally beautiful day, a gem found in the often rainy Dublin. Mind you, the raindrops caressing my face have their own soothing charm - remember, identifying pluviophile here.

Trinity College has a long list of renowned alumni. Oscar Wilde, the Irish author, poet, and playwright, known for gems like "The Picture of Dorian Gray" and "The Importance of Being Earnest," walked these very

halls. And then, there's Bram Stoker, whose "Dracula" sends shivers down my spine. Not forgetting Samuel Beckett, the Irish novelist, playwright, and poet who bagged the Nobel Prize in Literature in 1969. It's pretty amazing when you think of it.

Tossing my coat onto the grass, I slide out of my heels and stretch my legs, sighing contentedly as I gaze at the clear blue canvas above me. The autumn sun's warmth seeping into my skin, I can't help but feel lucky for this surprise sunny day in Dublin. Lying on the grass of Trinity College, my mind sets sail to far-off lands, drenched in endless sunshine and brimming with romantic adventures.

Assuming my best posture, I dig into my bag and fish out the novel that's been monopolizing my free time. It's a literary cocktail - one part dark, two parts intense, a splash of romance, and a generous pour of smut. No sooner do I plunge back into its tantalizing pages than I feel a prickle on my skin - someone's eyeballing me from somewhere in this urban wilderness.

It's like I've stumbled into a chapter from my favourite book. Across the manicured chaos of Trinity, a figure flickers into my view. There's this guy, looking like he's stepped straight out of a noir film. He's gone full autumn chic with a dark overcoat and matching turtleneck, black trousers that scream 'tailored' and boots that probably cost more than my rent. He's lounging on a park bench like he's king of the squirrels.

His aura hits me like a catchy pop song - it's charismatic, mysterious, and I can't get it out of my head. And let's not forget that gaze, so intense it could laser-cut diamonds, paired with a grin that's probably illegal in several states. That combo sends shivers down my spine like an ice cube down the back of my dress.

Our eyes meet, and it's like someone just cranked up the volume. His stare is a wordless conversation, a secret whispered across the grassy divide. Suddenly, I'm not just a girl in a park with a book. I'm a heroine in a twisty plot, at the precipice of an adventure with Mr. Mysterious. The story of my life is about to take a turn for the exciting, mirroring the thrill that my cherished novel offers with every turn of the page.

Doing a remarkable impression of a wallflower, I make a big show of fumbling with my camera as if it's the first time I've held it. The reality is, I know this piece of tech better than the barista knows my coffee order - large skinny cappuccino, extra shot (or two) of espresso, two pumps of sugar free vanilla syrup, not too hot, please.

With the panache of a secret agent on a covert mission, I subtly bring my camera on level. I feel like James Bond, only instead of a Walther PPK, I have a Nikon. I manage to snag a picture of the intriguing specimen in front of me. If there's a female version of a spank bank, then this picture would be sitting in the VIP lounge, sipping on a cosmopolitan.

Despite my best impression of a stoic statue, my eyes betray me. They're like overexcited puppies, bouncing around trying to catch every detail. All attempts at keeping a poker face are gone. It's like my eyes have taken on a life of their own, soaking in the view, leaving me to play the part of the hapless spectator. And just to add a cherry on top, Chloe Adam's 'Dirty Thoughts' starts serenading my ears. The timing is so spot on, I almost expect Chloe to pop out from behind a bush, reading my thoughts aloud.

The song's saucy lyrics, brimming with suggestive winks and nudges, mirror my unspoken musings. It's a moment of such comical alignment that I almost choke on my surprise. My cheeks flush a hue that would give ripe tomatoes a run for their money. The universe, it seems, is having a grand old time at my expense.

The mysterious man's sun-kissed skin stands out against the lush green Irish backdrop like a perfectly toasted marshmallow in a bowl of mint ice cream. His disheveled ebony hair frames a face that could give Greek gods a complex. And that well-groomed beard? It only serves to accentuate the smoldering intensity of his gaze. It's as if he's sauntered straight out of the pages of my favourite romance novel and plonked himself down in front of me. I half expect him to start reciting soul-stirring poetry any minute now.

As I continue to gawk, my curiosity amplifying faster than a pop song on the radio, it appears he's spotted me too. Time decides to take a coffee break as our eyes lock in a stare duel. With a smile that oozes mystery and charm, he rises, artistically drapes his coat over his arm - like he's about to perform a magic trick, and begins to saunter in my direction.

Holy shiteballs!

A wave of anticipation is doing the samba through my veins, I abruptly shift my attention back to the book in my grasp - a pitiful attempt to project an image of nonchalance. The lines of text do a merry jig before my eyes as the noise of his advancing steps resonate, grinding against the gravel path, growing closer with each nerve-wracking second. My heart is thumping like a hyperactive drummer at a heavy metal gig.

The sound of his steps comes to a screeching halt and boom! There he stands:

this sun-drenched stud muffin, throwing a shadow over my lap so long it could compete in a summer day length contest. And we're talking about a summer day in a toasty place, not in Ireland, where summer days are more like rain bingo. He looms over me, probably about 6 feet tall, if I had to guess. The sun, clearly his number one fan, puts a spotlight on him, forcing me to squint and shield my eyes from his blinding dazzle.

"Need anything?" I manage to squeak out, attempting to keep my voice from betraying my internal chaos. His smirk is like a gravitational pull, the kind that comes with complimentary heart palpitations. "Could you recommend a decent museum to visit in Dublin?" His accent is the symphony my ears never knew they needed. Despite feeling like I've been targeted by Cupid's sniper, I attempt to maintain my composure. "Sure. Uh... The National History Museum of Ireland is a solid choice. It's pretty close by. If you're interested in natural history and, um, stuff." His grin is mischievous as he quips, "Yes, I'm interested in stuff, all types of stuff." Oh dear lord, I bet you are.

I mentally headbutt myself to stop gawping at him like a crazed fan at a surprise Beyoncé concert. Clearing my throat - more like a car engine sputtering to life - I realize my intense gazing is likely making me appear less like a casual observer and more like a wannabe psychic. "OK, so, it's just a 10-minute jaunt. Head back towards those arches and hang a left. Just keep trucking straight until The American College Dublin pops into view and take a right before that. It's so big you'd need to be Mr. Magoo to miss it."

"Thank you," he retorts, his smile setting off fireworks as he swivels to depart, gravel protesting under his mammoth boots. He tosses a roguish grin over his shoulder, leaving me to decipher the cryptic crossword that is this intriguing stranger.

His parting nod, dusted with an extra layer of cheerfulness, begins his departure. I find myself yearning for a moment of pause in the universe, a desire to savor this unexpected rendezvous a little longer. But then, he abruptly halts. My eyes follow him as he pivots, retracing his steps towards me. "Would you care to join me?" he ventures, his voice awash with daring self-assurance.

By Nicky Ireland

A playful smirk dances its way across my face, and I find myself responding with a surprising, "Uh... yeah, sure, OK." He plants himself squarely in front of me, extending his left hand. I can't help but admire his slender fingers, kissed by the afternoon's golden glow. His nails are flawlessly groomed, and notably, devoid of a wedding band. I let out a silent sigh of relief.

Suddenly, my attention shifts from his hand. I accept his assistance to rise, albeit a bit clumsily. The comforting warmth of his hand and his firm grip sends my imagination spiraling... his secure grasp ignites an exhilarating image in my mind... of his hands around my neck. I shake my head, admonishing myself for such bold fantasies. I'm practically a stranger to him. It's high time I got a grip on myself.

His towering stature leaves me feeling petite, given my modest 5ft 5" height. A thrill courses through me as I realize that I barely reach his shoulders. My gaze shifts to his mouth, and I'm immediately captivated by his full, rosy lips. I find myself daydreaming about their touch.

As I smooth my dress over my thighs, he gestures forward with an inviting hand. "Ladies first," he offers in his captivating accent. I hardly feel like a lady in this moment, but I manage to articulate a "thank you" and step ahead of him.

I attempt to shake off the worry that he's scrutinizing my backside. My dress ends just a few inches below, and I hastily reach back to adjust it. The fear that my dress is creeping upwards, my ass greedily swallowing the hem, is all too real.

Our walk is blanketed in silence, and it feels like it's stretching into eternity. Overly dramatic? Absolutely. But I can't help it.

Then, an idea strikes me. I turn to face him, a mischievous grin on my face. "You know, I never thought being a tour guide would involve guiding handsome men around. I should consider adding 'heartbreaker tour guide' to my resume," I joke.

His laughter rings out, warm and hearty. It's contagious, and I find myself laughing along, the sound of our shared joy filling the air. This unexpected encounter just took an unexpectedly fun turn.

"I'm Santiago, Santi for short. And you?" he inquires. "Oh, I'm Nicky. Nic, Nickerless... whatever you like," I babble, immediately wishing I could retract it. His laughter echoes around us, and I steal a glance at him, utterly entranced. This man is a vision.

"Nicky, you're quite a character. I like that," he remarks, a teasing edge to his voice. Why does that make me blush? It's probably because I'm not accustomed to compliments from such a good-looking man.

As we amble alongside each other, I can't help but take in his striking features and wonder what it would be like to share a private moment with him. We exchange witty quips and casual conversation, both of us visibly pleased with each other's company. With each step we take, I find myself increasingly drawn to him and intrigued by his charismatic personality.

We inch closer to our destination and I quickly realize that Santiago is not just any Joe soap. He's a dashing foreigner hailing from Barcelona, who's landed in Dublin for work. The city lights twinkle as we stroll through the streets, while he spins tales about his hometown. Stories of sun-kissed beaches, electrifying nightlife, and a cultural history as rich as a chocolate cake. I drink in his words, getting lost in daydreams of adventuring to Barcelona one day, perhaps with him as my guide. Whoa, slow down!

A whirlpool of thrill and trepidation stirs within me as we finally arrive at the towering spectacle of The Natural History Museum of Ireland. Snugly tucked away on Merrion Street Upper, locals endearingly refer to it as the 'dead zoo.' But trust me, it's far from an ordinary museum. It's a veritable treasure chest brimming over with 10,000 animal exhibits from every nook and cranny of the globe, encompassing mammals, birds, fish, and all sorts of creepy critters.

This venerable institution first welcomed the public in 1856 to showcase the Royal Dublin Society's collection. As years rolled on, the state took the reins, becoming the proud keeper of this architectural marvel and its numerous inhabitants. The museum is a living time capsule, virtually untouched for over a century. Entering its premises isn't just a stroll into a building; it's akin to stepping onto a time machine. Some dub it a 'museum within a museum', others a 'palatial residence of death'. To me, it's a magnificent testament to worldwide biodiversity!

As we venture into the Irish Room on the ground floor, we come face-to-face with Ireland's native fauna. Towering skeletons of giant Irish deer loom over us amidst a diverse assortment of skulls and bones. We marvel at the taxidermy displays of mammals, birds, fish, and other creatures that call Ireland home. Some of these exhibits, like the badgers, hares, and foxes, have been here for over a century, and there's even a basking shark hanging from the ceiling!

"Isn't it amazing how these animals have been preserved?" I say, pointing at the shark. Santi nods, his eyes wide with fascination. His interest, so palpable, adds a fresh layer of intrigue to our surroundings, making everything feel undiscovered. It's as if his curiosity is breathing new life into the museum, and I'm utterly entranced by his reaction.

As we navigate the lower gallery, a medley of bird calls from across the globe fills the air. We are dwarfed by the skeletal remains of a humpback and fin whale suspended from the ceiling, their formidable presence creating a spine-chilling aura.

"Now, did you know," I begin with a playful twinkle in my eye, "that a single humpback whale can produce up to 400 gallons of sperm at once?" Santi raises an eyebrow, a smirk pulling at the corner of his mouth. "I mean, talk about a whole ocean of love right there!" I continue, beaming with pride. His laugh echoes throughout the room, a sound that never ceases to warm my heart. As he throws his head back, I find myself captivated by the intricate tattoos on his neck, my heart fluttering uncontrollably at the sight. Damn!

As we continue our exploration of the museum, I can't help but nudge Santi playfully, "An expert on Spanish gastronomy, huh? So, what's your specialty? Paella or tortilla de patatas?"

He grins at me, "Ah, you're putting me on the spot! But if I had to choose, I'd say the traditional tortilla. It's simple yet comforting. It's all about the perfect flip, you know."

I laugh, "The perfect flip, huh? Sounds like my eyeliner application in the morning. One wrong move and it's a disaster."

He chuckles, joining in on the light-hearted comparison. "Well, you've certainly mastered that art, if I may say so. Just like the perfect tortilla, it's all in the detail."

Our banter continues, a delightful back and forth filled with laughter and shared stories. I find myself drawn to his passion for cooking, and he seems genuinely intrigued by my work as a makeup artist. The ease with which we converse feels as natural as the flow of a river, each topic a stepping stone guiding us further into the depth of our connection.

"Santi," I say, pointing towards the Glass Sea Creatures, "if you were one of these creatures, which would you be?"

He looks thoughtfully at the display before pointing to a delicate glass jellyfish. "I think I'd be that one. It's a wanderer, freely drifting with the currents. Plus, it's transparent, and I believe in being open and honest."

I laugh, "And here I thought you'd choose something more... culinary-related. Perhaps a glass lobster?"

Santi chuckles, "Too predictable! But what about you? Which creature embodies the spirit of a freelance makeup artist?"

I ponder his question and my eyes land on a vibrant glass clownfish. "I think I'd be that one. It's colorful, adaptable, and stands out amongst the rest. Just like a good makeup artist should."

Our laughter continues echoes throughout the gallery, a testament to the ease and comfort that has blossomed between us. It's an afternoon filled with

By Nicky Ireland

enchanting glass art, intriguing wildlife, and a sprinkle of flirtation that adds an extra dash of sparkle to our banter. This museum adventure with Santi has proven to be much more than a simple outing; it's a shared journey of discovery, laughter, and connection.

Moments later, I find myself entrenched in a deep contemplation of a badger family display, my mind wandering through the artful complexities of taxidermy. Suddenly, I sense Santi's presence as he subtly aligns himself with my back. I come to a full stop, his aroma wrapping around me like a cocoon. He's a seductive blend of worn leather and exotic spices. As he leans in, he whispers, "You know, the one good thing is that we can't smell them," his hushed voice causing a shiver to dance down my spine. I turn to face him, immediately ensnared by the emerald depths of his eyes, framed by lashes as dark as a raven's feathers. A lump forms in my throat, our silent exchange resuming once more through our locked gazes. What on earth is going on here?

With a gulp, I manage to respond, "You know Santi, even the most pungent beast wouldn't hold a candle to the aroma of my housemate!" His features scrunch up in an adorable display of confusion, triggering a wave of laughter from me. "I've got a housemate," I clarify, shrugging nonchalantly, "he has a unique...understanding of personal hygiene." His eyebrows shoot up in surprise. "You're not solo then?", he queries, a note of intrigue weaving through his tone. "Not quite, the sky-high rents in Dublin and my salary aren't exactly on the same page. But hey, the company can be quite entertaining at times."

I meander away from the badgers, journeying towards the exhibit dedicated to female peregrine falcons. The placard informs me of their hefty build and their deadly dive-bombing tactics, talons prepped for the kill. Talk about a fierce matriarchy! These femme fatales are not to be underestimated!

We plunge headfirst into the tapestry of art, culture, and sheer wonderment that each exhibit has to offer. Our initial giggles and playful banter steadily evolve into profound discussions about life, love, aspirations, and the whole nine yards.

"Soooo, Nicky, any special someone in your life?" His question hits me out of the blue. Wowza! We're diving straight into the deep end much faster than I anticipated.

"Ah, no. My ex and I parted ways some time back," I confess, managing a semblance of a grin. No need to delve into the ex's eccentric lingerie collection just yet. It does feel strange, sharing this part of my life, but I'm hopeful we can steer clear of this topic for the time being. "I'm sorry to hear that Nicky," he offers, a glimmer of relief seeping into his tone. "No worries," I reassure him, "We just weren't right for each other. Best for both of us, really." I smile sincerely, the authenticity of my words shining through.

"Hey Santi, anyone special you're, well, 'connected' with?" I carefully select the word 'connected', avoiding any assumptions about his preferences. A silent wish floats up to the universe, crossing my fingers he's on my team.

Santi doesn't reply immediately, taking a moment to process as we leisurely explore the museum. His gaze is steady, lost in contemplation. My heart races, waiting on pins and needles for his response. After what feels like an eternity, he opens up, "My former girlfriend and I split under bitter circumstances. She was unfaithful."

His candid admission renders me mute. I do what I can to offer solace, lightly touching his arm and mirroring his previous sentiment, "That's tough, Santi." He glances my way, a gentle smile gracing his lips as he covers my hand with his, murmuring, "I appreciate that."

As our shared adventure deepens, the sun kisses the horizon, casting a warm, golden sheen on our escapades. The day's close creeps up on us, and we agree it's time to bid adieu, but not before arranging a cocktail rendezvous for the next day. Inside, I'm celebrating with a mini happy dance.

This isn't your everyday farewell. It's loaded with light-hearted teasing and wordless promises, leaving a tantalizing anticipation for our ensuing rendezvous. Our laughter merges, initiating a vortex of exhilaration for tomorrow. As we take

By Nicky Ireland

our leave, the prospect of another day together adds a silver lining to our collective memory. An implicit challenge lingers in the air, silently concurring that our next gathering will only fortify our bond. Here's hoping!

"What's your poison then, Santi? A martini man, or do you prefer a classic old-fashioned?" I ask, breaking the silence as we meander out of the museum.

He chuckles, "I'm a man of simple tastes—whiskey on the rocks, and I'm all yours."

I grin, "I'll remember that for tomorrow. And just so you know, I'm a sucker for a good dry martini."

His laughter echoes through the quiet street, "I guess it's a date then."

Indeed, Santi, it is.

I head home, feeling like a brand new me. My heart is overflowing with hope and excitement for what the future holds. Even under Dublin's trademark rain clouds, I've got my very own pocket of sunshine. I'm brimming with the comforting reassurance that chivalry isn't dead after all.

I decide I need to get out some energy with a spot of housework. Today has been a wild roller coaster ride without a seat belt. And now, would you look at the time! It's late, but hey, this carpet isn't going to vacuum itself, right? So, here I am, about to wage war against dust bunnies, night owls be darned.

Now, there's Ben. Sweet, probably snoring, Ben. I reckon he's upstairs, lost in dreamland. I could march up there, knock on his door and give him a fair warning, but the thought of performing the scratch and sniff test near his room... let's just say it's as appealing as hugging a cactus.

So, what's a considerate roommate to do? Well, I'm about to compose an epic text message, something along the lines of "Brace yourself, the vacuum cleaner is coming!" Let the chips fall where they may!

Me: Hey Ben! Guess what? The sound you're hearing is not an alien invasion, it's just me and my faithful dust-busting buddy!

Ben: Seriously? At this ungodly hour, you're wrestling with the vacuum.

Me: Oh, Ben, you surprise me! I had no idea you were acquainted with the concept of a vacuum. Colour me impressed!

Ben: I've got an early start tomorrow. Can you give it a rest?

Me: But Ben, it's a laughter-filled cleaning party down here! You're missing out on my epic dance moves. Picture this - me, the vacuum, and a little bootie shake as we conquer the dust bunnies!

Ben: Enough! I'll take over the vacuum duties after work tomorrow. Just please, stop!

Me: It's a deal, Ben. Sweet dreams to you and your oh-so-sensitive ears!

Sitting on my bed with a hot cup of tea in hand, I can't stop my mind from replaying the day's events. My overactive imagination is having a field day right now.

Specific tastes

Chapter Eight

Specific tastes

Chapter eight

NICKY

The clock is ticking down to my reunion with Santiago tonight, and I can't contain my excitement! The day has been a whirlwind of wardrobe selection, finally settling on a knock-out, curve-hugging cobalt blue dress. It's got a daring neckline that gives just a peek of what's underneath, and it flares out just right at the waist, taking a page out of an old Hollywood starlet's playbook.

My hair is swinging in a lively ponytail, adding a dash of fun to the whole ensemble. I've gone light on the makeup, just enough to bring out my natural beauty without laying it on too thick. A touch of blush, a hint of mascara, a subtle gloss on my lips - it's all about balance, baby!

I've picked out a cosy little bar smack in the middle of the city for our rendezvous. It's usually a chill spot, perfect for leisurely chats while soaking in the inviting vibe.

This bar is a haven of warmth, with its rich mahogany interiors and comfy leather seats. I snag a booth right next to the crackling fireplace, an oasis of heat against the cool autumn night. The air is alive with the smell of seasoned wood and a comforting hint of peat smoke from the fire, blending beautifully with the faint aroma of traditional Irish whiskeys.

I beat Santiago to the bar, giving me a chance to sit back with a quick drink. I order my go-to, a sharp, dry martini, and a side of warm, buttery soda bread. As I settle into the soft leather seat, sipping on my delightful cocktail, I can't help but revel in the soothing hum of the bar's chatter and the distant strum of a fiddle, setting the stage for what I hope will be an unforgettable evening. Everything crossed!

By Nicky Ireland

As the soulful tune of 'Blackbird' by Séamus and Caoimhe Uí Fhlatharta reverberates around the room, I'm all ears. Just at that moment, Santi, the man of the night, rolls in. He's got this alluring vibe, like a magnet pulling everything towards him, me included. Here he is, sauntering confidently in my direction. Our eyes lock, his full of warmth and promise, and he shoots me a grin and a wink that sets the room ablaze.

His get-up is a total knockout: sleek black pants, boots to match, and a navy blue button-down, casually undone at the top. The shirt's open neckline offers a sneak peek into his ink collection, each piece revealing a slice of his journey. His earrings, catching the soft fireplace light, stir my curiosity. I'm barely holding back the impulse to stroll over and give those earlobes a playful nibble.

Santi steps in, his hand, large and warm, cups my face with a gentle certainty. Suddenly, it feels like we're in our own universe, a bubble away from the surrounding buzz. I tilt my head back, looking up at him with wide, starry eyes. His grin broadens, suggesting inside jokes and whispered secrets. Leaning in even closer, he lands a swift peck on my cheek before murmuring, "You look beautiful, Nicky."

He slides into the seat next to me, every move as smooth as a ballet dancers. With a casual flip of his wrist, he flags down a waiter to order his poison. I'm on tenterhooks, can't wait to hear his pick. "What's your poison tonight?" I ask, my voice laced with a thrill of anticipation. "I've got a soft spot for a solid whiskey," he reveals. His choice draws a chuckle from me, "Lucky you. This place is known for its killer whiskey collection."

As our server approaches our table, Santi, the epitome of nonchalance, makes his beverage selection, "A Suntory Hibiki 21 Mount Fuji, thanks." Our server appears as though he's just encountered an apparition. "Might I suggest some top-tier Irish whiskeys instead, Sir," he ventures, aiming to nudge Santi towards a more traditional choice for an Irish pub.

Unswayed, Santi courteously holds his ground, "Appreciate the suggestion, but my palate leans towards the Japanese variety. The Suntory Hibiki 21 Mount Fuji will do just fine, if that's not too much trouble." Our server's reaction resembles that of a man who's just received a verbal slap, and he scuttles off, evidently thrown off by such an audacious request in this emerald isle watering hole.

With an air of nonchalance, Santi pivots to address me, no trace of embarrassment etched on his features. "You do realize you might have just given the entire Irish community a mini heart attack with that order," I playfully jab, both tickled and somewhat star struck by his brazenness. "I'm a man of specific tastes, Nicky," he retorts, an intriguing twinkle in his eye suggesting a deeper meaning to his words. An electric wave of exhilaration courses through me.

As he reclines in the booth, his muscular silhouette testing the limits of his shirt, my eyes are irresistibly drawn to him. His gaze remains unwavering.

Matching his relaxed demeanour, I swivel to face him, folding one leg over the other and settling into the plush seat. "You do understand that the Irish are practically the godfathers of whiskey, don't you? The term 'whiskey' is derived from the Gaelic phrase uisce beatha, translating to 'water of life'," I counter, my heart racing at the prospect of catching him off guard.

Our light-hearted banter is disrupted by the reappearance of the server, who places Santi's chosen poison on the table, his scowl barely concealed. "Your Japanese whiskey, Sir," he grumbles, his tone seething with resentment. "Thank you", Santi replies, his unwavering composure unperturbed by the server's evident distaste. His authenticity is strangely captivating.

I observe him as he lifts his glass, savoring the whiskey's aroma before indulging in a slow, deliberate sip. Leaning back, a mischievous gleam in his eye, he announces, "There's no denying the appeal of Irish whiskey. The triple distillation process lends it a smooth, captivating flavor that sets it apart from its Scotch counterpart, which typically undergoes double distillation." I hang on to his every word, entranced by his impressive knowledge.

"But," he continues, "Japanese whiskey is renowned for its intricate and refined palate, a tribute to the premium ingredients and painstaking distillation technique. Both Irish and Japanese whiskeys have their unique allure and enjoy a venerable status in the spirits realm. Ultimately, it boils down to personal preference. As you may have surmised, mine are rather distinctive, Nicky."

I find myself unable to resist a cheeky quip. "Well, well, if it isn't a whiskey aficionado in our company," I tease, a playful twinkle lighting up my eyes. "I must commend you, your command over the complex art of distillation, the subtleties of tasting, and your profound admiration for the craft is nothing short of impressive. You've evidently dedicated a significant portion of your existence to the art of whiskey consumption. Could it be that you're secretly harbouring a wee bit of that Irish in you?"

The edges of his lips curve upwards, forming a self-satisfied smile at my teasing remark. I find myself compelled to extend my playful banter. "Should I consider addressing you as 'Santi the Sensational Sommelier', kind Sir?" I suggest, maintaining a light-hearted ambiance. He inhales deeply, his chest undulating with the rhythm of his concealed laughter. His enjoyment of my playful banter sends an electrifying thrill coursing through me.

"Just continue to call me Sir, Nicky," he retorts, his voice a rich, low timbre, "and it won't take you long to acquaint yourself with the affectionate nicknames I've been considering for you." His words send a wave of anticipation surging within me. There's an undeniable spark between us, a sense of mutual understanding, perhaps he even understands me better than I understand myself.

As we savor the smooth Japanese whiskies and crisp Dry Martinis, we exchange stories and share warm laughter, creating our own intimate universe. We're deeply engrossed in an animated conversation about our mutual passion for music, and how beautifully melodies can echo life's myriad experiences. Give me any song, and I'll expertly intertwine it into the narrative of my current circumstances. It's a skill that I'm quite proud of!

There's a strange yet comforting sensation, as if our paths had intertwined in a previous life. This elusive aura of trust and empathy is challenging to put into words, but it's undeniably present, quietly weaving its enchantment around us.

Rising from our cozy booth, Santi extends his hand towards me, his broad smile lighting up his face. "Shall we embark on a little adventure, Princesa?" he proposes, his tone teasing. I accept his hand, and with a shared chuckle, we bid our adieu to the bar. His hand, a comforting anchor, guides us through bustling Grafton Street, our destination the enchanting Saint Stephen's Green park.

As the crisp wind playfully nips at us, Santi casts a worried glance my way. "I hope you're not turning into an icicle, Princesa," he quips with a playful frown. His unexpected humour sends ripples of laughter between us, the affectionate nickname he's given me, 'Princesa,' causing my heart to flutter. With a theatrical flourish, he drapes his heavy, dark wool coat over my shoulders, pulling me closer. His coat provides a shield against the chilly air, but it's his soft kiss, planted on my forehead, that sends a delightful warmth coursing through me.

Our stroll through the park mirrors the pace of a lazy Sunday afternoon, the setting sun casting a vibrant canvas of oranges, yellows, and reds across the sky. It's a perfect reflection of the cozy fireside we'd left behind. Santi's occasional gentle touches on my arm punctuate our quiet exploration, his warmth seeping into me. Our shared silence, filled with understanding and care, creates a bubble of tranquility around us.

Upon discovering a secluded bench by a large pond, we're greeted by the spectacle of the setting sun's reflection dancing on the water surface. As if in a rehearsed play, Santi plops down first, then playfully beckons me onto his lap, wrapping his coat around me. Nestling against his chest, I find a comfortable spot at the crook of his neck, his scent - a captivating blend of leather, rich spices, and subtle sweetness - enveloping me.

"Santi," I begin, lifting my gaze to meet his. His eyes, soft and knowing, lock onto mine. He responds with a teasing, "I know, Princesa, you can't resist my charm." His words, laced with humour, acknowledge the silent conversation between us, addressing my bubbling uncertainty and longing. As he plants a soft kiss on my head and rests his chin on my hair, we soak in the enchanting sunset, time seemingly standing still. I hold onto him, desperate to etch this precious memory into my mind, our shared giggles echoing into the fading light.

SANTI

As I guide Nicky towards a waiting cab, an unexpected wave of attachment washes over me. There's something about her that arouses a sense of comfort and familiarity within me, as if we've known each other for more than just this brief encounter. I've always been a man who trusts his instincts, and they're pulling me towards her.

An intense need to ensure her safety sparks within me, urging me to accompany her all the way home. I want to cocoon her in my warmth, to stand as her guardian against the often harsh realities of the world. My heart is an overflowing fountain of yearnings and emotions, and I crave to show her the depths of my feelings. There's this wild hope inside me that she might understand, reciprocate, and maybe even bask in the glow of these shared sentiments. However, I am aware that it could be too soon, and Barcelona waits for me with the promise of a new dawn.

As she prepares to step into the taxi, I pull her back into a warm hug. It's a silent plea for her to sense the profound yearning that's pulsating within me. I want my fervour to seep into her, to stir any dormant desires she may secretly nurture. Her response is welcome, her arms encircling me with a strength that leaves me gasping for breath.

I release her for a brief moment, my eyes soaking in her features. Our gazes intertwine in a silent conversation, my hands tenderly cradling her face in a gesture that surprises even me. I lean closer, my eyes still locked onto hers, and my lips brush against hers in a gentle, lingering kiss.

Our lips meet in a revelation of softness and sweetness, tinged with the remnants of the Martini she had earlier and the cherry essence of her lip balm. As our lips part slightly, I seize the opportunity to gently nibble on her lower lip, our breaths ebbing and flowing in perfect harmony. I gently tug at her lip with my teeth, her soft moan resonating against my lips. The taste of her, the sensation of my tongue softly caressing hers, is pure bliss.

The sudden honk of the cab driver breaks our intimate bubble, bringing us back to the reality of the moment. I raise a finger, asking for just a little more of our stolen time. I tell her about my upcoming travels, my voice heavy with unspoken feelings, "I hope to see you again," I confess, each word resonating with hope.

Her smile lights up the night as she replies in a voice barely above a whisper, "please, I'd really love that." I plant a gentle kiss on her forehead, a soft promise, "I'll be in touch. Dream sweet, Princesa."

As the cab disappears into the distance, I'm left standing there, a strange sense of emptiness tugging at my heart. But I hold onto the hope that this isn't our goodbye, but rather, the opening chapter of a magical journey together.

NICKY

It's the heart of the evening, the time when night has fully claimed the day. The clock strikes ten, a peal that reverberates through my cozy abode. I'm deep in the throes of an Australian 'Married at First Sight' binge. They've got the melodrama nailed to perfection, each episode a tantalizing dance of emotions.

By Nicky Ireland

Suddenly, the silence is ruptured by the familiar creak of the door. In saunters Ben, my housemate. Ben, the man for whom personal hygiene is a once-a-month event. A man whose existence is perpetually accompanied by the scent of week-old pizza. But wait! He's not alone. Accompanying him is a young woman, pushing a baby pram. The plot, it seems, just took an unexpected twist!

With a complete disregard for the theatrical masterpiece unfolding on the screen, they plunk themselves right beside me on the couch, their presence casting a shadow over the escalating drama on TV. Well, there goes my 'Married at First Sight' marathon, cut off in its prime.

However, being the model of gentlemanly behavior that I am, I rise to the occasion, and introduce myself. Because in all honesty, Ben's manners are as lost as a ship in the Bermuda triangle. "Oh yeah, sorry, this is Sarah," Ben mumbles, the introduction falling out of his mouth like an afterthought.

"Hey Sarah," I greet her, my voice a beacon of light in the awkwardness. "Is this little munchkin yours? Anything you need?" I ask, my eyes bouncing between Sarah and the baby, trying to solve the mystery that just strolled into my living room.

"No thanks, I'm good. Yeah, she's my little one. She'll be turning half a year old in a few weeks. Hope we're not causing a disturbance? Ben mentioned you were cool," Sarah replies. Her voice is soft, a gentle melody that stands in stark contrast to Ben's gruff tone. I wave away her concerns with a nonchalant shrug. Ben may be a bit of a chaos magnet, but beneath the grime and pizza smell, he's a decent guy. And tonight, it seems, he's brought a new chapter into our sitcom of a life.

Time ticks by, and there's Ben, fumbling through an awkward attempt at snuggling up with Sarah. I can't help but feel a twinge of sympathy for the girl. She must have a severely impaired sense of smell if she's not repulsed by Ben's perpetual funk. I decide it's high time to make a swift exit, stealing a glance at the peacefully sleeping baby in the pram - a pocket-sized nugget of adorability.

With a parting grin at Sarah and a subtle nod to Ben, I make my escape to the haven of my bedroom, leaving them to their evening. Ben, with his signature eau de who-knows-what, Sarah exuding her quiet charm, and the baby, the only guilt-free participant in this unexpected sitcom.

Just as I'm about to board the rapid transit to dreamland, my phone chimes. A text from Ben, most likely lounging with Sarah, no doubt engrossed in some trashy TV show in the living room.

Ben: Hey, you still among the conscious?

Me: Only because of you, yes.

Ben: Sorry about that. Sarah just had a question, do you have a morning-after pill by any chance?

Me: Now why would she be pondering over that at this ungodly hour?

Ben: Err... we got a bit carried away and didn't have any protection.

Me: I'm at a loss for words, truly. And believe me, that's a rare occurrence.

Ben: She's just a smidge worried she might be cooking up a mini-me.

Me: You're joking, right? The wriggling infant in the pram didn't serve as a hint of the possible repercussions, no?

Ben: So, umm, do you have any?

Me: No Ben, I don't operate a pharmacy from my boudoir. She'll need to see her GP tomorrow, or pop into a pharmacy, or perhaps consult a sorcerer. I'm not the expert here.

Ben: Alrighty, thanks.

Me: Here's a friendly tip - prevention is definitely better than a midnight text to your drowsy housemate!

Good grief! What in the world is up with that man? Honestly, if there were a Bad Decisions Olympics, he'd be donning a gold medal by now.

As I try, and fail, to unravel his latest escapade, my eyelids start to defy my determination to stay awake. The struggle is real, but sleep, like a sly ninja, ambushes me and soon I'm out for the count.

Now, get ready for the dream I found myself in - it's the kind of dream that would make Freud redden and Picasso drop his palette in awe.

I'm amidst the hustle and bustle of Barcelona, enveloped by the heady scent of paella and the heart-tugging twangs of a flamenco guitar. And there, right in front of me, is the very definition of Spanish deliciousness - a man whose sun-kissed skin could make a bronzed Greek deity green with envy. His eyes, oh those deep emerald eyes, they're like precious gems twinkling with mischief and magnetism, luring me in like a flame tempts a moth.

And the tattoos, sweet heavens, the tattoos! They're not just any body art, they're the kind of tattoos that shout 'rebel' yet murmur 'I pen sonnets on Sundays'. Each inked masterpiece is a tale, a riddle waiting to be decoded.

I mean, seriously, if deliciousness took human form, Santiago Maspinco would be it. And all I can think is... Delicious! Now that's what I call a dreamy dessert - someone hand me a feckin' spoon!

Heaven is a place on earth

Chapter Nine

Heaven is a place on earth

Chapter Nine

NICKY

As the first light of dawn breaks over Dublin, I know Santi has already set off on his journey back to Barcelona, leaving me behind. I decide that in his absence, I'm going to dive headfirst into my career. Suddenly, the thought of giving my makeup artistry website a fresh, new look seems exciting. I even contemplate reaching out to a few creative agencies for potential collaborations. Today, I'm all about getting things sorted and organized. Keeping my racing mind occupied is key here.

Splashing through a reviving shower, I decide it's time for a shampoo party! As the warm water dances through my hair, it's like a magical worry-rinse - "Does he really like me? Will I see him again?" Yes, we're talking about those butterflies-in-the-stomach sort of worries.

With my hair still dripping wet and swaddled in a cozy towel, I make my way down the stairs to my kitchen. A comforting cup of coffee is just what I need to jumpstart my day.

Just as I'm about to start the coffee machine, my face lights up at the sight of Santi's face on my phone screen. Responding with a gentle "hey you", I'm met with a surprise. "I've changed my flight. I need to see you," he admits. His confession sends a wave of shock and excitement through me.

I'm about to shower him with a barrage of excited responses when a sudden knock at my door interrupts me. Keeping the phone pressed to my ear, I navigate my way to the front door. Opening it, I'm met with the bright beam of Santi's smile. "How about now?" he asks nonchalantly. Without a moment's delay, I bolt towards him, my heart pounding with anticipation. As I leap into his welcoming embrace, our lips unite in a fervent kiss that sets my soul ablaze. His powerful hands cradle my face, his fingers delicately tracing a path to the nape of my neck, gathering up my damp locks in his grasp. With an assertive yet tender shove, he directs me back into the sanctuary of my home, using his foot to kick the door closed behind him, shutting out the world.

His hand, like a caress of a summer breeze, gently strokes my neck, guiding me with an unwavering certainty towards the staircase. Using his firm grip as leverage, he gradually nudges me down onto the plush carpeted steps. The softness of the carpet cushions me, a stark contrast to the electrifying desires coursing through my veins.

The fervent yearning I harbor for him is an uncontainable wildfire, a tempest of passion threatening to consume me whole. I'm teetering on the precipice, caught between restraint and surrender. The time has come to let myself be swallowed by the inferno. It's time to dance in the flames!

As my towel tumbles from my grasp, his lips embark on a heated exploration of my neck, leaving a trail blazing with passionate kisses in their wake. His hand, like an adventurous explorer, ventures further, discovering the curve of my bare breast. A sudden nip on my neck sends a bolt of electrifying pleasure rippling through me, igniting a blaze that reaches the furthest corners of my soul.

I watch, my breath hitching, as he sinks to his knees before me. My legs instinctively wind around his waist, pulling him closer. Even the tiniest gap between us feels like a chasm too vast. The anticipation of this moment has been simmering within me for the past forty-eight hours, and I'm dangerously close to boiling over.

Swept up in this intoxicating whirlwind of passion, I revel in the warmth of his mouth as he tenderly teases my nipple between his lips. Our breaths mingle, a palpable testament to the lust-charged tension that binds us. He begins to shrug off his jacket, the fabric sliding off his broad shoulders at a tantalizingly slow pace. His fingers, with the precision of a skilled pianist, make their way to the zipper of his pants, pulling it down in a suspenseful motion that leaves me utterly

By Nicky Ireland

breathless.

With an urgency that pulses through our very beings, my fingers find their way to his luxuriant, dark locks, pulling him nearer with a fervor that sends currents of raw desire coursing through my body, magnetizing me to his. My gaze is ensnared, caught in the breath-taking spectacle that unfolds as he unveils his seriously large cock. Holy feckballs! It stands tall, powerful and commanding, a testament to his virility. The pulsing veins that trace its length are like paths on an explorer's map, and the glistening tip, covered in delicious pre-cum, promises untold delights, a thrilling preview of the euphoria that is yet to engulf us. I'm utterly entranced, held captive by this sight. His body is a living work of art, a testament to the unparalleled beauty of the masculine form.

Seizing control with an effortless grace, his sturdy hands tenderly guide my legs apart, baring my pussy to his intense scrutiny. A journey commences as his gaze travels down the landscape of my body, finally coming to a halt at the intersection of my thighs. Our eyes meet in a profound exchange of understanding, a silent testament to the shared intensity of this moment. A playful smile graces his lips, and in an almost conspiratorial whisper, he murmurs 'mi diabla'. The words ignite a wild blaze within me, a fiery need that threatens to consume me whole.

I silently thank my lucky stars for the Spanish classes I chose to take in secondary school. The language lessons have now become a tantalizing tool in our arsenal of desire, adding an extra dash of spice to our passionate encounters. And the colorful Spanish slang I've picked up along the way? It's the cherry on top of this delectable sundae of seduction!

His head descends, drawing ever closer to my eager pussy, his tongue embarking upon an enchanting journey through my now soaking wet folds. This isn't a hurried affair, no. It's a patient, conscious survey, as if I'm a rare, costly delicacy that he's intent on savoring. I have no hope of repressing the sounds of pleasure that escape my lips. The longing coursing through me is unlike anything I've ever experienced, a ferocious tempest of pure, unrefined desire.

His fingers gently part my pussy lips, carving out a trail for his tongue to delve further, to uncover the very core of my being. The sound of his satisfied groans sends delightful shivers through my body, a heavenly feeling that leaves me trembling. Two of his fingers locate my entrance, plunging deep within and emerging drenched with my wetness. He removes them from my pussy, his eyes locking with mine, a determined, unyielding expression on his face.

Guiding his wet fingers over my erect nipples, the contact feels like a spark setting my skin aflame. The sensation of my own arousal being smeared over their sensitive tips sends a wave of pleasure crashing through me. His fingers continue on their journey, ending up at my mouth. "Open," he commands in a low, rumbling voice that leaves no room for argument. Obediently, I comply.

His fingers, slick with my own essence, trace a tantalizing path over my lips before he slowly pushes them into my mouth. "Taste yourself," he directs, his voice husky with desire. I obey, swirling my tongue around his fingers, savoring my own taste, relishing every drop. His attentive stare, his deep green eyes clouded with longing, intensifies the entire experience.

"Are you on birth control, mi princesa?" His inquiry, a blend of concern and desire, hangs in the air between us. I catch my breath, nodding, and manage a whispered "yes". Our eyes meet, a spark of relief ignites in his gaze as he reassures me, "I am clean". Exhale! The feeling is mutual. My last relationship ended with a comprehensive medical examination and since then, it's been just me, myself, and I. Apparently, Santi has been on a similar solitary journey.

With our concerns discarded as easily as an old pair of socks, his lips find mine in a slow, deliberate kiss that sends a frisson of anticipation down my spine. His tongue embarks on a journey around my mouth, savoring the lingering taste of our shared desire. He teasingly captures my lower lip between his teeth, sending a thrill of joy zipping through me. This is an incredible, passionate moment, filled with an urgency that has us both entranced, enveloped in a world where only we exist.

I can feel the insistent pressure of his rock-hard cock nudging against my pussy.

By Nicky Ireland

His hips, strong and determined, gently urge forward in a noiseless entreaty. As he begins to fill me, slowly, deliberately, a gasp escapes my lips, a testament to the anticipation of being completely consumed by him. My fingers, like talons, dig into the solidness of his shoulders, pulling him closer, compelling him deeper inside me.

He displays a patience that speaks volumes, allowing me to adjust to him, inch by measured inch, even as our lips remain fused together, our breaths stolen in quick, irregular bursts. His hand, bold and curious, ventures into uncharted territory, fingers dancing over my skin in a quest to discover my throbbing clit. His thumb embarks on a rhythmic journey, tracing tight, methodical orbits around it, sending bolts of electrifying pleasure coursing through my veins.

Our lips part, and our gazes, weighted with desire, lock. A silent conversation is shared, a mute dance of longing that leaves us gasping for air, our mouths agape in a tableau of raw, unchecked desire. The tempo of his movements quickens, each thrust a testament to his strength, stretching me, filling me. We surrender ourselves to the sensation, our heads thrown back in the throes of passion. The promise of our impending release lingers in the air, tantalizingly within our grasp. I'm on the brink of cumming, yearning to crest the summit of this rapturous symphony alongside him.

When his climax arrives, it's like a runaway freight train, unstoppable and powerful. A deep, primal growl escapes him, a roar of satisfaction echoing in the stillness. His eyes, twin pools brimming with pleasure, remain locked onto mine. He fills me with every drop of his cum, and in reaction, my own climax washes over me, my body contracting around him in a vice-like grip. Our shared climax mingles together, a silky testament to our mutual arousal that tickles our senses and trickles down our throbbing thighs.

In the aftermath, our bodies lie entwined, our breaths ragged and uneven. I'm certain of only one thing: heaven isn't merely a destination you reach at the end of life's journey. No, heaven is in the here and now, in the warmth and comfort of his arms. Every moment spent with him is a slice of heaven, a testament to our shared intense passion.

The following morning, the golden rays of the morning sun stream through the window, bathing my living room in a warm, glorious light. It feels as if we're two wide-eyed kids waking up to the rush of Christmas morning. We're nestled comfortably on the couch, the inviting aroma of freshly brewed coffee filling the air, our hands gently knotted in a moment of tranquility.

Santi's flight to Barcelona is scheduled to take off in a matter of hours, and from there, he'll be jetting off to Dublin airport. Eager to savor every precious moment we have together, I volunteer to play chauffeur. But Santi, in his stubborn charm, insists on sticking to his cab plan.

We're so engrossed in each other, our conversation flowing effortlessly, punctuated by bouts of laughter and moments of shared silent glances. Each kiss feels like a dance, passionate and fervent, stirring memories of the previous night. Let's just put it this way, sleep wasn't a high priority on our agenda. Santiago Maspinco, what a whirlwind of an adventure it's been! His infectious energy has me completely swept up. Discovering our desires are so exquisitely matched is more than just satisfying. The realization that Santi leans towards the dominant side sends thrilling shivers down my spine.

He's just as thrilled, if not more, to learn of my inclination towards the submissive side. We spent last night delving into our past relationships, discussing what was lacking, particularly behind closed doors. Our narratives are startlingly similar, our wants and needs mirroring each other. It's hard not to believe that our meeting was anything short of destiny.

As I stoke the fire, adding more logs and watching the flickering light play around the room, Santi playfully snatches my phone. He offers to save his work and home numbers himself, while I tend to the fire.

The moment he punches in the passcode, an unexpected silence descends upon the room. I glance over to find him smirking at me, an eyebrow raised in amusement as he flips my phone in my

direction. My heart skips a beat as I spot the impromptu photo I had taken of him during our first encounter at Trinity. In that moment, I wish for a sinkhole to appear and save me from the wave of embarrassment washing over me!

Feeling the heat rise in my cheeks, on par with the flames crackling in the fireplace, I stumble over my words. But Santi, always the tease, drops to his knees, his contagious laughter ringing out in the room, basking in the moment of my discomfort. He manages to choke out, between bouts of laughter, "desnúdate." Without a second thought, I comply. His next words, "I'm about to make your ass as red as your cheeks, mi diabla," send a rush of anticipation coursing through my veins, a thrilling promise of what's to come.

SANTI

With a sense of authority lingering in the air, I signal for Nicky to rise and undertake the ceremonious shedding of her clothing. Her compliance is immediate, commencing the striptease as I leisurely make myself comfortable on the couch. The anticipation is palpable, as she has developed an uncanny knack for turning the ordinary into a tantalizing spectacle.

Finding my place amidst the plush cushions of the couch, I lean back, indulging in the spectacle unfolding before me. She reveals herself with a slow grace that is nothing short of captivating. Once the final garment falls to the floor, she stands still, her hands clasped demurely at her front, her eyes eager, and awaiting my next command. So obedient, so wonderfully compliant. With a playful grin, I pat my knee, a silent invitation for her to lay across my lap. She moves with graceful obedience, her eyes holding mine captive as she drapes herself across my lap. The contact sends a thrill of anticipation through us both. A quick, playful slap to her ass elicits a startled cry, followed by a giggle that echoes through the room.

"Lift your ass up, mi putita," I instruct, a faint smile playing on my lips. She complies, and I take a moment to appreciate the sight. Her skin, bare and inviting under my gaze, has me drawing a deep, appreciative breath.

Owned — A BDSM Erotic Romance

Brushing my hand over the curve of her ass, I ask in a low voice, "Do you understand your punishment, mi putita?" She nods, a glimmer of mischief in her eyes.

"And why is that, Nicky?" I inquire, the playful note in my voice apparent.

With a giggle, she replies, "For secretly capturing your handsome face on camera." Her confession sends us both into a fit of laughter, her body shaking with mirth on my lap.

A light smack on her ass brings her giggling to a halt, replaced by a gasp of surprise. I shoot her a teasing smirk, "You know, mi amor, paparazzi activities are no longer permitted."

She nods, a mix of amusement and understanding crossing her face. "Understood, no more covert photography of strange, yet irresistibly attractive men," she says, her tone playful.

We share a moment of laughter, the room filled with a sense of intimacy and shared humor. It's these moments of light-hearted banter, paired with our passionate connection, that sends waves of joy and pleasure coursing through us. This is our world, a blend of fun, passion, and an undeniable bond.

"I'm going to spank you ten times. Understand?" I ask with a twinkle in my eye. She grins and nods. "I want you to count each one, can you do that for me?" She responds with a playful roll of her eyes, "I can count, you know." I laugh and start the playful punishment, setting a light, ticklish pace.

By the time I reach the fifth smack, I've increased the strength a bit, and she's wriggling underneath me, trying to stifle her soft moans. I lean close and whisper, "Everything alright, Princesa?" She turns to look at me with a mischievous grin, "Oh, absolutely!" The playful tension between us is electric, and it's clear we're both enjoying this.

The seventh smack lands and I can't help but feel a rush of desire. "Are you counting?" I tease, to which she gasps in faux shock, "I lost track, you'll have to

81

start over!" I laugh, pulling her in for a passionate kiss. It's a moment teetering between laughter and longing, and it's absolutely perfect.

As we pull away from the kiss, I unzip my pants, and she looks at me with a knowing smirk. "What's this?" She asks, feigning innocence. I smirk, "Well, I was hoping you could help me out with something...". "Always needing help, aren't you?" Before I can respond, she leans in, and I let out a sigh of pure pleasure.

My eyes never leave her as she teases me, her blue eyes sparkling with mischief. When she pulls away, she runs her finger along the head of my rock-hard cock, swirling her fingertips around my pre-cum and with a raised eyebrow asks, "Is this what you wanted help with?" Then, she brings her wet fingers to my lips, slowly watching as she covers my lips in my own arousal before we share a playful, passionate kiss.

I reach up to tangle my hand in her hair, pulling her back down towards my cock sharply. As she returns to her task, I can't help but let out a low moan. But I'm also concerned for her comfort. "You alright, mi amor?" I ask, lifting my hand from the top of her head and she nods, a wicked grin on her face, "Better than alright. But don't get too comfortable, I'm just getting started." The boldness of her statement sends a thrill through me, and I can't help but let out a groan.

As we continue, she guides my hand back to her hair. It's an unspoken invitation to keep up the intensity of our play. The sensual tension between us is punctuated by soft breaths and teasing, a perfectly passionate moment we're both lost in.

The tension between us is palpable, a sizzling power play threatening to boil over. The mischievous glint in her eyes speaks volumes, she knows exactly what she's doing and the effect she has on me. "Drink Papi's cum, mi diabla," I command, and she obeys. As I hold her head still, her lips engulfing me completely, firmly at the base of my cock.

She flashes me a cheeky grin, her response a playful challenge, "Careful, you might just get what you're asking for." Her lips, lusciously soft, envelop me fully, completely. A sensation so divine, it sends me spiraling and I cum with a guttural roar, shooting cum into the back of her throat and like the good girl she is, she swallows every single drop.

The room fills with a sense of satisfaction, of fulfilment. I can't help but let out a satisfied sigh. "You're a fiend, you know that?"

Her glimmering eyes meet mine, a spark of wicked delight dancing within them. "And you wouldn't have me any other way," she retorts.

This is bliss. Pure, unadulterated bliss. And in that moment, I know without a shadow of a doubt that I am irrevocably hers. She has cast a spell on me, one that binds and holds me captive in the most pleasurable way.

This moment, this connection—it's an intense passion that sends surges of pleasure coursing through us both. It's a dance of desire, a playful exchange, a passionate encounter that leaves us both breathless. It's everything we are, everything we're becoming, and everything we will be. Pure, utter heaven.

Love letters

Chapter Ten

Love Letters

Chapter Ten

NICKY

Days are whizzing by since Santi hit the road, and boy, does a chock-a-block work diary come in handy for a welcome distraction! The pang for him seems cuckoo, but hey, that's just the crazy maze I'm navigating right now. Our day is crammed with ping-pong text messages and quickie phone chats, each brimming with more than just a casual 'hey' or a mushy line.

Every 'hello' we toss isn't just a hi-fi, it's our personal lighthouse, a nudge reminding us of our footprints in this vast world. Our texts are sprinkled with goofy emojis mirroring our mood du jour - a grinning one when we're on cloud nine, a glum one when the day's been a bummer.

The whispered sweet nothings aren't nothing - they're our everything. Each one is a cozy virtual hug, a digital squeeze. We swap chucklesome snippets from our day, narrating the tiniest, supposedly inconsequential tidbits that paint our individual worlds. We chinwag about the page-turners we're devouring, the music we are loving, the grub we're digging into, even the zany dreams from the previous night.

These messages are our lifeline, our umbilical cord to each other. They're the threads sewing together our bond's tapestry, making the miles between us shrink a tad. As we sail this sea of distance, these glyphs on a screen, the voices in our ears, morph into more than mere words - they're our intimacy, our shared slice of life in a world that insists on playing keep-away.

Later that day, as I step into my castle, a sea of letters sprawls across the "welcome" mat, cheerfully waving hello to my toes. A dramatic sigh slips out as I gear up for the inevitable paper showdown. Diving into the pile, my fingers

By Nicky Ireland

freeze on a cream-colored treasure, its elegant script whispering "To Mi Princesa, Nicky". A wave of feels crashes over me, but I quickly surf it away, clutching onto hope.

Deciding a cup of piping hot herbal tea is in order before I dare to unlock the secrets of this handwritten time capsule, I let the suspense simmer. Fingers crossed it's not a Dear John letter, with the familiar ghost of rejection spookily floating around my mind.

As I tango with some deep-seated worries, a twosome of fears keeps cutting in - the fear of rejection and the fear of being left alone. These fears, like pesky poltergeists, pop up, casting a gloomy cloud over my sunny disposition. For years, they've been holding me hostage, putting a damper on my emotional growth and well-being.

These fears, born from past heartbreaks, have often had me clinging like a koala to relationships that were about as fulfilling as a diet of eucalyptus leaves. The horror of solitude, the fright of isolation, had me stuck in emotional quicksand, making me stick around in relationships that I knew, in my gut, weren't my happily-ever-after.

But, plot twist! Ever since I found myself flying solo, I've been wrestling these ancient fears and worries. Every week, I've been teaming up with a super therapist, mustering all my courage to shove away these pesky feelings that have been calling the shots in my life for far too long. With each new sunrise, I'm on a mission to vanquish these fears and seize back control of my joy and my journey.

I plop down into a comfy chair, excitement now bubbling in my chest. In my hands, the envelope unfurls, each crease whispering tales of my special bond with Santi. I can't help but hope it means as much to him as it does to me.

My heart does a little jig as I spot his handwriting. The faint aroma of him wafts from the pristine cream paper, a unique blend that's so Santi. It's like a cocktail of soft leather and a zesty punch of tobacco. It's like being wrapped up in a warm

Santi-hug.

This scent, a sensory postcard from Santi, is pure magic. More than just an aroma, it's a time machine. His words suddenly feel amplified, as if he's right here, whispering softly in my ear. With this sensory anchor, I dive deeper into the present, ready to soak up his penned-down thoughts.

Mi Princesa, Nicky

You're all I think about, awake or asleep.

I hope I'm as much on your mind.

I can't wait to see you again. That's a promise.

Until we're together again.

Te necesito,

Santi XO

Holding the precious letter close, a goofy smile takes over my face. This isn't some run-of-the-mill email, or a text message, it's a love letter, brimming with affection and attention to detail. Every word isn't just ink splashed on paper, it's an echo of a heart that beats in tandem with mine.

I pull the letter closer, taking a deep breath. The spiced-leather scent fills my senses, almost overpowering, yet soothing. More than just a smell, it's him, it's us, it's a silent witness to our shared laughter and secret whispers.

Eyes shut, I let nostalgia take over. My mind saunters through a memory lane bathed in the soft glow of a shared sunset, as fresh as if it happened yesterday. I remember his woolen coat, a shield against the crisp autumn air and the world.

Every word, every scent, every memory sparked by this letter finds a home in my heart, a testament to the love that refuses to be dwarfed by distance. This letter is more than just words on a page, it's a lifeline, a lighthouse in the storm of his absence. It's a piece of his heart in my hands, a symbol of love that stands strong across miles. It's more than a letter; it's Santi with me, a priceless comfort that means the world to me.

Snuggled up in the pillowy sanctuary of my top-choice seat, cradling a cozy cup of fragrant herbal tea like it's my most treasured possession. I give myself a beat to soak in the tranquil scent that's dancing in the air before daring to take a sip. The instant it hits my lips, a sigh of pure bliss escapes me. Nestled in my lap is my phone, my magical portal to a universe of rhythm and rhyme. I flip it open and waltz right into the Spotify app, running my thumb over a treasure trove of tunes that have become the background score of my existence. Seeing one of my current favourite tunes, I can't stop my finger from hitting play.

Just like that, the room's awash with the spellbinding start of Ruth B's 'Dandelions'. I kick back, letting the plush chair cushion my head, and shut my eyes. It's as if someone hit the pause button on the world, leaving just me and Ruth B's soul-stirring serenade.

As the lyrics weave their way into the quiet, I find myself diving headfirst into each word. Every verse, every chorus, rings true to my own experiences and feelings. I can't help but get swept up in the raw, unfiltered truth of the song.

Cozied up in my cushy chair, cradled by the warmth of my tea, I'm in a state of absolute Zen. The music washes over me, bringing a tidal wave of pure, uncut joy. This is my happy place. This is pure bliss.

As night falls, cozily cocooned in my bed, I figure it's prime time to slide into a cheeky text banter with Santi.

Me: Hey from the land of fluffy marshmallow clouds and rainbow unicorns! Guess what's causing a ruckus in my head?

Santi: Hey there, mi Princesa. The anticipation's killing me!

Me: You're so bold, Mr. Maspinco!

Santi: Just kidding. Spill the beans.

Me: It's you! All you. Every delicious bit of you is throwing a rave in my mind, you absolute charmer.

Santi: Princesa, you're making me wish I could pop over there and give that gorgeous ass a hard smack for getting me all riled up here.

Me: Oopsie! I seem to have misplaced my halo.

Santi: My sassy little devil!

Me: Sweetest dream my beautiful man, xoxo.

Santi: Sweet dreams Princesa, xoxo.

I put my phone down only to be disturbed once more. A text from my BFF, Liam.

Liam: We've got a predicament here.

Me: Oh Jesus, what's occurred?

Liam: I believe I've crossed over.

Me: Excuse me?

By Nicky Ireland

Liam: I've never been so high in my life. I feel like I'm dying. Or perhaps I'm already dead. I can't tell, Nic.

Me: Alright, cookie monster.

Liam: Who's that?

Me: Never mind. Are you capable of moving?

Liam: For what reason? Am I in the way?

Me: I'm referring to your limbs. Can you move them?

Liam: They're dancing on their own.

Me: And your location would be?

Liam: I believe I'm in paradise.

Me: Any celestial portals in sight?

Liam: Certainly not.

Me: Are you experiencing warmth?

Liam: Indeed, and I'm perspiring profusely. Oh lord, what's the situation, Nic!

Me: I knew it, you're in the underworld.

Liam: Oh Jesus H Christ, Nic!

Me: Wrong deity for your current locale, Liamo.

Liam: Shite! Do you have a key to my apartment?

Me: I do. For what purpose?

Liam: You need to get rid of my 'novelty' items. I can't be 'that guy' when they find my body.

I can't contain my laughter, but I know I need to take action. So, I decide I'd better hop in my car, to check on Liam. But before I hit the road, I make a quick pit stop at the local shop. I pick up some food, hoping it might help to 'sober' him up. I'm not sure if it works the same way with weed as it does with alcohol, but who knows. The whole situation is just too funny.

So, here I am, having an impromptu sleepover at Liam's place. You'll never believe what I walked into. Liam, sprawled out on the kitchen floor, stripped down to his grundies, gazing intently at the ceiling as if he's having a deep, philosophical conversation with the light fixtures. You'd think he was auditioning for a role in a low-budget, avant-garde remake of 'The Starry Night'.

With a sigh, I gather him up, tuck him into bed, and hope he sleeps off whatever cosmic journey he's on. He's as high as a kite that broke its strings and is now drifting somewhere over the Antarctic. And can you guess the culprit? Weed-laced cookies.

Morning comes, and Liam is still floating somewhere in the stratosphere. Honestly, I have no clue how much cannabis he crammed into those cookies, but if I had to guess, I'd say he used a whole marijuana plantation. A mental note is quickly scribbled in my mind: 'At Liam's, bring your own cookies and tea. You don't want to end up having a heart-to-heart with the toaster!'

So, there you have it. My unexpected sleepover at Liam's. Who knew a Tuesday evening could be this eventful?

My sanctuary

Chapter Eleven

My sanctuary

Chapter Eleven

SANTI

Just a few weeks ago, I waved goodbye to Dublin and hello to my home in Barcelona. Yet, the effervescent spirit of a certain Miss Nicky still sparkles brightly in the chambers of my heart. It's like I'm playing a never-ending game of hide-and-seek with her in my thoughts, a welcome interruption from the daily grind.

My apartment, nestled like a hidden treasure in the heart of Barcelona's Gothic Quarter, is my refuge from the storm of professional life. It's my hideout where I escape after the culinary battles in my restaurants, a place to recharge and refresh. Further south, in the whisper-quiet neighborhood of Bellamar, I've a mansion that's my secret haven for tranquility. I can almost see Nicky there, her vibrant presence adding a new dimension to the tranquility, sooner, I hope, rather than later.

In the culinary universe, I've carved my name with a constellation of Spanish restaurants and bars studded across Europe. But my love for food and cooking didn't just pop up like a mushroom—it's a legacy, a culinary baton passed to me by my dear grandfather, José. His footsteps were my roadmap to becoming a celebrated chef, and his passion for food became mine. His departure in my early twenties was like losing a compass, but he left me with not just memories, but also a hefty inheritance.

With that inheritance as my starter dough, I leapt into my culinary adventure. After honing my skills at the esteemed Culinary School of Barcelona, a breeding ground for world-class chefs, I wisely poured my resources into my passion. Now, at a sprightly 32, I bask in the pride of owning a successful chain of restaurants. I can almost hear José's hearty laugh, his eyes twinkling with pride at how I've risen using the love for food he cultured in me.

Even with my pockets filled from my inheritance and the flourishing of my restaurants, I've kept my feet on the ground. I've never let the clink of coins muffle my values or distort my view. In fact, the wealth has only added more logs to the fire of my passion for food, and strengthened my resolve to create indelible dining experiences. I firmly believe that success isn't about the weight of your wallet, but the weight of love and passion you put into your work—and by that scale, well, I'm tipping it over!

In the heart of Barcelona's old city, right in the thick of the Gothic Quarter, there's my apartment and I'm absolutely head over heels for it. Why? You might ask. Well, for starters, its location is beyond compare - nestling between the vivacious La Rambla and the bustling Via Laietana, and tucked between the picturesque Mediterranean seafront and the Ronda de Sant Pere. It's like the heart in the body of the Ciutat Vella district.

The Gothic Quarter is like a bottomless goodie bag of the city's most ancient parts - it's got bits of Barcelona's Roman wall and a whole bunch of medieval landmarks that can make any history buff squeal with delight.

Now, nestled in this historic goldmine is my beloved apartment, a radiant sanctuary that is a beautiful mish-mash of traditional Spanish allure and slick, modern aesthetics. Splashes of colour in the form of Spanish art and colorful rustic furniture jazz up the place, making it a vibrant canvas of creativity and warmth.

This apartment is no shoebox - with a generous 146 m² (or 1572 sqFt) of space, it's more like a mini mansion. It boasts two bathrooms, one of which is ensuite to the master bedroom, five fabulous rooms including a kitchen, dining room, living room, an office, and a TV/music room, and four additional cozy bedrooms. And as if that's not enough, there's a terrace, a lift for when your feet need a break, and a caretaker who's always ready to lend a hand. Oh, and did I mention the south-facing orientation that ensures sunlight pours in all day like an invited guest?

And FYI, the apartment's terrace offers a killer view of the breath-taking Gothic Quarter, adding a dash of magic to the place. It's not just a living space, but a source of endless inspiration and a love letter to Barcelona's rich history.

As the day's hustle and bustle winds down, I retreat to my private nook on the terrace. Settling into my trusty old chair that's been my silent companion through countless evenings, I drink in the night air. It's crisp and slightly chilly, but it's a refreshing contrast to the day's heat and commotion. And just like that, with the cool breeze on my face and the vibrant city at my feet, I'm smitten all over again.

I nestle into my plush chair, my fingers dancing over to snatch a Cohiba. The promise of its bold, hearty taste is a thrill in and of itself. The practiced ceremony of setting it aflame is slow and deliberate, a nod to countless similar nights basking in my own company. As the initial wisp of smoke twirls upwards, the day's pressures seem to evaporate. The urban jungle stretches out under my watchful eyes, a spectacle of shimmering lights and hushed whispers. I look on, captivated by the sight, the cigar's scent weaving itself into the evening breeze.

Cradled in my hand is a glass of Westward Whiskey, Pinot Noir cask finished - an ideal libation for a serene night such as this. Each gulp is relished, the silky liquor blazes a warm trail down my throat, kindling a cozy glow from within. The distinct fusion of flavors is a sensory expedition, each mouthful a tribute to the artisanal skill embedded in its creation.

In the backdrop, the soothing strains of Matthew and The Atlas's 'Gutter Heart' permeates the apartment. Each chord is a tender murmur, reverberating through the rooms and spilling out onto the terrace. The music is my steadfast ally, its rhythm seeping into the silence of the evening. The symphony of the instruments, entwined with the potent lyrics, magnifies the peace of the night. The world recedes, and in these instances, I am in harmony, submerged in my own snug bubble of satisfaction.

As the evening unfurls, drenched in peaceful tranquility and a sense of accomplishment, I find myself leisurely strolling towards the haven of my bedroom. The gentle drone of the bustling city beneath my apartment serves as a soothing background score to my solitude. I nestle into the cushy comfort of my bed, with the phone nestled in my hand like a lifeline. My fingers, almost on autopilot, punch in Nicky's digits. An undeniable yearning for her voice rings inside me.

"Hello, princesa," I drawl, my words a gentle whisper as she picks up. My voice, laced with a warmth and familiar fondness, lingers between us in the air.

"Santiago?" she queries, her voice tinged with surprise and a hint of bemusement. "Is it really you?"

"Indeed, it's yours truly, Nicky," I confirm, a soft smile gracing my face. "What's up?" I inquire, a genuine curiosity for the minutest details of her day, her thoughts, her emotions.

A brief pause ensues, the silence punctuated only by the rhythm of our shared breaths over the line. "I'm good, didn't expect your call tonight, we chatted so much today. Not that I'm complaining, mind you." she chuckles, her laughter a soothing antidote to my longing. "And what about you?" she returns the question.

"Feeling better," I confess, "much better now that I'm listening to your voice, mi princesa." I can almost picture her, miles apart, blushing at my words. Her soft gasp echoes through the phone, tugging at my heartstrings. "Same here, Santi. Same here," she whispers back, her sigh echoing with a hint of relief and affection.

With a heart filled with hope, I ask, "How about planning a trip to Barcelona soon?" The question, pregnant with potential, fills the air.

A short pause follows before her voice rings with an unmistakable excitement, "Yes, yes, absolutely, Santi!" Her joy mirrors on my face as a wide grin. "I'll sort out everything for you, princesa," I propose, keen to facilitate her travels.

"Really, Santi? Are you sure?" she probes, her voice wavering with a bit of uncertainty.

"Absolutely," I confirm, my words brimming with confidence. "I'll ping you all the details. Come over, spend some time with me. I miss you," I confess, my voice thick with longing and desire.

Her reply is a mere whisper, "Oh Santi, I can't shake you off my mind. I know it sounds bonkers. I just..." Her voice peters out, the silence echoing with her vulnerability.

Cutting her off, I assure her, "I'm right there with you, Nicky. You're always on my mind. The last face I see before I drift off to sleep, and the first thought as I wake up. You've become a permanent resident in my thoughts."

Her enthusiasm is palpable, practically bouncing off the walls in her declaration, "Santi, I'm practically counting down the seconds until I see you!"

"You'll see me before you know it" my voice a cocktail of calm and desire in one.

The call wraps up, and I soon sink into a serene sleep, my heart light with the confirmation of our mutual affection. She's on her way to join me, and that thought sends a delightful shiver of anticipation running through my veins. I can't wait to catch a glimpse of her twinkling eyes, to feel the comforting heat of her touch, and to let her into my universe.

Downward dog

Chapter Twelve

Downward dog

Chapter Twelve

NICKY

I'm still grinning from ear to ear, thanks to a surprise call from Santi last night. Fast-forward to this morning, I crack open my email at 9 sharp and boom! There it is - my flight details from Dublin to Barcelona, courtesy of the ever-efficient Santi. In just seven days, I'll be soaring through the skies to meet the man who's got me head over heels. The Barcelona escapade countdown is on, and the butterflies in my stomach are doing somersaults!

Moving on to the next item on my to-do list, a yoga session with my partner in crime, Liam. We're religious about hitting the studio thrice a week - it's our workout of choice. It keeps us fit and sane, and with Liam around, it's always a hoot.

Our Dublin yoga haunt is a picture of quaint charm, and we've claimed our regular spots in the class. Despite being yoga veterans, some poses still give us a run for our money. But our all-time love remains the Downward Dog - the poster child of yoga poses. It's the first pose you learn when you dip your toe in the yoga pool, and it's a staple in most sessions.

I'm a Downward Dog devotee as it stretches my hamstrings and calves, a blessing for someone who's up on their feet all day. Plus, it's good for strengthening arms and legs. Liam, ever the melodramatic, swears by this pose as it eases his perennial backache, a condition he never misses a chance to whine about. My snappy comeback? "Spend less time flat on your back, and you might dodge the backache bullet!" His indignant glare is met with my cheeky challenge, "What's up, Liam Murphy, ready for a showdown?" His mock horror always has me in splits.

By Nicky Ireland

As we gear up for our pose, we get down on all fours, aligning wrists with shoulders and knees with hips. We curl our toes and push back through our hands, lifting our hips and straightening our legs. We fan our fingers, rotate our upper arms and broaden our collarbones, letting our heads hang loose and guiding our shoulder blades towards our hips.

With Liam's nose nearly brushing against my ass, I spot an opportunity for some mischief. I whisper, "Hey, Liamo, guess what?", and he looks up, retorting, "What, witch?". Keeping a poker face, I give him a cheeky wink and say, "I downed a pint of Guinness for breakfast!" He loses his balance and tumbles out of his pose, and we're both laughing our heads off, much to the chagrin of the other class members.

We're indeed a pair of cheeky yoga pranksters. We're far from being the teacher's pets, but hey, we wouldn't want it any other way!

That evening, we decide it's time to shake things up. The weekend is here and we're ready to plunge into the lively city nightlife, sip some mouth-watering cocktails, and move to the beat. Dressed to the nines, we're off to the acclaimed Cocktail Club in the heart of Dublin. Liam, looking dashing in his dark shirt unbuttoned just enough to show off his tattoos and toned body, his jeans highlighting his athletic physique. He's clearly ready to turn his chronic back pain into a dance partner!

As for me, I go for slim dark jeans coupled with a sparkly silver top. My favourite choker adds just the right touch to the plunging neckline. Liam, ever the joker, teases me about whether the choker reminds me of Santiago. And he even tries to pull off a Spanish accent - so bad it's funny! I reward him with a friendly punch on the arm and strut off to our waiting cab, his laughter trailing behind me.

Liam's always been supportive, especially now when it comes to Santi. He knows all about my disastrous relations past. Now, I can't help but hope he finds someone special - he deserves all the happiness in the world.

Upon entering The Cocktail Club in Dublin, we are immediately swept up in the infectious energy of the pulsating crowd. This hidden gem, nestled behind an elaborate art deco door in the heart of the city, morphs into the ultimate hotspot when the sun goes down. Stepping through its threshold is akin to a time-travel journey, transporting us back to the glittering allure of the Roaring Twenties. A clandestine haven boasting an impressive array of spirits, a myriad of award-winning cocktails, and delectable nibbles is revealed to us.

As the sultry tones of Rita Ora's 'Praising You' featuring Fatboy Slim waft through the air, we comfortably settle into the vibrant atmosphere. Naturally, we gravitate towards our beloved cocktails. Mine, whimsically named 'The Wibbly Wobbly Wonder', is a divine concoction of Absolut grapefruit vodka, fernet branca, lbv port, fresh citrus juice, and vcc 3 sugar syrup, elegantly served over crushed ice in a wine goblet and adorned with fresh mint, orange zest, and a cherry. Liam, on the other hand, opts for the 'Curly Wurly', a rejuvenating fusion of Beefeater gin, apple, rhubarb, and vanilla that's served over crushed ice and soda water in a highball glass.

Hours melt away as we toast, laugh, and sip our way through the cocktail menu. "Ya know, I reckon I could swim in this 'Curly Wurly'," Liam slurs, his Kilkenny accent growing thicker with each passing drink. I laugh, "Just don't drown in it, we'd have a hard time explaining that to the bartender!"

As the DJ seamlessly transitions to 'Joe La Taxi' by Two Many DJ's, our smiles broaden. We're massive fans and have lost count of the nights we've spent dancing away to their beats. "Ah, this is a tune," Liam exclaims, his accent now a thick Irish brogue, "Moves like Jagger, I have!"

Without any hesitation, we bolt from our seats and commandeer the dance floor. Our dance moves, a humorous blend of unbridled joy and a dash of tipsiness, are as infectious as the evening's energy. We draw amused glances, but we're too engrossed in our world of rhythm, laughter, and unadulterated fun to care. "Ya know, Liam," I jest between breaths, "Your dancing's as wobbly as your accent!" To which he retorts, "And you're as wibbly as your wonder, witch!"

By Nicky Ireland

Indeed, the night at The Cocktail Club is one for the books, filled with sparkling banter, laughter, and high spirits. Just thee best!

One size doesn't fit all

Chapter Thirteen

One size doesn't fit all

Chapter Thirteen

NICKY

The day is finally here, I've packed my bags for Barcelona, and the excitement is about to burst through me!

As I finish off my morning makeup gig and give my work station its final sanitization before I head out, one of the chaps from the Ad Agency pokes his head into the makeup area. "Hey there, can I help at all?" I inquire. "No, um, this is somewhat uncomfortable," he mumbles, his face etched with discomfort. My mind races - what could I have possibly done to upset the apple cart this early in the day? I wrestle with my composure, trying to avoid jumping to conclusions. "Don't worry, I'm always receptive to constructive criticism..." I start, attempting to defuse the situation, but he interrupts me. "No, no, it's not that. You haven't screwed up anything."

I give him a puzzled look. "Alright then," I respond. He proceeds, his tone somewhat hesitant, "I happen to work with Jake O'Sullivan." "I see," I reply, my curiosity piqued at where this conversation is heading, and I raise an eyebrow in question.

"You seem like a genuinely good soul, and having observed you at work today, I thought it only fair to let you know that Jake is on some sort of rampage. He's been spreading unkind words about you to our key clients, and I'm sure it's impacting your work opportunities."

This catches me off guard. Why on earth would Jake, my ex, be doing such a thing? While I had a hunch something might be off, I'm still grappling with understanding his motive. I take a deep breath, deciding it best not to delve deeper at the moment. Instead, I mull over how best to send a clear message back to Jake - one that'll make him button up.

"That's regrettable. I suspect he might be a touch bitter," I reply. "Oh really? Did you two part ways on bad terms? I recall you being a pair for quite some time," he inquires. I lean in, my voice dropping to a whisper, "In a manner of speaking. You see, I believe he's still irked because I walked away with all his favourite lingerie." His face turns a shade of crimson, and I quickly add, "Oh, not in the way you're thinking! It's just that it means he'd have to shop for his own for his virtual adventures with random men." I inhale sharply, my teeth clenched. "One size doesn't fit all, after all," I shrug nonchalantly.

He just stares at me, completely taken aback. Then, out of nowhere, he bursts into laughter and I can't resist joining in. "Oh my God. The guys back at the office will have a field day with this," he guffaws. And in that moment, I can tell my plan has hit its mark. Take that, Jake, you little shite!

I'm breezing into Dublin airport this fine afternoon and lo and behold, Santiago has pulled a fast one and bumped me up to business-class. The lady at the check-in desk does a double-take at my astonished face when I ask her to double-check. But yep, that sneaky man has gone all out and snagged me a business-class ticket for my swift two-and-a-half-hour flight to Barcelona.

I step onto the Aer Lingus flight, feeling like a Hollywood diva, channeling my inner Elizabeth Taylor. My royal journey begins as I make my way to my opulent business class seat. An exclusive cabin, decked out with lie-flat seats, is my throne for the flight. The moment I sink into my spacious seat-bed, the steward swoops in with a complimentary amenity kit. Talk about a pamper session! It's packed with flight socks, an eye mask, ear plugs, toothbrush and paste, mints, plus Voya toiletries like lip balm and hand cream. Take that, Sephora! They even toss in a pillow and blanket for good measure.

Before me lies a 16-inch HD touch screen paired with noise-reducing headphones. It's like I've hit the entertainment jackpot with over 120 hours of movies, TV series, comedies, documentaries, interactive games, music albums, and an audio library of podcasts and world music. Holy guacamole!

By Nicky Ireland

Once settled, I decide to doll myself up a bit. Nothing too flashy, I don't want to look like a drag queen upon landing. But going bare-faced? Uh-uh, not happening. After all, I've got to look my best for my dream man.

An hour into the flight and I'm as chill as a cucumber, thanks to a couple of glasses of white wine. The food arrives and I figure maybe it's time to lay off the booze... do women even get a form of brewer's droop? Who knows. I go for the salmon, light and delectable, just what the doctor ordered. Plus, it's the perfect sponge to soak up the alcohol.

Touchdown! After retrieving my weekend luggage, I take a deep, grounding breath. A quick mirror check reassures me - I look good and ready to face the arrivals hall. My heart is playing a drum solo, thoughts of what awaits with Santi at his Bellamar mansion sends waves of heat coursing through me. One thing's for sure, I'm in for a wild ride. And I can't frickin' wait!

"Amor y fuego"

Chapter Fourteen

'Amor y fuego'

Chapter Fourteen

SANTI

The buzz of excitement crackles through me as I stand in the lively arrivals hall at Barcelona airport, eagerly awaiting the arrival of the one and only Nicky. It feels like a lifetime since our last rendezvous, and I'm practically buzzing with the thought of her warm, playful touch.

Every tick of the clock dials up my anticipation, painting vivid images of her making her grand entrance into my stately abode for the first time. The prospect of having her there, in our private hideaway, all to myself, sends a jolt of pure, unadulterated thrill through my veins.

Then, there she is, emerging from the arrivals hall like a burst of sunshine, her eyes finding mine in an instant. Her face transforms into a radiant smile, and her laughter, light and bubbly, bounces off the walls. She abandons her bag and sprints towards me, launching herself into my waiting arms. I scoop her up with ease, our bodies melting together like two puzzle pieces designed to fit just so.

Encircling her waist, I draw her closer, a sense of wonder washing over me at the sensation of her pressed against me. I lean in, pressing a gentle kiss to her lips that sends a shockwave of electrifying bliss down my spine. This moment - the sweetness of her lips, the fragrance of her hair, the melodious sound of her laughter in my ears - is utterly intoxicating. The sheer joy of having her here, with me, is a tidal wave of emotion, and I can't wait to dive headfirst into this new chapter of our story.

Despite the trek from Dublin to meet me, she is the epitome of radiant beauty. Every element of her outfit has been meticulously selected, underlining her innate charm. Her blue jeans, clinging to her like a second skin, sketch the contours of her captivating curves. The cute Aran jumper she's sporting, a soft cream hue, fits her like a glove, highlighting her immaculate figure and the gentle rise and fall of her breasts. Each glimpse of her sends a visceral surge through me, a desire to stake my claim, to brand her as mine.

Our adventure kicks off from the buzzing Josep Tarradellas Barcelona–El Prat Airport. We're darting through the lively city of Barcelona, aiming for my tucked-away mansion in the tranquil neighborhood of Bellamar. As we zigzag through the city's maze, Barcelona's stunning visuals roll out like a giant, mesmerizing poster. The city's architecture, a jumble of Gothic and modernist, strikes a pose against the vivid Mediterranean sky. This is Nicky's first-time gate-crashing at my place, and the buzz of having her here is absolutely electric.

My Audi A7 is our chariot for this picturesque journey, giving us a cozy bubble as we soak in the scenery. As I steer through the winding roads, our fingers play a teasing game of tag, each touch adding a jolt of excitement to our journey. The buzz of seeing each other again, the sweet promise of time yet to be spent, adds an extra jolt to the air, making our hearts do a synchronized happy dance. Once we roll up at the mansion, I draw her in smoothly, dropping a low "bésame" into her ear. She fires back with an enthusiastic lip-lock, a smooch so passionate and intense that we're both left gasping for breath.

Stepping out of the car, the midday sun throws a welcoming party, casting a golden glow that's hard to resist. I glance back at her. Her eyes go wide, and I can see a masterpiece of awe being painted on her face as she soaks in the monument to my pride and joy. My Spanish mansion, christened "Amor y Fuego," stands tall and proud, a physical embodiment of my spirit and a tribute to my refined tastes. It's architecture, a love letter to my roots, encapsulates my essence and serves as my hideaway from the world's noise. Tucked away in its serene corner, it's a private paradise that's as mesmerizing as it is exclusive.

Her eyes dance over the intricate details of the mansion, twinkling with silent admiration. I catch a smile playing at the corners of her lips, my sanctuary mirrored in her gaze. The grandeur of the mansion seems to have won her over, and I can't help but bask in a sense of satisfaction.

By Nicky Ireland

Around us, the mansion's setting unfurls like a breath-taking Spanish painting, with majestic mountains striking a pose in the background. Nicky is visibly impressed by the beauty wrapping around the house, the splendor mirrored in her gaze.

A surge of anticipation wells up within me, particularly when I think about her reaction to the surprises that lie within my personal pleasure dome. My playroom, a realm crafted for pleasure and discipline, is something I can't wait for her to discover. The thought of her gasps of delight and the aftermath of the intense pleasure I plan to unleash, whips up a storm of excitement within me.

My heart picks up its pace, anticipation making my palms a touch clammy as I fantasize about unveiling even more of the depths of my desires to her. The secret room, my sanctuary is brimming with promises of shared intimacies and unchartered territories. The thrill of the unknown, the adrenaline rush of the impending exploration, fans the flames of my anticipation, morphing it into an almost tangible energy. It's a space where we can blur the lines between pleasure and pain, a realm where every sensation takes the center stage. I anticipate her reaction, and I have a feeling it will be nothing short of spectacular.

Holding her petite, playful hand in mine, I guide her with a gentle touch towards the formidable threshold of my home. The substantial gateway to my castle, both impressive and majestic, swings open with an air of understated elegance, revealing my own universe. Mi princesa, my treasured co-adventurer, now officially my partner in crime.

Her eyes, as wide as saucers and sparkling with a blend of fascination and mischief, take in the grandeur of the entrance hall. 'Love and Fire' it's called; a tribute to the harmonious fusion of age-old tradition and contemporary chic. Its towering ceilings and immaculate, white walls are a nod to a glorious past, while the strategically placed wooden features add a dash of the here and now.

The ambience exudes a sense of warmth and a homely comfort, a feeling further amplified by the captivating Spanish art pieces that embellish its many nooks.

Bold, energetic furniture, audaciously juxtaposed against the white walls and wooden highlights, mimic the pulsating energy of life itself.

Her delight knows no bounds as she tightens her grip on my hand, her tiny feet bouncing with unrestrained glee. Her beaming smile lights up her face and in that smile, I see the brilliance of my castle - the happiness, the warmth, the dynamism. All of it now shared with her, my witty princess, finally by my side.

"Do you have a craving, mi amor?" I ask, my gaze meticulously seeking out her response within her eyes. "I'm starving Marvin," she retorts, her voice gentle yet humming with expectancy. I lead her, with a composed tenderness, towards the kitchen - the core of my abode where my two passions, her and cooking, will seamlessly blend.

Our mutual enthusiasm for gastronomy fuels a spirited chat. We find ourselves immersed in the world of recipes, ingredients, and the sheer joy of whipping up something delectable from nothing but raw materials. The idea of showing her how to prepare one of my top choices, a true Spanish banquet, fills me with an eagerness that's rare even for me.

Nicky's zeal is contagious; her eyes glitter, reflecting my own thrill at the thought of a day dedicated to exploring the culinary arts. She's over the moon about diving into the nuances of Spanish fare, about unveiling the delicate equilibrium of spices and ingredients that morphs plain grub into a gourmet wonder.

The vision of her delight is as heady as the most refined vino. Each giggle, each banter, each moment of connection, amplifies the joy of our encounter. The idea of delving into this mosaic of Spanish cookery, of savoring the end product of our efforts, lends an exclusive charm to our mutual expectancy. We're cooking up more than just a meal; we're concocting a memory, fusing our love for food and our affection for each other in a delicious blend.

The mansion is a mirror of my soul, and my obsession for Spanish cuisine is one of the many reflections it captures. Amidst the traditional Spanish architecture lies my extravagant culinary kingdom, a place where rustic allure shakes hands

By Nicky Ireland

with contemporary grandeur. The kitchen is a canvas of chilly steel and cozy, aged timber, a picturesque and practical space.

The walls, decorated with a plethora of pots and pans, tell tales of my culinary conquests. They hang like badges of honor, speaking volumes about my commitment and zeal towards gastronomy. They're not mere utensils; they're my warriors, each holding stories of past feasts and promises of future celebrations. From the cast-iron skillet, a veteran of countless steak searing battles, to the copper saucepans, seasoned with the aroma of countless simmering sauces, each piece holds a chapter of my gastronomic journey.

Together, we chop and change a medley of vegetables, dress the Spanish meats that had been marinating since dawn, and manage the catch of the day, handpicked by yours truly from the local fish market. The kitchen transforms into an orchestra of odors, a symphony of spices, as the pan starts to sing under the heat, crafting our delectable Paella de Marisco.

This dish, brimming with fresh shrimp, clams, mussels, and an assortment of other seafood, is more than just food. It's a masterpiece, a product of our shared love and precise skills. We swirl around the kitchen, tasting the simmering paella and savoring the dancing aromas.

Each spoonful is a shared secret, a silent cheer to our culinary adventure. A stray drop of the rich sauce escapes her lips, and my thumb instinctively reaches out to catch it. A mischievous smile forms on her lips, her eyes sparkling with delight and love. In a surprising yet tender moment, my lips trace the path my thumb just took, tasting the divine sauce from her mouth. It's a sweet exchange, our laughter and witty exchanges fill the air, as tasty and warm as the dish we're crafting.

At dinner, I am giddy with excitement as I spill the beans about my dream, a restaurant in Dublin that combines my Spanish roots with Ireland's culinary delights. It's a thrilling prospect, and it feels like the stars have aligned to bring us together at this perfect moment.

Nicky, ever ready to embrace her artistic abilities and newfound independence, is my muse. She's the spark that ignites my ambition to make the Dublin restaurant idea a reality. Our first encounter in a Dublin museum, filled with ancient Irish fauna and intoxicating aromas, was the starting point of this incredible adventure.

She talks about her love for photography with a wit that lights up the room. She loves to snap moments in time, preserving memories as images that she carries with her. Her passion inspires me, just as my dreams inspire her. We're each other's cheerleaders, our bond growing stronger with every shared experience and conversation.

As the night progresses, we dive into deeper waters, discussing love, past relationships, and the quest for the perfect partner. The electric chemistry between us is palpable, pulling us closer to each other since our paths first crossed.

We find ourselves enveloped in the serenity of my veranda, each holding a glass of Albariño - a delightful white wine with roots in the lush vineyards of Northwestern Spain. It has a unique character, a fresh and revitalizing harmony of flavors that dances on our taste buds, a medley of citrus and stone fruits like peaches and apricots.

We cuddle up in the swing seat, the fading sunlight casting an enchanting glow around us. I bring out my prized Mantas de Grazalema blanket, a tribute to the art of handcrafting. With fringes rolled by hand and made of pure merino wool in natural colors, it cocoons us against the creeping evening chill.

A mesmerizing panorama unfolds before us as the sun starts its descent, setting the sky on fire with colors. The horizon blazes with shades of fiery orange and soft pink, the clouds tinged with a purple glow, all beautifully reflected on the calm surface of the nearby lake.

As our first evening together draws to a close, I find myself wishing I could stop time. I long to wake up to her radiant smile every morning and have her calming presence be the last thing I feel every night. I can only hope she's as eager to start this journey with me, sooner rather than later.

Mi sala de juegos

Chapter Fifteen

By Nicky Ireland

Mi sala de juegos

Chapter Fifteen

SANTI

As daylight breaks, radiant beams of the sun pierce through the window, casting a warm, golden glow across the room. The spacious bedroom, my sanctuary, is bathed in the warmth of daybreak, summoning us to embrace the new day. An enormous bed, the centerpiece of the room, sits comfortably in this sanctuary, its soft, inviting covers hinting at the comfort it provides.

Turning, I find Nicky in peaceful slumber, undisturbed by the morning's call. Last night, we reveled in the slow dance of our bodies, celebrating our reunion by exploring the familiar yet exciting contours of each other. The morning light dapples her flawless face, her tangled curls forming a cascade down her back. The sheets, draped low, offer a glimpse of her beautifully curvaceous ass.

I extend my hand, tracing a path down her spine. It elicits a smile that slowly blooms on her face, a smile that I find myself mirroring. Her joy is a contagion that I willingly succumb to. I don't believe I've ever experienced such profound happiness. "Good morning, mi amor", I whisper, and her eyes flutter open, revealing a vibrant blue, sparkling with an array of playful schemes.

"Good morning, my handsome man. What exciting adventures do you have in store for me today?" she asks. "Well...", I reply, the anticipation of the surprise I have for her causing my heart to flutter, "I have something important to reveal to you." Her eyes widen with intrigue as she regards me, her complete trust in me causing a swell of affection in my heart. "Soon, mi amor, soon", I promise.

After a quick, refreshing shower in the ensuite bathroom, I gently take her hand in mine, leading her upstairs. We ascend towards a special room, a room that has never seen any visitors, mi sala de juegos. My heart pounds with excitement as I prepare to share this intimate space with her, this space that will soon become ours. A place where we can freely express our desires, and surrender to the wild love that binds us.

Cracking open the door to my chamber nestled within the mansion, a flirtatious blend of vanilla and musk winks at us, luring us in with a coy smile. The room is a playful mashup of sensual whims and restraint, a sanctuary for indulgence and discipline alike. Delightfully intricate furniture, hewn from robust dark, stained black mahogany and draped in plush velvet and leather of the deepest blacks and greys, punctuate the space, their metallic trims winking mischievously under the soft, romantic lighting.

Restraints, playful tokens of dominance and submission, are arranged in a cunning game of hide and seek, setting the stage for exhilarating power play. An assortment of toys, each bearing its own unique badge of pleasure or retribution, are neatly tucked away in a locked cabinet like a box of mischievous secrets. A sex swing, with a large canopy and plush velvet cushioning, featuring a robust chain pully system for height adjustment, dangles from the lofty ceiling, swaying coyly and adding a dash of excitement to the room's charisma.

Let's not overlook the grand Saint Andrew's cross, a signature piece in the thrilling world of BDSM. This sensual apparatus is designed with precise points to gently but firmly secure the ankles, wrists, and waist. Once fastened to the X-cross, Nicky will find himself in a wide, standing spread-eagle stance, a position that induces a rush of anticipation. The prospect of her being bound face-first to the cross brings a flutter of excitement, as it often preludes a thrilling whipping session. Of course, being latched to the cross with her back offers a different kind of pleasure, a position often used for tantalizing sexual teasing or for more intimate bondage experiences. The anticipation and longing for what's to come is a feeling like no other.

The room's centerpiece is a magnificent four-poster bed, its majesty is a spectacle to behold, draped in a teasing layer of black satin. This bed, an emblem of luxury and pleasure, stands majestically, casting a shadow of decadence. A sleek black leather chair with a canopy, akin to a throne, sits confidently across the bed, elevated on two steps. The thought of admiring Nicky from that strategic spot sends a ripple of thrill through me, her finally becoming my unsuspecting, enticing prey.

The throne is flanked by steel bars that stretch from the high canopy to the floor, providing an excellent support for my primal instincts. My treasured collection of whips, canes, and floggers adorns the back of the chair, always prepared for their moment in the spotlight. A diverse range of spanking tools, each with its own style and weight, are ready for action, stashed away in another locked cabinet.

The room is awash in deep, dark hues from its décor and fabrics, creating a fun, seductive riddle to be solved. As I idly flick a switch on the wall adjacent to my throne, the room gets washed by a hypnotic, pulsating red light, echoing the rhythm of a heartbeat, setting the stage for intense anticipation.

Beside the light switch, a button solely dedicated to orchestrating the room's soundtrack waits. A gentle tap and it fills the room with ambient tunes, transforming the space into a harmonious serenade of sound.

As the room gets invaded by the tunes of 'Marianas Trench' by Cosmic Space Traveler, it's clear we're not dealing with your run-of-the-mill Spotify playlist here. Oh no, it's a celestial jam that's hitchhiked its way from some far-off cosmic corner. It's more ethereal than your grandma's homemade apple pie, carrying a transcendent quality that screams "heavenly orchestra". It's a cocktail of melodious notes, hushed yet powerful enough to echo around the room, and ricochet straight into your heart.

This music doesn't just give you the feels, it's an orchestral hypnotist, spinning a soundscape so intoxicating, that the room's ambiance blushes. It doesn't just hum in the background, but dances with the room's vibe, shaping and being shaped by it. The symphony from this cosmic fiddle seeps into every air molecule, turbocharging the already tipsy atmosphere.

The room is painted with a heady mix of musk and sweet scents, knitting a tantalizing tapestry of incense and vanilla. This olfactory concert isn't a fluke; it's more calculated than a physicist at a billiards table, designed to ignite the senses and raise the anticipation bar. Scent is one of my passions and each scent, painstakingly chosen, plays its part in this room's irresistible charm.

Vanilla, the 'black gold' of the fragrance world, wraps around you like a warm hug from a long-lost friend. It signals an open invitation to chill, weaving an ambiance of peace.

Then there's sandalwood, with its creamy, woody aroma acting as the anchor in this heady scent storm. It's known for its Zen-like qualities, helping to clear the mental fog amidst the fragrance fiesta.

The scent of white musk, a note that used to be sourced from the secretions of Tibetan deer (before we decided to synthetically produce it), gives off the vibe of clean skin. It's like stepping out of a fresh shower, light and comforting. This fragrance is the calming agent in this scent symphony, triggering a Zen state and dialing down anxiety.

The mingling scents in this room whip up a cocktail that's both intoxicating and calming, crafting a sensory playground that's primed to ignite passion while offering a magnetic allure. The room itself is a shrine to luxury and hedonism, its deliberate design and ambiance transforming it into a carnival for the senses, a sanctuary for auditory, visual, and tactile indulgence.

As Nicky steps into this room for the first time, her eyes bloom wide like a nocturnal flower in awe and thrill. She's like a kid in a candy store, curiosity dancing in her eyes at the prospect of what lies ahead. I catch her gaze, my eyes a reflecting pool of anticipation, eager to pilot her on this maiden voyage. The reins are in my hands, but the ride, that's for both of us to enjoy.

Guiding her with a tender touch, we drift towards the more private lounge corner of the room. We've dabbled in the discourse of Dominant and submissive dynamics before, but now, it's time for a deep dive before we plunge further into this territory.

"Mi amor," I begin, my voice a serious undertone cutting through the room's sensual symphony. "It's vital that you grasp the dynamics of D/s, particularly within the realm of kink and sexual exploration. It can be incredibly rewarding, offering a fresh lens to view your sexuality and intimate experiences. But it's equally important to understand the delicate intricacies and the fine shades that accompany the roles we're about to step into."

Her grip on my hand tightens, her eyes locking onto mine with a genuineness that blankets me with warmth. "Santi," she starts, her voice a steady stream of certainty. "I get that our intimate encounters can unmask hidden aspects of who we are. Although I'm a newbie, I'm not naïve. I know that the bedrock of a successful D/s relationship is heart-to-heart communication and consent. I'm game to let you steer this ship. I trust you."

I lift her hand to my lips, planting a kiss on her knuckles as a seal to her understanding. "Absolutely, mi princesa, it's crucial that we keep the lines of communication wide open about our wishes, our boundaries, and our comfort zones. This is a willing exchange of control - a Yin Yang affair, so to speak." Her grin infuses a lightness into our conversation. I tap my knee softly, a silent cue for her to make herself comfortable in my lap.

As she nestles into my lap, her arm snakes its way around my shoulder, her fingertips sketching soothing doodles on my back. Our other hands intertwine on my lap, anchoring us as our conversation flows on.

"Persistently, we must aim to be honest, open, and considerate in all our interactions," I emphasize.

"There might be times when I'll want to introduce a little twist in our dynamics, say, bondage. It can play different roles – a mode of discipline, a reward, or even a sensory journey to assert my dominance, but with your safety always in mind. Yet, bondage is but a single facet in the myriad of escapades we're going to dive into. Sensory play, elaborate role-playing scenarios that don't necessarily involve pain, and a spectrum of other experiences will mark our adventure. The scenes we devise will always be a collaborative endeavor, a melding of our desires and fantasies. Hence, our journey will be uniquely ours, a tribute to our special connection and shared understanding."

Digging deeper into the conversation, I elucidate, "When we immerse ourselves in the roles of submissive and Dominant, there's a chance we might stumble upon a high that's reminiscent of the effects of certain substances. Our senses will be sharpened, emotions might overflow, and we may even feel like we've been transported to a different plane of existence." She's all ears, soaking in every word.

"These scenes can act as a form of profound meditation, and they can be immensely therapeutic. However, given the intense emotions involved in reaching such a meditative state, we need to account for the aftermath of our play. It's crucial that we give ourselves some time to gently return from these scenes. Are we on the same page?"

She nods, her eyes sparkling with enthusiasm. "Absolutely, I get it. I'm over the moon that we can talk about this so openly and easily. This exploration is something I've been yearning for, but I've never experienced this level of connection or safety with anyone else. Every bit of this feels right, Santi, and I couldn't be happier that it's you I'll be embarking on this journey with," she cozies up to me, and we share a few moments of silent connection before resuming our chat.

"Post-scene care will be our indispensable bonding time, Nicky. We might spend it cuddling, maybe I'll fetch you a glass of water, or we could discuss everything that just unfolded. We'll figure out what type of aftercare suits us best, and it will be a top priority. It's crucial because it aids us in returning to a state of equilibrium and calm after particularly intense scenes, while also nurturing a deeper bond and trust between us."

As our dialogue progresses, I address any questions Nicky has, and we establish some boundaries. We agree to revisit everything as required. Her trust in me at this moment is paramount, and I reassure her that I will always honor it.

By Nicky Ireland

Finally, with a glint of anticipation in my eyes, I quip, "Are you ready, mi putita hermosa?" Giving her a playful wink, she giggles, blushes, and retorts, "I was ready before I was born, and you know it."

Play with my chaos

Chapter Sixteen

Play with my chaos

Chapter Sixteen

SANTI

Nicky lights up the playroom like a curiosity-laden lighthouse, her vibrant presence compelling me to observe her antics. My gaze follows her every movement with a zealous admiration that teeters on the brink of idolization. Each breath she takes becomes a silent symphony that echoes through the room, her slight gasp revealing a shared sense of wonder. I can't help but get lost in the sight of her; her black silk robe barely skimming over her enticing silhouette is an intoxicating sight, sending waves of desire coursing through me. My body responds instinctively, a testament to her charm, yet I remain as still as a statue. Composed and in control.

I stand with a calculated calmness – arms folded, one hand absentmindedly running over the curve of my bottom lip, while my gaze never strays from her. Our silent exchanges, this tantalizing tango of glances and unvoiced promises, only fans the embers of anticipation within me.

Dressed in nothing more than blue jeans slung low on my hips, I present her with an unhindered view of my physique. Her eyes rove over the intricate tattoos etched on my skin, each design a tribute to a life lived passionately. She takes in the sight of my nipple piercing, a favourite toy of hers. The memory of her tongue flitting over it, her teeth gently nipping it, sends a thrill of anticipation through me, a teaser of pleasures yet to unfold.

I find myself caught between an eager yearning and the restraint required of her Dominant. "Mi Princesa," I assure her in a calming baritone that pierces the quiet atmosphere, "I'm here for you."

"Should anything seem unclear, don't hold back from asking. 'Fuego' is your safe word. It's as crucial as it gets," I emphasize, the weight of the safe word hovering palpably between us. "This word is your safety net, your safeguard, your instant respite from any unease. It's a potent tool and I encourage you to use it without any trepidation. If things get too intense, everything will stop the moment that word crosses your lips."

"But remember," I gently nudge her, "If you can't voice your discomfort, you have a backup. Tap my leg, or any part of me, twice. And just like that, everything comes to a standstill."

Her returned smile and a soft "Yes. Thank you," floods me with reassurance. It's crucial that she comprehends her safety and comfort top my priority list. She must know that nothing will be imposed on her, that her consent to submit is not only a gift to me, but a testament of her trust.

Her playful surrender - it's a prize I value, one I crave. Her eagerness to learn and readiness to comply sends thrills of excitement coursing through me. Each stride she makes on this path, each act of giving in, is a testament to the faith she has in me, the power she willingly relinquishes. It's a gift I treasure, and equally, a responsibility I'm keen to shoulder.

A raw hunger stirs within me, a dire thirst for her acquiescence. An insatiable longing to both devour and be devoured by her. The very core of me quivers on the brink of a release that poses to fracture my poise. Yet I hold onto my self-control, a thin curtain distinguishing the gentleman from the beast within. I need her to step into my world, to dance with my disorder, to soothe the fierce tempest that roils within me. The anticipation is a tangible torment, a delightful torment promising a climactic end. I wait, every fiber of my being crying for release, yet I'm bound by my own discipline, restrained by my determination to protect her, to adore her. To wait for her.

She swivels towards me, her gaze holding mine hostage. "I ache to lose myself entirely in you," she murmurs, her eyes scrutinizing me with an intense, adoring curiosity. Gradually, she lets her silky robe slip off her shoulders, pooling in a heap of fabric at her feet. She's a sorceress, a mermaid beckoning me to her.

By Nicky Ireland

Her body is a captivating mix of soft curves and ghostly whiteness, her skin a canvas I long to discover. A recollection of a beauty spot, nestled on her inner thigh, snags my attention, sparking a fervent desire to explore it, to appreciate it once again.

I cross the room, each stride a measured dance of anticipation. Making myself comfortable, I sit at the foot of the bed, I keep my gaze locked on her. I spread my legs wide, creating a welcoming space for her. My breath catches, yearning for this moment to extend endlessly, to hang suspended in the air. The sight before me stirs a tempest within, and I find myself mapping out our afternoon. A blueprint of what I desire to do with her, to her, and for her starts to form in my mind.

"Your innocent heart, contrasted against your delightfully wicked thoughts, is fast becoming my most cherished vice, mi putita," I admit to her. A beat passes, and then she purrs, though with a dash of nervousness, "I scratch and I bite too."

A smirk plays at my lips, "Oh, mi chica ardiente, you'll crawl and you'll beg too. On your knees. Now!" The order echoes in the room, the dominance in my voice firm and decisive.

And just like the obedient slut she's proven herself to be, she elegantly descends to the floor. The tension is tangible, the heat between us a sentient being. Our actions are a ballet of surrender and control, each one stoking the flame that threatens to engulf us both.

She's inching forward in a fun, playful crawl, each move as delightfully calculated as the next strategy in a high-stakes game of chess. I watch her, feeling an unusual quickening of my pulse, a sign of the captivating charm she radiates. She's the riddle I yearn to solve, and the urge to map the mystery of her skin with my fingers is overpoweringly strong.

As she reaches my space, I guide her to spin around, now showing her back to me. She settles into a kneeling position, hands upturned on her thighs, creating a picture of playful surrender. This is her witty way of saying, "Game on."

I pick up the collar from its resting place on the bed, an item carrying an ocean of unspoken words. It's a thick black leather band, carrying the Spanish inscription 'puta obediente'. I secure it around her neck, the leather feeling cool against her skin. It might appear as a simple accessory, but this collar is a powerful symbol of our intriguing connection, a physical representation of the bond we share. "Remember, a collar itself is just an accessory," I tell her. "It's the two souls it unites that make it a symbol. You, mi amor, are my 'puta obediente'."

I then proceed to bring her up to speed with the rules of our unique game in this room. Once inside, she's to play her part on all fours. Standing is off the table, only crawling is allowed. "Address me as Sir and nothing else within this room, got it?" I say. She nods in response. "Speak up, Nicky," I encourage her. A soft, "Yes, Sir" is her reply. "Good girl," I commend her, my lips curving into an appreciative smile.

In my hand, I hold a blindfold, as dark as the night and as smooth as the satin it's made of. An exciting wave of anticipation washes over me as I gently cover her eyes with it, taking her sight and immersing her in a world of mysterious darkness. She gasps softly, a sound so delicate that it cuts through the silence of the room. It's a sign, a testament to her trust and her submission that ignites a surge of desire within me.

I connect a leash to her collar, the metal feeling cool and solid against my hands, a physical representation of my control in our game. I hear her breath hitch, and the delicate chain of the leash grows taut between us. The sensation sends a shiver of excitement through me, the mental image of her, on all fours, following my lead, stokes the fires of my desire. I rise, my command firm yet intrigued, "Crawl."

She shifts onto her hands and knees, once again, humor glinting in her eyes. The leash, wound tightly around my wrist, becomes our mutual guide. A light pull and she's sidling over to the bed's edge. I offer the invitation for her to ascend, to remain on all fours, my tone a cocktail of calm control and eager curiosity.

She plays along, a smirk dancing on her lips. "Mi putita," slips from my mouth, my heart doing a little jig at her playful compliance. I assure her that an inspection of my 'property' is imminent, the phrase tinged with a promise of intimacy and a hint of ownership. My directive is simple - spread your legs wider, make yourself fully visible to my gaze.

My position at the bed's foot grants me a perfect view. Her figure, a masterpiece of curvaceous lines and soft spots exactly where they should be, is laid out before me. Every inch of her is a new territory waiting to be discovered, cherished, adored. I take it slow, my eyes drinking in the sight of her beautiful ass and pussy, savoring the enticing panorama.

Deciding to join her on the bed, I position myself just behind her shapely ass. My attention is drawn to her pussy, glistening with anticipation. The sight is captivating, hypnotic, and I'm filled with an almost overwhelming need to touch her, to taste her, to smell her.

My hand lifts, fingers charting the terrain of her, delving into the intimate folds and crevices of her cunt. My index finger orbits her entrance, a teasing touch that coaxes a soft, pleased hum from her. The sound sends a ripple of desire coursing through me.

I lean closer, pressing my nose against her cunt, drawing a deep breath. Her scent is heady, a sweet, tangy perfume that whispers of temptation and allure. It's delightful, addictive, and I can't help but crave getting lost in her. My tongue makes contact, delving deep into her pussy, tasting her heated response as she shudders beneath me, a living testament to my effect on her.

But I hold back from granting her the release she so clearly desires. My voice, firm and authoritative, echoes in the quiet room, "From now on, you'll only cum at my command, got it?" Breathless, teetering on the precipice of ecstasy, she manages to respond, "Yes, Sir."

Grasping the leash with a firm grip, I playfully call out, "Up!" She takes the cue, positioning herself in a kneeling stance, her back snuggly aligned with the warmth of my body. There's a comforting weight to the leash in my hand, a tangible testament to the dynamics of our unique game. I unfasten my jeans, freeing my eager cock from its denim restraint. It stands to attention, aroused and glistening with pre-cum. A wave of pleasure sweeps over me, causing me to recline my head and let out a low, rumbling moan as my hand slowly works its way along my stiffened cock.

Adjusting her upward gaze, I ensure her slender neck is in alignment with my crotch, my grip guiding my rock-hard cock along the front of her throat. The head of my cock firmly placed against the edge of her neck, my hand gripping firmly I grab the engorged head and I draw back, the pressure of my long cock across her throat causing a slight constriction in her breath. She gasps, but I steady her, softly reminding her of her safe word. It's our pact, a sign of respect and trust that she can call halt when it gets too overwhelming.

But she shakes her head, a spark of defiance in her eyes. No words spoken, yet her resolve is clear. The sight of her resilience, her determination to continue, leaves me breathless. My own breathing becomes more rapid as I watch her gracefully contend with the unfamiliar sensation, my length adding to her challenge. It's a sight that fuels my desire, the enthralling dance of power and surrender pushing me to the edge of pleasure. This, I fathom, is the zenith of ecstasy, a journey beyond the typical spectrum of arousal.

Releasing my cock's chokehold on her neck, I tilt her head back until she is directly beneath me, her nose nestled against the underside of my heavy balls. I instruct her to take a deep breath, to immerse herself in my unique scent before commanding her to "taste me". I seek to engage every one of her senses, to have her crave my distinct taste, my unique scent. "Suck!" I command, and she obliges, her lips encircling my balls. She tends to me with an intensity as if it's the only thing that matters. Her attention sends a shiver through me, my cock responding to her touch, with a pulsating throb. The anticipation of release building. Guiding her with a firm hand, I hold her chin firmly against my balls, my hips pushing downwards, ensuring her mouth is pressed firmly against my aching balls. The sounds of her delight echo around us, coaxing a satisfied moan from me.

With a swift jerk on the leash, I twirl her around in a neat arc, her movements guided by my confident hand. Down she cascades onto the bed, meeting the soft surface with a muted thud that punctuates the quiet room, a surprised gasp slipping past her lips. I start my calculated approach, anticipation crackling in the air as I inch forward on my knees, one after the other, in a deliberate rhythm, tracing a path along her torso. I station myself on either side of her, my body radiating a cool composure as I hover just inches from her face. Her mouth opens in an enticing mix of excitement and surrender, offering a silent invitation that sends a shiver of thrill through me.

Grabbing the base of my heavy cock with my hand, I begin to tease her mouth with it. "You're going to beg for me, my obedient slut. Beg for me!," I instruct, my voice a deep, smooth rumble. My hand twines in the silkiness of her hair, pulling just enough to coax a soft whimper from her.

"I want your cum, Sir. I need it. Please, give me your cum, please," she replies, her voice a sultry whisper that shoots a wave of desire straight through me. There's something about her, a perfect cocktail of innocence and mischief. With a lazy roll of my hips, I press my throbbing cock against her inviting mouth, pushing inside a little, before removing myself again, painting a tantalizing image of what's to come.

With a playful tug of my hand, I tease her mouth again with my cock, pulling it away from her lips only to return it again with a sharp slap against her mouth. A delightful whimper escapes her, a sweet siren song of submission that pulses through me. Finally, I slide my thick cock all the way into her mouth, her warm breath against me creating an electrifying sensation.

Her moans fill the room, a harmonious symphony that amplifies the tantalizing sensation. Her tongue dances over me, tasting, exploring, reveling in every inch of me. She seems to relish the experience, an eagerness that leaves me wanting more.

"Share with me how I taste, mi chica ardiente," I command, the anticipation making me draw in a sharp breath. She releases me with a wet pop, her words tumbling out breathlessly. "You taste like every delightful sin, Sir. Everything I've ever desired, ever needed, and ever craved." Her words hit me harder than expected, stoking my interest and igniting a fire within me. A low sound of approval escapes me, an instinctual reaction to her words.

I reach out, my fingers gently lifting her chin. I lean in, pressing my lips onto hers in a lingering kiss, a silent promise passing between us. "I love how I taste on your lips," I murmur, savoring our shared flavor, a taste of the desire and the promise of what lies ahead. The potent mix of lust and excitement courses through me, a thrilling prelude to the symphony we're about to craft.

With an air of playful urgency, I gently guide her head back onto the soft cushion of the bed, finding my position above her. A thrill of anticipation races through me as I reintroduce my cock to the inviting heat of her slightly parted lips. My movements commence, my hips dancing to the rhythm of our mutual desire, gliding in and out of her mouth, allowing her to savor the full length of me. She eagerly receives me, her throat opening up to accommodate me entirely. With a firm hand, I pull at her collar, bringing her face so close to the base of my pulsating cock that a whispered secret wouldn't find its way between us.

"Play with your cunt for me mi chica sucia," I demand, my voice akin to velvet in the humid air. Her legs respond by parting, her knees sinking into the soft mattress as her hand embarks on a journey towards her thighs. I feel her hips dance beneath me, her chest rising and falling in tandem with mine, our breaths composing an orchestra of escalating symphony, resonating our ascending pleasure.

As our breaths quicken on the brink of precipice of climax, "Oh mi amor," I exclaim, my words a bare request. "cum for me, give me everything you've got," I instruct, and she replies with a muffled moan, stifled by my deeper exploration into her welcoming throat. Her submission is my triumph. We shudder as we cum simultaneously, our voices weaving together in a melody of satisfaction, her muffled exclamations around my pulsing cock as she swallows every last

By Nicky Ireland

drop of me.

In the ensuing tranquility, our heartbeats slow and I gently settle onto her, our bodies merging as we snuggle into each other's embrace. I find myself captivated by the rhythmic rise and fall of her chest, a calming antidote to the rawness of our intimate connection. We gasp together, our mutual breathlessness reverberating in the room.

With a tender gesture, I reach for her blindfold, lifting it from her eyes. As her gaze adjusts to the dim light, she directs her attention towards me, a playful smile dancing on her lips. The sight sets off a symphony of emotions within me.

She moves closer, clinging to me, our bodies a testament to our shared passion, painted in sweat and desire. Our fragrance fills the room, a potent reminder of our sensual dance. As I press a gentle kiss to the top of her head, I murmur into the silence, "Te adoro," and she answers by gripping me tighter, a silent commitment to cherish this moment, to treasure us.

A Fuego Lento

Chapter Seventeen

By Nicky Ireland

A Fuego Lento

Chapter Seventeen

NICKY

I'm getting my first-ever tour of Santi's kitchen kingdom, and I'm practically bouncing with excitement. We're at A Fuego Lento, a restaurant that's not just a name but a pun with layers. Santi explains it to me with a twinkle in his eye: it's about slow-cooking or simmering food to perfection, and it's also about slow-burning, intense love. I feel a shiver run down my spine as he lifts my hand to his lips, planting a gentle kiss on my knuckles. A cheeky wink from him and my heart does a somersault.

Santi's been spinning yarns about his culinary baby, A Fuego Lento, and I've been hanging onto his every word. This place is a Spanish Restaurant and Bar, but with a modern twist that sets it apart. Santi's the big boss in the kitchen, but he's got a powerhouse team backing him up. It's comforting to know that his labor of love is in good hands even when he's not around. In turn it means he can choose exactly how much time he spends in the kitchen or his office.

As we saunter down Del Parlament, in the vibrant Sant Antoni neighborhood, A Fuego Lento stands out like a diamond in the rough. Its entrance is a beacon of mystery and promise, a doorway to a universe of tantalizing tastes. The modern exterior is marked by a logo surrounded by a fiery halo - a nod to its name.

The façade, a mashup of dark wood and broad windows, gives any curious bystander a sneak peek into the world inside. Deep red drapes cascade down the windows, adding to the mystery. We step through the door into a snug, dimly lit space that feels instantly welcoming. With Santi's hand firm in mine, I'm guided into his culinary utopia.

Everything about A Fuego Lento screams Santi: his joy, his passion, his love for his craft. This place is classy, yet warm and inviting. It's a perfect blend of traditional Spanish charm and chic modern vibes. The air is electric - you can tell it's a crowd favourite. The blend of old and new in the décor gives it a sophisticated feel without losing its roots. The restaurant is alive with the sound of happy customers, adding to the mesmerizing charm of this amazing place.

On a bustling Friday night like tonight, the energy is palpable. It's clear that this is where the locals come to unwind and enjoy good food with good company. The maître d', Camila, greets us with a genuine smile. The staff's faces light up at the sight of Santi, their respect for him evident in their smiles. Standing here next to him, I can't help but swell with pride.

I'm chatting with Camila, a woman in her prime who's the epitome of elegance and allure. Check out that refined nose of hers, sitting pretty on her light-tan face like it's nobody's business. Standing at, I would imagine, a solid 5ft 6", she's no slouch. And that hair, oh-la-la, it's glossy black and slicked back into a neat bun. Her eyes, a deep, warm brown, are the kind that give you a friendly nudge and say, "Hey, come on in." And her wardrobe choice? A killer black pencil skirt and crisp white blouse, complemented by some sweet flat pumps. She's rocking her curves and turning heads left and right — the woman's a knockout.

We're treading deeper into the restaurant now, and boy, is the vibe electric. Camila's weaving through the crowd like a pro, trading niceties with the regulars and giving a warm welcome to the newbies. She's a smooth talker, keeping the chat alive with no sweat.

The restaurant? Picture a cozy cabin meets modern hotspot. Wooden beams crisscross overhead, tables come complete with their own selection of twinkling candles, and lights are hanging low, bathing the place in a warm, inviting glow. The seating arrangement's a mix and match of foursomes and long benches, perfect for a communal feast. And don't get me started on the tall, industrial-style heaters scattered around, their flames dancing and adding a touch of magic to the room.

My nose is going wild with the aroma of food in the air. It's like a symphony of spices, fresh ingredients, and perfectly grilled meats and fish — my stomach's throwing a tantrum in anticipation.

And there's the bar, right at the far end, calling out to me. It's stocked with every kind of alcohol you can think of, and then some. The high-end whiskey, the cocktails, they're all singing my name. And the bar stools? High and tan leather, fitting right into the warm vibe of the room. The bar staff are having a good time, their friendly banter and laughter adding to the buzz in the room. It's the perfect spot to kick back and enjoy a drink amidst all the hullabaloo.

Meanwhile, Santi's gaze is burning a trail on me, a scorching mix of desire and heat that makes my skin tingle. His arm is around my waist, leading me through the maze of tables and chairs. And his earlier whisper, his command for me to skip the panties tonight, is still ringing in my ears, making my heart race with excitement and anticipation. This is going to be one heck of a night!

Daringly stepping out of my fashion comfort zone, decked out in a dress that sparkles like the cosmos, its metallic sheen playing a lively game of peek-a-boo with hints of baby blue. This getup is the perfect blend of classy and subtle, the floaty fabric whispering around me as I move. The sleeveless cut pairs nicely with a choker-style neckline, injecting an air of sophistication. Under the warm, ambient lighting, I'm twinkling like a fairy. I feel radiant.

My silver heels tap a catchy rhythm against the hardwood floors, their sound disappearing into the harmony of tunes filling the air. The familiar chords of 'Play with Fire' by Sam Tinnesz ripple from the speakers and I can't help but grin. I catch sight of Santi guiding me to our table and I erupt into a fit of giggles. His fingers squeeze mine in a comforting response.

My blonde curls cascade down my back, playfully concealing the daring cut of my dress. It plunges low, revealing a secret patch of skin that only Santi and I are privy to. Each step, each hip sway, cranks up the thrill of the evening, Santi playing the perfect guide on this magical night.

I can't take my eyes off Santi however. He's a powerhouse, his presence dominating the room. Decked out in dark navy pants, they're tailored to perfection, hugging his muscular thighs and firm ass. They showcase his athletic build, a tribute to his discipline and strength. His crisp white shirt is buttoned low, revealing the intricate tattoos adorning his chest. The ink swirls upwards, following his neckline and creeping towards his chiseled jaw.

Every nuance of his outfit emphasizes his masculine aura, from the straining fabric over his muscular chest to the tantalizing glint of his nipple piercing. The sight of it, the metallic shine against his skin, sends a thrill through me, sparking an urge to trace my fingers over it.

His scent hangs in the air, a potent cocktail of musk and cologne, leaving a trail of desire wherever it goes. His touch is assertive, his hand holding mine in a quiet assertion of control. His grip is a silent promise, an unspoken testament to his commanding aura. Every single detail of his appearance underscores his irresistible charm and allure.

Cozied up at a table right next to the bar, Santi and I find our spots, and he casually pulls my chair closer to his. It's a smooth move, timed perfectly with the arrival of our waiter. The guy's in his early 20s, rocking short, dark curls and a well-groomed beard. A little flash of metal winks at me from under his lip - a piercing, smack in the center. His black shirt and pants scream 'staff member'.

"Sir, ready for me to put through that order you mentioned earlier?" he asks Santi, all professionalism. I whip my head around to Santi, eyebrows shooting up. When did he decide on our meal? But instead of feeling side-lined, I'm actually more relaxed.

"Absolutely, thanks, Andres," Santi replies, not missing a beat. He swings his attention back to me, eyes glinting. "What's your poison, mi princesa?" My heart does a little flip. "Ooh, a cocktail, please!" I exclaim. Because nothing screams 'celebration' more than a fancy cocktail. "Cuba Libre for both of us," Santi tells Andres.

In no time, here comes Andres, our drinks balanced in his hands like he's done this a million times. The aroma of the cocktails wafts over to me, and I can hardly wait. "What's in it, Santi?" I question, lifting the glass to my lips. "White rum and cola, mi amor," he answers, "but the lime wedge is the secret weapon. Gives it that unique kick."

And boy, is he right! The drink is a dream. The sweetness of the cola contrasts with the tangy lime, creating a delightful play of flavors. And the rum? It's like a cozy hug, warming up the mix without overpowering it. Santi, you've nailed it. I look up at him, grinning from ear to ear.

He's observing me, eyes sparkling, clearly pleased with my reaction. His take-charge attitude, his confident choices, send a thrill through me. I'm not just excited about the food, I'm excited about the man who's pulling all the strings, making sure everything is perfect. And it's heady, just like the cocktail he's chosen for us.

Right now, we're about half an hour into waiting for our food, when our server Andres makes his grand entrance with our dishes. The sight and smell of it all instantly has my taste buds doing a happy dance. There's a rich, smoky scent that fills the air, a nod to the traditional Spanish way of roasting ingredients over coals that gives the food an irresistible depth of flavor. Sharing plates, loaded with an array of culinary treats, each dish a vibrant emblem of the city's eclectic food scene.

The plates are a visual treat, arranged with a keen eye for aesthetics and carrying local favorites steeped in Spanish tradition. They're a colour carnival for the eyes with their bold hues and modern presentation. There's pà amb tomàquet, a Catalan classic, with ripe, juicy tomatoes rubbed onto crusty bread. The vivid red of the tomato makes a striking contrast against the rustic brown of the bread. Alongside this, a melody of roasted peppers, eggplant, and onions, each vegetable cut finely and shimmering under a generous pour of fresh olive oil. A hint of fresh garlic adds a zesty punch that sends my senses into overdrive.

There's also the stewed oxtail, a comfort food favourite in Spain, looking very tempting with its glossy sofrito sauce and fragrant herbs, promising a flavor explosion. It's a vision in shades of deep browns and greens, the herbs adding a fresh twist to the hearty dish. Fresh bread, golden and crusty, stands by, all set to mop up every bit of the irresistible, savory sauce that comes with the oxtail.

Then there's the esquixada - a salt cod salad. It's a riot of colors with red peppers, ripe tomatoes, crisp onions, and black olives. A generous pour of extra virgin olive oil gives a glossy finish to the salad, creating a dish that's as refreshing as it is substantial. The vibrant colors are a delicious teaser of the salad's equally vibrant taste, making it a tempting part of the meal.

Of course, what's a Spanish feast without jamón Iberico? The cured Iberian ham, a dark, luscious red, sliced thin and arranged gracefully on the plate. Its look is as tempting as its taste, a clear testimony of the artistry that goes into Spanish charcuterie. In addition, there are bombas - a variety of potato croquette - and more pà amb tomàquet, each dish a tribute to the delightful complexity of Spanish cuisine. Each plate is an open invitation to savor the genuine flavors of this diverse city, and I'm all in.

Diving headfirst into this epicurean escapade, Santi escorts me through dish after dish, each melody of flavors seizing my senses. Amidst this sensory extravaganza, I suddenly become aware of Santi's firm, warm hand sliding up my inner thigh. A wave of warmth radiates from my core, ignited not just by the magnificent food and wine, but also by his touch.

His gaze is unblinking, meticulously monitoring my reactions to his intimate touch. As I draw in a shaky breath, I lose myself in his deep green eyes, bordered by thick, dark lashes. Despite being in the heart of a bustling crowd, we're ensconced in our private world, oblivious to our public setting. I feel secure, confident that Santi would never place me in an uncomfortable situation. He's my guide, helping me discover desires I never knew I possessed.

Underneath the table, his palm and fingers continue their expedition up my leg, inducing a surge of moist warmth between my thighs. As his hand meets my pulsating core, he skillfully maneuvers his knuckles between the folds of my pussy, grazing my already stimulated clit and coaxing a low moan from my lips.

His fingers explore my slick folds until two of them find my entrance, slipping inside as I grasp his wrist, suddenly gasping for air.

"Keep your eyes on me while I'm deep inside you, mi amor," he commands in a low, husky voice. "I want to feel your body tremble under my touch." As he dives his fingers deeper into me, his thumb orbits my sensitive clit, and I can't suppress the wave of pleasure that swamps me. The euphoria drenches his fingers as I clench around him, gyrating my hips against his hand, pulling him deeper, surrendering to the shuddering climax that rips through me. His gaze unwavering, watching my every pant, every stifled moan.

As the aftershocks of my climax subside, he synchronizes with my rhythm, tempering his previously relentless pace. He leans in close, his breath blending with my panting exhales, and kisses me with a slow, deep intensity. Our tongues twirl in a tantalizing tango, our lips lightly nibbling at each other, craving more.

He culminates the passionate kiss, withdrawing his fingers from me. Then, with a seductive flourish, he glides his wet fingers across both of our conjoined lips, staining them with my arousal. The scent and taste of my own cum on our lips draw a groan from him, amplifying the electric connection between us.

As the clock ticks towards our exit, Santi, the maestro of this magical night, gets up from his chair. The air is thick with suspense, just as potent as the lingering aroma of our delicious dinner. He shoots me a cheeky wink and whispers, "Time to get you home, mi chica sucia".

The staff are still all smiles, even at this late hour, their goodbye wishes echoing around us. Santi reaches out and I take his hand. I feel his strong hold, our fingers interlaced, a silent vow of protection and closeness.

We make our exit, the cool night air wrapping around us like a welcoming shawl. The city lights twinkle like far-off stars, painting our path ahead with a romantic glow. This amazing night still has so much more in store for us, an untold story ready to unfurl under the moon's watchful gaze. We head off with the guarantee of more laughter, more whispered secrets, and unforgettable moments yet to come.

As the evening transitions into night, Santi and I find ourselves cozily nestled in bed. The enchanting whispers of the evening continue to weave their magic, transforming our night into a delightful adventure. Say no more.

Amidst all the fun, a buzz from my phone breaks the spell — it's a text from Liam.

Liam: Hey witch! I've been missing you

Me: Oh, Liamo, I've been missing you too!

Liam: Alright, don't get creeped out. But I've been snuggling up at night with that shit you left at my apartment the last time you visited.

Me: Wait, what???

Liam: It carries your scent and it's oddly comforting to cuddle with.

Me: Liam, that's frickin' disgusting!

Liam: Oh, for feck sake!

Liam: I just can't with this Autocorrect!

Liam: I swear, I meant shirt! I've been sleeping with your shirt!

Me: Dying here!

Lady in red

Chapter Eighteen

Lady In Red

Chapter Eighteen

NICKY

I'm still buzzing from last night's antics at A Fuego Lento, followed by an intense night in Santi's apartment. Yes, I'm a little worn out, but I'm also practically glowing with happiness. My trip to Barcelona for the first time is proving quite the experience and I'm loving every second of it!

Today, Santi has to pop into his office to tackle some unexpected work. We'll meet up later at the restaurant and head back to his apartment - 'home', as he calls it, making me feel like I belong too.

In the meantime, I'm planning a thrilling expedition to Barcelona's makeup stores. Oh, the anticipation! Even if I don't buy anything, just swatching the colors and feeling the textures will have me squealing with excitement. Point me in the direction of Sephora - a beauty haven we sadly lack in Ireland - and I'll be in skincare and makeup paradise!

As I sit on Santi's bed, I decide now's the perfect time to put on a bit of light makeup. Walking into a makeup store bare-faced? That's practically sacrilegious! From the ensuite, I hear Santi stepping into the shower, and I can't help but grin, remembering his tatted, muscular physique. Yum!

Suddenly, music floods the room from the bathroom. It's Two Many DJ's "9 to 5", and I can't help but let out an excited 'YES!' at full volume. I can hear Santi chuckling at my reaction and belting out the tune.

As the song keeps playing, I start to wonder what's taking Santi so long. Feeling a little mischievous, I sneak into the bathroom and switch the song on his phone. He shakes his head and bursts into laughter as Two Many DJ's "I'm Waiting for My Man" starts playing. I giggle at his reaction - I can be quite cheeky, but he

By Nicky Ireland

loves it.

When he finally emerges, I'm perched on his plush bed, waiting like an excited puppy. He looks divine, dressed in a slick pair of dark suit pants, a crisp white shirt, and a stylish tie. I can't help but swoon. He winks at me while adjusting his cufflinks, and I rise to help him with his tie. It's just another excuse to touch him. As I fix his tie, he gently circles my neck with his hand, and we lock eyes. He gives my neck a light squeeze and tugs my bottom lip with his teeth. I'm floating on cloud nine.

Shortly after, Santi waves me goodbye in the heart of Barrio Gótico, his words of caution echoing in my ears — "Stay safe, eat snacks, and keep yourself hydrated." His adorableness is through the roof, I swear!

Now, I find myself on a beeline for the grandest beauty boutique in sight. I feel the comforting weight of face wipes in my purse, a silent reminder of the inevitable makeup-removal mission that will follow my upcoming swatch-frenzy. Oh, the joy of painting the back of my hands with a kaleidoscope of makeup hues!

As I push open the doors to "La Esencia de Belleza", my eyes twinkle with excitement. I offer a silent apology to my credit card, knowing it's about to have quite a workout. This place, it's a breath-taking paradise. It's grandiose and absolutely enchanting. It's a treasure chest brimming with irresistible goodies. Countless rows and counters are laden with a vibrant array of products — creamy skincare potions, colour cosmetics and perfumes that smell like a dream. I can already tell, I won't be leaving this spot anytime soon.

Later that day I'm heading to Santi's Restaurant. I am famished, laden with way too many shopping bags and can't wait to see my man. Despite it being only a few hours since I saw him and he's text me repeatedly throughout the day. Ensuring I am safe, asking me if I need anything, telling me once again to have a snack and drink fluids. Secretly, I am loving his over protectiveness.

I make myself comfortable at a spot by the window. I can't get over how beautiful and unique the Gothic Quarter is. I settle in, order a cup of tea, come on, I'm an Irish woman! and enjoy the views out of the window. I'm a people watcher. I enjoy watching people interact, wondering what their life stories are.

Shortly after I get settled Santi arrives and heads straight to me. I stand and he whisks me up into an embrace. My feet lifting off the floor and I giggle. "Mi chica ardiente" he whispers in my ear as we embrace. I'm giggling like a little girl.

Our embrace is suddenly interrupted when I hear a woman's voice. "Santiago. How are you?" she says and I watch as she places her hand on his arm. He turns and she leans in and kisses him on both cheeks, her eyes staying with mine. He seems surprised and a little uncomfortable. What's going on?

He steps away from her, pulling me protectively into his side and says "Nicky, mi amor, this is Arcenia." and boom! My heart sinks. His ex-girlfriend! Holy shite she is beautiful! Long dark silky locks, bright blue eyes and tanned skin. Like a golden bloody goddess that's just stepped all over my not so fancy outfit. Damn!

"I just popped in for a bite" she says, eyes glued on me. Keep that bitey mouth to yourself lady! Wow I'm feeling more than a tad protective right now.

She's wearing a red sleeveless dress, matching her perfect red lipstick on her perfect face, with her perfect bone structure. Feck sake!

Santi quickly tells her "Well enjoy, Arcenia. This is Nicky, by the way. My partner." and he strokes my back reassuringly. She looks a tad bit unhappy at that statement. "Well...", she fakes a smile, "Enjoy your food" and she turns on her perfect expensive heels and sways off towards her table with her perfectly toned legs.

'This will not ruin my perfect day, this will not ruin my perfect day' I chant in my head. Taking deep breaths as Santi settles in beside me at our table.

"Hey there, mi amor, you doing okay?" Santi asks, his chair scooting back a bit as he taps his knee invitingly. Without hesitation, I crawl onto his lap, well aware that being in the same room as his ex-girlfriend leaves me feeling just a little rattled. "I'm fine," I muster, and feel his hand take mine, his lips pressing a gentle kiss to my knuckles. It's comforting. And as I nestle into him, his scent and the tight circle of his arms around me create a cocoon of safety that immediately soothes the turmoil in my head.

"I last saw her months ago when I called it quits, mi princesa," he assures me, his voice steady and sincere. "I have no interest in seeing her again. Why she's here is a mystery to me. But I don't care enough to cause a fuss. All that matters is that you're here with me... and, I bet you have a whole host of things to show me," he teases, eyeing the assortment of shopping bags scattered around us.

I can't help but chuckle at this – perhaps I did let loose a little too much on the retail therapy today. Brushing off the thought, I focus my attention back on Santi, making a conscious effort to ignore the icy stare from across the restaurant. I can practically feel her eyes trying to sear a hole through me.

As always, our meal is delicious. Santi insists that I stay on his lap, making me feel cherished and protected, like a kid again, and I relish every moment of it. We share mouthfuls of food, gushing over the exquisite blend of flavors and exchanging affectionate glances.

Finally, it's time to leave for home, our home. A smirk plays on my lips as I think about the little surprise I picked up during today's shopping spree. I know it's going to make Santi's night. I can hardly wait.

SANTI

I'm barely containing my surprise at Arcenia, my ex, strolling in unexpectedly today. I'm left scratching my head, wondering what she's up to. If it weren't for Nicky's presence, I would've shown Arcenia the door of the restaurant without a second thought. But I didn't want to ruffle feathers with my beloved. So, I bit my tongue and turned my attention to what truly mattered - cherishing my moments with Nicky and ensuring her comfort always.

Owned – A BDSM Erotic Romance

The night is rolling in, and mi princesa, Nicky, is freshening up with a shower before we call it a day. I've already had mine and find myself propped up in bed, idly scrolling through our restaurant's social media feed. That's when Nicky saunters into the room nonchalantly. My jaw drops more than a notch at the sight of her. The mischievous sprite has donned the most tantalizing cat outfit I've ever laid eyes on! My heart skips a beat at her sight.

She playfully raises her hands to her chin, mimicking a cat's paws, and licks the back of one hand while purring a playful "Meow" with a giggle. I can't help but chuckle along. The outfit is a daring array of black leather straps tracing her curves, a choker around her throat and suspender style straps at her thighs. The pièce de résistance is a black leather cat mask, her bewitching eyes accentuated with dark makeup peeking through. The red lipstick she wears is incredibly captivating. I'm intrigued to see what those lips have in store for me.

I rise, leaving the comforts of the bed, and her eyes widen at the sight of my large cock standing tall and erect, practically pointing at her. With a composed coolness, I take hold of it, giving it a quick stroke as I approach her and take her hand. With a firm yet gentle pull, I guide her out of the bedroom, heading towards the stairs leading to our play room. Yes, kitty, you're definitely going to be the cat that got the cream tonight.

In our vibrant playroom, she elegantly drops to her knees, adopting a playful crawling stance. She's well-versed in the rules of our game, and her compliance brings a smirk to my face. I circle around her, my steps leading me directly to the cabinet that houses an impressive collection of our playthings. I select one that I've been eagerly anticipating introducing her to. Right now, it seems, is the ideal time.

I stride over to the wall and flick a switch, filling the room with the gentle melody of ambient music. A second tap on the switch swaths the room in a pulsating, deep red light, fabricating an atmosphere that oozes allure. I can't help but think, this is going to be an entertaining night.

I saunter back towards her, concealing our new toy behind my back. Her eyes, sharp and curious, never leave me. As I reach her, I lower myself down to her level, tapping her mouth with my free hand. "Time for your snack, mi gatita," I suggest in a teasing tone. She complies without hesitation, her obedience never failing to impress. From behind my back, I present the novelty: a bushy cat's tail butt plug. Her eyes widen in fascination, traveling from the plug to my face, her anticipation almost palpable.

Holding the plug before her, I ensure it's well-prepped, I spit down on it, my saliva coating its sleek, dark metallic surface. As it glistens, I bring it to her lips, prompting, "Now, be a good kitty and suck." The command rolls off my tongue, firm yet filled with anticipation.

She takes it into her mouth, her tongue twirling around the plug with a sultry grace. I feel my body responding in kind, a jolt of excitement coursing through me. I stifle a groan, reminding myself that we are just at the beginning of this delightful journey.

Once I'm confident that the plug is adequately lubricated, I rise to my full height, her eyes following my every move with an intriguing blend of mischief and obedience. I position myself behind her, taking a moment to admire the tantalizing view before me. Using my free hand, I trace a slow path along her cunt. She's already drenched for me. I can't help but comment, "Always so ready for me, my little kitten?"

I begin to tease her with gentle strokes, my fingers exploring her further, eliciting an eager response from her. "Eager gatita, aren't you?" I tease, my tone dropping to a seductive whisper. Her moans echo through the room, a symphony of pleasure as I quicken my pace.

Gradually, I withdraw my fingers, moving upwards towards her puckered hole, I prepare her for our new toy. As I begin to slowly introduce the plug to her ass, her response is electric, her body pushing against me in anticipation. I stifle a groan of my own, my hand instinctively reaching for my cock, matching the rhythm of the plugs movements circling the entrance of her tight ass. "You're such a good kitty," I compliment her, my voice barely a whisper as her breaths grow more ragged.

As I slowly begin to push the plug inside her, her loud groan of delight fills the room. The slow introduction of the toy sends her spiraling into ecstasy, her scream of pleasure echoing off the walls. Oh, she definitely likes this.

In the blink of an eye, the plug is securely positioned. I rise to my feet, venturing to a separate locked cabinet to retrieve her collar and leash. As I return, I crouch beside her. She's a spectacle, her body glistening from the heat of her excitement as I secure the collar around her neck and attach the leash. "Oh, mi puta obediente," I murmur, standing upright once more.

With the leash firmly in hand, I leisurely make my way towards my throne, dropping the leash and instructing her to maintain her position on all fours. I settle into my seat, legs spread wide, proudly displaying my hardened cock and heavy balls to her and the need for release visibly straining within me. I cross one ankle over my knee as I lean back, my hand thoughtfully stroking my beard as she looks up at me, her eyes never wavering. Such a good girl indeed.

A few moments pass before my hand leaves the comfort of my beard, finding a new home around the base of my eager cock. "Lie back on the floor, mi gatito sucio," I command in a low rumble. I watch as she complies, her movements a graceful dance that ends with her sprawled on the floor. "Spread," I growl, and she does so without hesitation. Her knees rise before they fall to either side of her, making contact with the floor.

She watches me, anticipating her next instruction, her furry tail tucked between her legs in a submissive display. "Play with your pussy, pussy," I say, a hint of a laugh crossing both our faces before she obeys, her hand inching towards her wet cunt.

I watch, my hand following suit on my now extremely angry cock, and her eyes remain glued to me. Our breaths become ragged, matching in rhythm as we perform for each other, our bodies on full display. I listen for her gasps of pleasure, my own movements quickening to match hers. "I want you to cum for me, mi gatito obediente," I urge, and she quickens her pace, her actions mirroring my words, causing my own arousal to intensify.

"Fuuccckkkk!". My voice resonates powerfully within the expansive room as I reach the peak of my orgasm, her resonant cries mirroring mine as she experiences her orgasm in perfect synchrony. The evidence of our shared satisfaction warms my abdomen, a sticky, tangible mess. Covering me in ribbons of cum. As we regain our breath, I direct her, "come get your cream, my kitty cat."

Gracefully, she navigates towards me, halting her advance just before me, nestling between my legs. She adopts the seiza position, her legs folding neatly beneath her thighs while her ass finds comfort on top of her heels. With anticipation in her eyes, she brings her paw - the one soaked in her own cum - up to her mouth, and begins a slow, deliberate cleansing with the flat of her tongue. Each stroke is slow, calculated, and intensely captivating. I find myself spellbound, unable to tear my gaze away from her.

Once she is satisfied with her cleanliness, her hands demurely fold in her lap. She leans in to me, her eyes meeting mine, as she embarks on a slow and deliberate exploration of my cock. My head leisurely falls back against my throne. I watch her, captivated as she commences her journey, tracing the ribbons of cum that mark my body. With only her tongue, she teases, licks and slurps, sensually relishing every last morsel. Her soft moans accompany her movements as she savors every last drop, and I find myself groaning along with her, enthralled in this moment. She is without a doubt, the best gatita obediente.

It's not over 'til the fat lady sings

Chapter Nineteen

It's not over 'til the fat lady sings

Chapter Nineteen

NICKY

Tonight's the night! My last evening in Barcelona with Santi, and guess what? He's whisking me off to the Opera. Yes, the Opera! I pinch myself to be sure it's not a dream. Sneaky Santi has been keeping this a secret. The prospect of my first ever visit to an opera has me buzzing with a level of anticipation that's off the charts.

Exiting the spacious sanctuary of our ensuite bathroom, I take one last look at my reflection. My smoky eye makeup and bright red lips are on point, ready to dazzle the night away. I strut towards the bedroom, only to freeze in awe at the sight before me. There, lying elegantly on the bed, is a ravishing red, silk dress with a pair of muted gold high heels to complete the ensemble. Wowza!

Gently, I lift the dress, admiring its luxurious texture and the hint of its costly craftsmanship. I swallow a lump in my throat, a mix of raw emotions, as I start to slip into it. I gaze at my reflection in Santi's full-length mirror, I can't help but marvel at how the dress fits like a second skin, its silky red fabric flowing onto the floor in a cascade of elegance. The sleeveless design features a delicate lace bodice that adds an extra layer of sophistication. As I continue to admire my reflection, I sense Santi's eyes on me from the bedroom doorway.

And there he is, looking every bit the Latin God, in his black tuxedo, with the sun's glow making him even more irresistible. He's decked out in shiny dress shoes, a crisp white shirt, and a black bow tie, with a white handkerchief peeking out of his pocket. I feel my heart flutter at his divine appearance. My sun kissed Deus!

With his hands crossed over his chest and one leg casually resting in front of the other, crossed at the ankles, leaning against the door frame, he throws me a low, sexy whistle. "Mi princesa, you look like a goddess," he compliments. I return the compliment with a smile, my eyes meeting his in the mirror as I thank him for the beautiful dress. "Not a patch on you, mi amor," he responds, his tone filled with admiration. He strides towards me, his hand extended my way. As our hands meet and he playfully utters, "Let's go to the Opera, mi diabla."

SANTI

As we saunter towards the magnificently grand Opera House in Barcelona, a wave of anticipation washes over the throng of opera enthusiasts clustered at the entrance. For tonight's spectacle, I've opted for the 'Zarzuela' Opera - a Spanish concoction of lyrical drama that masterfully weaves spoken and sung scenes, garnished with a dash of dance, into a captivating tapestry. I'm banking on Nicky's penchant for sophisticated drama to have her smitten, and I'm practically buzzing with anticipation for her reaction to the evening's entertainment.

Upon stepping into the opera house's vast expanse, we're greeted by the buzzing chatter of eager patrons. The foyer is a breath-taking sight to behold, with towering beams, gilded columns, majestic pillars, and an architecture that can only be described as a love letter to splendor. I gently take Nicky by the hand - her eyes wide with awe - and guide her towards our reserved table nestled within the opera house's restaurant.

As we settle into our seats at an elegant table, swathed in pristine white linens and adorned with polished cutlery, I steal a glance at Nicky. Her eyes dart around in wonder, and I can't help but bask in the joy of sharing this experience with her. Her appreciation for such moments is palpable and fuels my own happiness.

The restaurant is a testament to fine dining, with luxury red curtains cascading down to the floor and dazzling crystal chandeliers casting a soft, warm glow over the room. Together, we take our seats at the shared table, where we're met by

By Nicky Ireland

the cheerful grins of our fellow patrons. A lavish golden candelabra stands proudly at the center of the table, contributing a flicker of enchanting light to the room's ambience.

As glasses are filled with exquisite wine by the adept sommeliers, the room dims to a hushed whisper. Suddenly, from behind a deep-blue curtain, a robust cantante de ópera emerges, standing in quiet dignity before unleashing a powerful performance that fills the room with haunting echoes.

Nicky, wide-eyed and awestruck, swivels to face me, her mouth agape. In classic Nicky fashion, she silently mouths the phrase 'holy cow balls', a trademark expression that never fails to incite laughter. Suppressing my own chuckle, I raise her hand to my lips for a gentle kiss, a silent promise of many more nights like this to come.

As our culinary parade of delights makes its entrance, we're greeted by a dish that can only be described as the epitome of Spanish cuisine. A delectable arrangement of fresh salmon reigns supreme, lounging comfortably atop a bed of borlotti beans, chorizo, and an eclectic mix of vegetables. The symphony of Flavors that ensues can only be described as utterly divine, stimulating an array of lively conversations around the table.

I can't help but notice a fellow diner's rather focused attention on Nicky, causing my fists to ball unnoticed under the table. Nicky, in all her radiance, is impossible to ignore, but there's something about this intruder's gaze that is a tad too appreciative of what is, quite frankly, mine.

As the grand finale of our meal approaches, I decide it's time to introduce Nicky to the next adventure of the night - an exclusive backstage tour designed for just the two of us. A perfect distraction from the unwelcome attention of our over-zealous dining companion.

We are escorted backstage and Nicky's excitement is palpable. With each step, her eyes widen and her witty remarks about the grandeur and history of the theatre keep me chuckling. Our guide, with enthusiasm matching Nicky's, narrates the theatre's rich history, adding to the charm of the evening.

We're privy to the behind-the-scenes magic, witnessing set designers immersed in their craft and performers warming up, their anticipation for the upcoming show tangible in the air. As we wrap up our tour, we pass the majestic curtain that earlier framed the powerful cantante de ópera. A spontaneous idea bubbles up within me, and unable to resist the temptation, I gently guide Nicky towards the curtain.

The sight of her in that dress has been a tantalizing image at the back of my mind since she had first graced it in our bedroom. Deftly, I position her so she's facing the grandeur of the curtain, my hand tracing a path up her leg as I wrap my other arm around her wait. A sharp intake of breath is her response, her head tilting back onto my shoulder as a soft moan escapes her lips when I start leaving a trail of gentle bites on her neck. As I hush her whispers, I lean in closer, murmuring "me calientas" into her ear, a cheeky grin playing on my lips.

A shiver runs through her as my other hand ventures further, discovering a delightful secret - she is as eager as I am. This realization fills me with a thrilling excitement, and I quickly free my eager cock from the constraints of my trousers.

With a swift, deft movement, I guide her panties to the side and I'm finally inside her, the force of my desire matching hers. She clings to the curtain and a nearby pillar for support, her body moving in rhythm with mine. The combination of my thumb playing a tantalizing melody on her clit and the depth of my thrusts has us reaching a crescendo rather quickly. Our shared climax leaves us both breathless, the heavy panting a muffled sound in the bustling backstage.

As we regain our composure, I gingerly smooth down her dress, turn her to face me, and looking into her eyes, I cradle her face and seal the memory of this already unforgettable evening with a passionate kiss.

By Nicky Ireland

NICKY

Oh boy, the show's starting now and I'm buzzing with excitement. My heart's doing somersaults, I'm telling you. This auditorium is nothing short of grand, and guess what? We've got our very own private box. The mammoth stage is decked with a deep blue curtain, and as it lifts, the live orchestra strikes up a tune. I'm on the edge of my seat here, no joke!

The curtain rises and there they are, the performers, frozen like statues on stage. Then, the most enchanting soprano begins to sing, 'La tempranica' zarzuela by Geronimo Gimenez. Her voice, it's otherworldly, echoing throughout the massive auditorium. I'm spellbound.

The dramatic story unfolds before us and I'm leaning forward in our box, my face cupped in my hands, utterly captivated. Santi, bless him, is right there with me, drawing small circles on my back, grounding me as I lose myself in the performance. Mind. Blown.

Next thing I know, it's intermission time. And boy, do I need to hit the ladies room! Guess that wine finally caught up with me. Santi, ever the gentleman, escorts me. As we navigate towards the restrooms, who do we bump into but that overly friendly guy from our table. Yuck. I keep my eyes front and center and march right into the restroom, avoiding his gaze.

After handling business, I'm touching up my lipstick when who should appear but dear Arcenia, smirking away. Great. My eyes nearly roll out of my head. She's there, washing her hands, all perfect fingers and manicured nails, and then she drops a zinger. "Well, well, well... Are you stalking me?" I almost want to kick her, even in these killer heels. I ignore her and keep applying my lipstick.

But she's just getting started. She launches into a monologue I simply don't want to hear. She sneers my name, "Nicky, you do realize that Santiago will return to me." I continue to ignore her. "Your days are numbered dear Nicky," she says, raising a perfectly manicured eyebrow, waiting for my response.

I slowly and calmly put away my lipstick, turn to her, and take a deep breath. Then, in the calmest voice I can muster, I say, "Oh Arcenia, darling, it's not over 'til the fat lady sings". Her perfect face falls, jaw dropping, mouth opening and closing like a stunned goldfish.

Sashaying out of the bathroom, with a wink to her over my shoulder, I walk to Santi, the ever-attentive bodyguard. His eyes dart to Arcenia appearing from behind me, a question forming in his furrowed brows. "All good, mi amor?" he inquires. I can't suppress a grin as I see Arcenia rush past us into the open arms of Mr. Overly Friendly. Well, well, well little Miss Perfect!

Holding Santi's hand, I reply, with the biggest smile, "Absofrickintootly, my handsome man." He guides me, hand in hand, back into the throbbing heart of the auditorium. This night just got a whole lot better!

SANTI

The night has been a grand success, a symphony of laughter, music, and the intoxicating thrill of everything that is the magic of Opera. Memories of Arcenia and her suspicious companion at the Opera House are set aside, their presence merely a footnote in an otherwise perfect evening. I wish them luck, for they might need it.

We return to the apartment, the city lights winking goodbye at us. I can't wait to be alone with Nicky, the taste of our stolen moment behind the theatre curtain still fresh on my lips. Our little rendezvous only made me want more. As if guided by an unseen force, I usher Nicky inside, our bodies drawn to each other like magnets.

In the lounge, I spin her around to face me. The glimmer in her eyes and the slight sway in her stance tell me the fine wine has charmed her. My gaze fixes on her, a seriousness replacing the playful glint in my eyes. I trace my thumb over her lips, the touch electric between us, "Your lipstick is almost gone mi amor, I think you need to reapply it." She looks at me, confusion clouding her sparkling eyes, "Aren't we just heading for dream land?" she questions.

Ignoring her query, I guide her back with slow, deliberate strides towards the edge of the plush sofa. I gently push her down onto the seat, our gaze never breaking. "Lipstick, Nicky," I instruct, my voice low and husky. She fishes out the red lipstick from her purse, her eyes never leaving mine. The lipstick nestles into my palm, a symbol of the passion between us.

As I begin to slowly remove my bow tie, her eyes watch every movement. I slide it out of my shirt collar and fasten it around her neck in one swift motion. "That's better mi putita," I murmur, a playful wink accompanying my words. A blush creeps up her cheeks, a sight that sends a thrill coursing through me.

My fingers work on the buttons of my dress pants, my eyes drinking in the sight of her. Her red satin ballgown drapes over her legs, pooling onto the floor between us. "Hitch your dress up," I instruct her and she obeys instantly. Her dress bunches up around her waist, the sight makes me growl, "Panties off. Now!"

She slides them down her legs and hands them to me. My command of "wrists together" is met with immediate compliance. I use her red lace panties as makeshift handcuffs, the gasp escaping her lips sending a low moan rippling through me. I know she loves this as much as I do.

Stepping back, I free my already rock-hard cock from my boxer shorts. Her gaze drops to my large cock, her breath hitching at the sight. I pump myself slowly, the sensation pushing me closer to the edge, but I want to savor this moment, for a while longer at least.

I uncap the red lipstick - my kryptonite. I watch her as I slowly begin to paint the already engorged head of my cock with the lipstick, turning it an even deeper shade of red. Her wide-eyed surprise fuels my desire for her even more.

I stride forward, the words "pucker up, mi puta hermosa" slipping from my lips. She obeys immediately. The lipstick falls to the floor as both my hands grip the back of her head. I guide her to my throbbing cock, using my hips to rub the tip all over her lips, painting her face with the red lipstick. The sight of her, all messy from my cock, is intoxicating. I can't get enough of her, my putita, marked by me and only me.

In the heat of the moment, my command echoes through the room, "Open wide." Without giving her a moment to react, I push my cock into the warm depths of her mouth. Her lips envelope the base of my cock, a sensation that sends an electric jolt through my body. I can feel her tongue venturing below, brushing against my balls, lavishing attention on them in a way that only she can. "Fuuccckkkk!" I cry out, my voice booming in the otherwise silent room.

I'm teetering on the edge, unable to hold back much longer. My hips move of their own accord, thrusting into her welcoming mouth. She chokes and gags on my length, yet the sensation only adds to my pleasure. I gaze down at her, her face a beautiful sight. Red lipstick is smeared across her lips, chin, and cheeks, while her mascara now paints a trail down her face. "You're such a beautiful mess, mi puta obediente," I murmur, my voice dripping with desire.

My need to be buried deep within her is overwhelming. Hastily, I push her back onto the soft cushions of the sofa. My hands find her ankles, lifting them high, while I grab a cushion to prop up her curvaceous ass. I lean into her, pressing her thighs into her chest, her ankles now draped over my shoulders. Her high heels, a seductive sight, remain on.

Her wrists, bound together, find their way over my head, her hands cradling the back of my neck. She grabs a handful of my hair, pulling roughly as I plunge myself into her hot, wet, cunt. The sensation of being sheathed in her tightness is mind-blowing. Our cries of pleasure meld together in a harmonic symphony. I lean in, capturing her lips with mine as I continue to claim her with a fierce primal urgency.

We lose ourselves in each other, our bodies moving in a sensual rhythm. The world around us seems to slow, our shared pleasure the only thing that matters. The taste of alcohol lingers on our tongues, adding to the heady mix of lust and desire.

We can't get enough of each other, our bodies craving the closeness that only we can provide. Our climax approaches quickly, our bodies trembling in anticipation. Our release washes over us in a powerful wave, leaving us breathless and sated.

A soft giggle escapes from her, pulling me from my post-orgasmic haze. Her thumb reaches out, tracing my lips in a tender gesture. "You've got some red lipstick on your lips, Sir," she teases, her voice sultry and provocative.

The sight of her, all disheveled and thoroughly fucked, is enough to stir my desire once more. She truly is a siren, luring me in with her beauty and sensuality. And I, a willing captive, am all too eager to lose myself in her once more. "I'm not quite done with you yet, mi diablita", I promise.

See you later alligator

Chapter Twenty

By Nicky Ireland

See you later alligator

Chapter Twenty

NICKY

Santi is currently behind the wheel, steering us towards Barcelona airport. Dublin is calling me back home, and if I were to put my emotions into words, 'devastated' wouldn't even begin to cover it.

The memory of our last night together at the Opera is still fresh - it was a night that defied reality, even with the Arcenia situation casting its long shadow. But I can't let that cloud the extraordinary experiences I've soaked in during my stay here.

As we navigate the roads leading to the airport, Santi's hand finds mine, cradling it on his knee while he drives. We're sitting in a thoughtful silence, each of us grappling with the impending sense of loss that's about to envelop us as soon as we step foot in the departure lounge.

Suddenly, Santi turns to me and winks before pushing a button on the car stereo. The familiar notes of Charlie Puth's 'One Call Away' fill the car. As the lyrics float around us, he gives my hand a gentle squeeze, silently assuring me that he'll be there for me always. A grin stretches across my face, wide as the Cheshire cat's. I'm fighting back a wave of tears, threatening to spill from my eyes.

As the departures hall comes into view, I ask Santi not to linger, even though every fiber of my being is screaming for him to stay. He seems hesitant but nods in understanding. A part of me secretly wishes he would join me on my journey back to Dublin.

He gets out of the car, his hands cradling my face as he lavishes me with kisses. My eyes betray me, spilling tears down my cheeks. He looks at me, his thumb brushing away my tears, whispering "I'm here, mi amor, I not going anywhere."

He seals his promise with a soul-stirring kiss. I practically breathe him in, wishing this moment could freeze in time.

Reluctantly, I pull away, forcing myself to walk through the gate without glancing back at him. But I can't resist. I steal one more lingering look, etching his image into my memory.

SANTI

As I peel off from the bustling airport, there's a sourdough-sized knot in my gut. Waving goodbye to Nicky? That's as tough as it gets for me. But let's get one thing straight – this isn't a tearful adieu. It's more of a cheery "see you later alligator", because I'm gonna make it my mission to get to her again as soon as possible.

With a quick pivot, I set a course for the office, ready to dive headfirst into the swirling vortex of work.

Nicky, the rascal, has been given explicit marching orders: first, a text once she's all buckled up on the plane, then another once she touches down in good old Dublin, and finally, a third once she's safely tucked away behind her front door. Overprotective? Absolutely. But that's just how I roll, and I wouldn't have it any other way.

To keep the ol' grey matter from churning too hard, I decide some tunes are in order. After all, music is the ultimate diplomat – a soothing balm in times of distraction. And so, the tantalizing beats of Diplo's remix of 'California Soul' fill the car, the rhythm riding shotgun with me as I navigate the road, lost in a labyrinth of thoughts.

I like clingy

Chapter Twenty One

I like clingy

Chapter Twenty One

SANTI

"Hola, mi hermosa madre" I exclaim, extending a flamboyant welcome to my mother on her occasional city visit. Nicky has been back in Dublin over a week now and to say I miss her wouldn't be true. I literally yearn for her with every breath I take.

Nestled comfortably in the peaceful embrace of the country landscape, my parents rarely swap their serene retirement for the bright lights of Barcelona. Yet today is an exception. Today, in honor of her city sojourn, I've drawn her to my culinary enterprise, A Fuego Lento, for a brunch as leisurely as a summer's day.

She cups my face with a motherly affection, planting a kiss on my cheeks with a playful, "Hola, mi querido hijo." Sofia Maspinco, my mother, is a remarkable spectacle of beauty. Her kindness shines around her like a halo, and she carries herself with a grace that is both mesmerizing and inspirational.

Her romance with my father, Alfonso, is a tale that never ceases to tug at my heartstrings. His dedication to her is as solid as a rock, unwavering and absolute. Their love story is as timeless as a classic novel, yet brimming with a fresh vibrancy in every interaction. They are a pair in perfect unison, each one filling in the gaps of the other in a dance of love that has been choreographed over the years. It's a testament to a love that has stood the test of time, a couple choosing each other, repeatedly, day in and day out.

Their connection is a blend of mutual respect, deep affection, and a spark that refuses to dim even after all these years. They are each other's pillars, sanctuaries, and best friends. Their love forms the cornerstone of our family, the

By Nicky Ireland

foundation on which my younger sister, Isabella and I were built.

As a child, their bond was my template for love — warm, nurturing, and unwavering. They've been my lighthouse in the storm, educating me on the essence of love and commitment. I owe them a debt of gratitude for the love they've bestowed upon me and Isabella, and for the principles they've instilled in us. Their love story fuels my quest, inspiring me to find a love as deep and enduring as theirs. A love I may just have found.

Reserving our spots at a table huddled near the window, we find ourselves immersed in the stunning panorama of the Gothic Quarter streets, while Elley Duhés 'Middle of the night' plays throughout the restaurant. The age-old cobblestone pathways, intricate architectural motifs, and the lively bustle of the crowd create a picture-perfect scene that is almost lyrical in its beauty. This city, I must admit, has a charm that's hard not to adore.

Positioned snugly into our plush seats, my mom begins to spin a yarn about her trek to this place. My dad, who opted for a day in, is conspicuously missing from her flank. It's like someone pressed the sad filter on a photo, his absence etching a somber shade on her usually cheery demeanor. I toss her a sympathetic grin, fully grasping the emotional tug-o-war she's engaged in. Nicky's absence has often left a similar void in my life, empty spaces that suddenly become profound reminders of our distance.

Nudging my musing mind back into the present, I turn to the gastronomical delights of my restaurant. I give my culinary maestros the green light for a selection of cured meats and picos; a renowned Spanish bread with a reputation for its crackly texture and unique taste.

In no time, our food parade begins. The tantalizing aroma swirling from the dishes is an irresistible call to our taste buds. Our first act, traditional tomacons; a Catalan specialty bread decked with a divine mix of ripe tomatoes, garlic, and extra virgin olive oil, makes its grand entrance. The luscious red of the tomatoes flirt with the golden-brown of the bread, creating a visually striking and toothsome curtain-raiser.

Sharing the spotlight is a hefty wooden platter, proud bearer of a medley of thinly sliced cured ham and sausage. The meat, flaunting an impeccable sweet-salty harmony, is a tribute to my chefs' culinary wizardry. Each mouthful is a flavor fiesta, the opulent taste of the meats finding a perfect dance partner in the tangy tomacons, weaving an epicurean tapestry of indulgence.

A wave of colossal pride sweeps over me as I scan my restaurant, my hardworking team, and the culinary masterpieces they've conjured. Mom and I dive into our feast, our chat seamlessly weaving through my booming business, family affairs, and the great canvas of life, painting a picture of a perfectly delightful evening.

As we chat, she fills me in about my younger sibling, Isabella, who's recently been hanging out with an individual of unpredictable nature. The image of Isabella mixed up with someone so erratic tightens my fists without thought.

Isabella, in her prime at 23, illuminates a captivating charm that simply can't go unnoticed. But alas, she's always had a soft spot for the rebellious sort, much to my bemusement. Her preference for "bad boys" over the more refined gentlemen has kept me uneasy since she dipped her toes into the world of dating at the tender age of 16.

Her selection of men is typically as wild and unpredictable as she is. Isabella, the unchallenged free spirit of our familia, appears to nourish herself on unpredictability's thrill. She possesses an uncanny ability to magnetize men who reflect her rebellious spirit, stoking the flames of her fiery, untamed personality.

Her past boyfriends are a gallery of varied characters, from inked musicians to thrill-seeking bikers, each one seemingly more defiant than the one before. It's as if she's constantly stirring the pot, eternally on the hunt for the next escapade, the next adrenaline rush. This wild streak, this relentless pursuit of thrill, is mirrored in her romantic endeavors, turning her life into a rollercoaster ride of high peaks and sudden drops.

Despite my calm demeanor, I can't help but be fascinated by her, even as I fret over her choices. It's a paradox that keeps my nights interesting, my worry for her striking a contrast with my admiration for her fierce independence. I find myself both intrigued and uneasy by her audacious spirit, as I continue to watch her whirlwind life unfold with an enigmatic blend of concern and respect.

The grand finale of our Sunday brunch is drawing near, the last, delightful drops of our café con leche being savored to the fullest. Suddenly, my phone, lying dormant on the table, springs to life with a sudden fervor that disrupts the tranquil symphony of our meal.

The screen bursts into life with the vibrant image of Nicky, her radiant face casting a glow across the room. With an almost instinctive swiftness, I pick up the phone, her call luring me like a magnetic force.

As I connect the call, my voice takes on a softer tone, "Mi amor," I welcome her, a smile spreading across my face like a warm sunrise. Out of the corner of my eye, I catch a glimpse of my mother's face lighting up, mirroring my own joy.

Her heart has always held a special place for the prospect of me finding someone, settling down, and starting a family. I can practically sense her thoughts racing with the thrilling idea of me being romantically involved.

The moment Nicky's voice echoes through the line, I can immediately detect a wave of distress. Her words tumble out in a hurried rush, the usually poised and witty woman replaced by an agitated whirlwind. I interject, reminding her to slow down, to breathe. "I'm here, mi Princesa. Tell me everything," I assure her, hoping to bring a sense of calm to the chaotic situation.

Through her teary words, Nicky unfolds the situation. "Molly has really gotten under my skin. I'm at my wits' end with her," she mutters. As she gathers herself, the source of her upset is revealed. Her elder sister Molly, in an unexpected move, visited the house Nicky rents from her and decided to hike up the rent, a financial strain that Nicky was already finding difficult to manage.

A wave of helplessness washes over me, knowing that my offer of financial assistance would likely be declined due to her fiercely independent streak. A thought flits across my mind, envisioning Nicky living with me in Barcelona, but I swiftly dismiss it. Maybe someday, I muse.

Nicky continues to vent, her voice filled with frustration. "She criticized our relationship and it really got to me. She doesn't even know you, heck, she barely knows me! And she's always jumping to conclusions. She thinks she's always right and I'm always wrong, and she's questioning my sanity for falling for a man living in another country. She said that we are spiraling and...", her voice breaks into sobs again.

"Nicky, mi amor, how can I help?" I ask, my heart yearning to soothe her. I'm itching to share my thoughts on her overbearing sister, but now's not the time for that. "Oh, I'm fine, Santi. Just one of those days, and I miss you. I miss you a lot. I'm sorry I'm acting so clingy. I get like this when I'm upset. I'm sorry," she admits, her words punctuated by her sobs.

"I like clingy," I retort, my words lightening the atmosphere. I can almost see the smile creeping back onto her face. "Te necesito, mi amor. Te necesito," I comfort her. Those words seem to wash over her, like a balm to her upset.

As the phone call concludes, I'm catapulted back into the realm of silence. I swivel around to catch my mother's curious stare. Her eyes twinkle with an adventurous glint, her hands clapping in a rhythm of giddy impatience. I can't help but chuckle, a grin seizing permanent residence on her face.

Hovering with suspense, my mother's voice dances through the air, "When do I finally get the grand tour of this mystery woman's world?" Her question hangs in the balance, and I release a robust laugh. "Hold your horses, mi hermosa madre," I comfort her, my hand nestling atop hers in a familiar gesture. Her eyes radiate a warmth that mirrors her anticipation, and she playfully nags, "Oh, Santiago, don't keep a lady waiting. The suspense is driving me up the wall!" I surrender to another round of laughter, her contagious excitement acting as the perfect mood elevator.

"Santiago, mi querido hijo," she interjects, her voice adopting a tone of gravity that briefly dampens our light-hearted banter, "it sounds like your mystery woman could use your company right now. Remember, the essence of our being is love and connection. Don't be shy to shower her with affection."

Her wisdom strikes a chord within me, a gentle reminder of life's most precious gifts - love, family, and connection.

She gathers her belongings in a swift, elegant motion, the rustling fabric breaking the silence. With a choreographed fluidity, we rise from the table. She pulls me into a comforting hug, her arms wrapping around me in a motherly embrace that brings both solace and strength.

Fire on fire

Chapter Twenty Two

By Nicky Ireland

Fire on fire

Chapter Twenty Two

NICKY

I'm sprawled across my bed, entangled in the battle-worn sheets, wrestling with the elusive specter of sleep. It's 10pm, the night's darkness presses up against the windows like an impatient visitor, a wild rainstorm is throwing a tantrum outside, its deafening cries echoing off the roof, drowning the world in its mournful melody.

Just hours ago, I was on the phone with Santi. The memory of my grumpy demeanor wraps itself around my thoughts like a mischievous snake, splashing my solitude with strokes of regret. Oh, how I miss him! I ache for his company, his voice, his touch.

My body squirms restlessly, my mind gets sucked into a whirlpool of yearning and frustration. Teetering on the brink of sleep, a sudden, muffled sound from outside shatters the peaceful silence. Irritation bubbles up inside me, morphing into a fiery annoyance that singes my frayed nerves.

With a disgruntled sigh, I sink back into the pillowy comfort of my bed, my eyelids weighed down by the heavy chains of impending sleep.

After a moment, I decide to surrender to the restive night. Yanking myself out of the cozy cocoon of my bed, I stomp towards the window, every step carrying the weight of my grumpiness. I'm primed to rain down my wrath on the source of the disturbance. But as I near the window, my anger evaporates like morning mist, replaced by sheer disbelief.

There stands Santi, drenched to the bone in the pouring rain, hoisting a boombox high above his head, a scene ripped straight out of the 1989 movie 'Say Anything'.

The sweet strains of Sam Smith's 'Fire on Fire' spill from the speakers, a melodious serenade embracing the stormy night. I rub my eyes in disbelief. Am I dreaming?

I fling open the window of my bedroom, propping myself up on the sill with my elbows. A broad smile stretches across my face, my chuckles bubbling up, mingling with the grand orchestra of the rain-drenched night and the music, turning it into a fun, lively concert.

Santi's face radiates joy, his eyes sparkling like distant stars, meeting mine from across the divide. The lyrics of the song pulsate through the air, acting as a mirror, reflecting the raw passion shared between us in this surreal moment.

As the song fades, I bound down the stairs, my heart pounding like a wild drum in my chest. I sprint towards him, my bare feet splashing through the puddles, the rain forming a curtain around us.

He places the boombox down, standing as still as a statue as I leap into his arms. I wrap my legs around his waist, my hands finding their home around his neck, and press my lips to his in a fervent kiss, the rain soaking us, oblivious to the tempest continuing to rage. The heat shared between us is intoxicating, the fire in our eyes reflected in our fervor.

Laughter rings from my lips as I tilt my head back, letting the rain wash over me. I can't help but let out a scream of pure joy into the stormy night. The world outside our cocoon of love is insignificant, my neighbors' opinions immaterial. This moment is ours, a bubble of love in the midst of the storm, and ours alone.

"Look who's here!" I exclaim, my voice bubbling over with joy. "Si, mi chica ardiente. Like I'd be anywhere else. You sent out an SOS, right?" he retorts. His words leave me with wide eyes and a surprised chuckle slips past my lips, "You're nuts, a simple call tonight would've done the trick." His grin widens, his words sending shivers down my spine, "Why aim for a mere spark, mi amor, when I can bask in your blazing fire right here?" My reply? A shower of kisses, my lips exploring his face, his grand gesture rendering me speechless.

By Nicky Ireland

Santi's contemporary serenade goes beyond a romantic display; it's a glowing testament of his love. He's here, just when I need him the most, his actions plunging me further into the love vortex. He's my world, my everything.

SANTI

Grasping Nicky's hand, I lift the retro boombox high as we plunge into her home with the thrill of adventure coursing through our veins. The rain has given us a proper soaking, leaving us both drenched to our cores. Nicky, mi Princesa, has caught the worst of it, her clothes bearing the brunt of the deluge.

I can't help but observe her oversized tee. It used to be a simple, opaque piece of clothing, but now, it clings to her form like an added layer of skin, made semi-transparent by the torrential downpour. It forms a snug fit around her, revealing more than it hides, and I feel a stir of arousal, the distinct hardness of my cock pressing against my jeans.

Earlier today, following our phone call, I managed to arrange a flight from sunny Barcelona to damp and chilly Dublin. Despite my jam-packed schedule, I was resolute in my decision to be here for her. It was clear as day to me that I needed to be by her side.

Choosing to be with her ignited a spark of joy that was far more intoxicating than any career victory. To make it work, I had to shuffle a few appointments I had lined up in Barcelona. The result? A clear slate, offering me an entire weekend to devote to Nicky.

The prospect of this exclusive time together, just the two of us once again, fills me with a joy that's hard to put into words. I'm practically buzzing with anticipation to see what the weekend holds for us.

Outside, the rain keeps up its relentless assault, each droplet colliding with the window in a symphony of nature's fury. "Time to warm you up, mi Princesa," I suggest, my voice a soothing whisper against the backdrop of the raging storm. We make our way upstairs, where I have a scheme to beat the chill.

Nicky is perched on the edge of her plush, queen-sized bed, wrapped in an oversized fluffy towel. It's a warm barrier against the cold seeping in from the storm brewing outside. Meanwhile, I take on the task of preparing a bath for us, adjusting the temperature until it's perfect.

The bathtub fills, the water frothing and transforming into a luxurious foam. I add more bubbles, their iridescent sheen adding a touch of enchantment to the scene. I light scented candles on the counter, their gentle glow casting dancing shadows around the bathroom, filling the air with a soothing blend of lavender and vanilla.

Then, I shed my own soaked clothes, the wet fabric a stark contrast to the warm air enveloping the bathroom. I dim the lights, creating an atmosphere of serenity and intimacy.

I return to her, my bare feet softly padding against the cold floor. I extend my hand towards her, and she rises to take it, the fluffy towel pooling at her feet as she steps towards me, an air of anticipation surrounding her.

Holding her hand, I lead her into the bathroom. A welcoming cloud of steam from the bath engulfs us, the aroma of the candles dancing through the air, composing a symphony of serenity.

Assisting her, she steps into the bath, her foot vanishing beneath the frothy, bubble-brimmed water. Once she's comfortably nested, I slide into the water behind her. The bath transforms into a sanctuary, warm water cloaking us, bubbles popping and fizzing, enhancing the calming aura.

In my hand, I grasp a large, plush sponge, saturated with the warm, soapy water. Gently, I glide it across Nicky's shoulders, the sponge's tender touch eliciting a satisfied sigh from her. She nestles deeper into my chest, her body radiating warmth, providing a comforting sensation. My heart drums rhythmically, a beat that echoes the pulse of my cock at the base of her spine.

As I continue to trace the sponge over her body, mapping a path across her collar bones and down to her breasts, her body reciprocates, her nipples tensing once more, a sight I observe over her shoulder. I'm captivated by the rhythmic swell and fall of her breasts as I continue to coax her nipples with the sponge.

A playful whisper slips from her lips, "mi diablo," she says, triggering a deep laugh from me. My mirth reverberates in the steam-filled room, a jubilant interruption to the tranquil atmosphere.

Nicky, with her quick wit, has a knack for catching me off-guard, and I can't help but admire her spirited charm. It's a moment of shared laughter, a testament to our connection, and I find myself intrigued by her even more.

Her curly hair spills between my fingers as I gather it into a high ponytail, tugging gently to tilt her gaze up towards mine. "On your knees, mi diabla. Now!" I say, my voice a rumbling command.

Quick as a flash, she's down, presenting her ass to me, a glance tossed over her shoulder that promises mischief and delight. Minx!

As I lower my face towards her tantalizing curves, my tongue commences a relentless dance of seduction on her ass. She squirms beneath me, her body a live wire of sensation. My hands, firm and unyielding, grip her hips, holding her still as I surrender myself to the intoxicating scent of her ass. She's a potent brew that leaves my senses reeling.

Her moans harmonize with mine, a symphony of desire reverberating against her, stoking the fires within her.

Rising to my knees, I position myself, my rock hard cock pressing against her, a throbbing echo of her own desire. As I glide the tip along her pussy lips, our shared groan is a testament to the raw intensity of our connection. "Oh, Santi," she breathes, her voice a siren's call that sends shockwaves through me.

With my cock poised at the entrance to her soaking wet pussy, I take hold of her hips, and with one decisive thrust, I'm enveloped by her.

Pleasure ripples through us, our cries echoing off the tiled walls. We move in rhythm, the bathwater and bubbles splash around our sensual playground, our bodies slick and heated in the steamy bath.

I see the yearning in Nicky's eyes, a mirror of my own craving for her ultimate release. "Play with your pussy, mi princesa," I order, and she complies eagerly, her fingers dancing over her sensitive clit.

My hands part her ass cheeks further and I spit down onto her ass, my saliva adding to the slickness. I remove my throbbing cock from her aching pussy and I slide it upwards, teasing her asshole, our panting breaths filling the bathroom with the sound of our unspoken desire.

In one swift movement, I push my cock deep into her puckered hole, our mutual gasp a testament to the intensity of the sensation. Leaning forward, my chest pressed against her back, I move with a depth and rhythm that leaves us both breathless.

Catching her hair in my grasp, pulling her head back forcefully, "You love when I fuck your ass, don't you mi puta obediente?" I assert. It's not a question but a statement of fact, yet she nods, her breath coming in short gasps.

Together, we climb towards the precipice, our bodies in sync.

With one final, deep thrust, I give her all of me, our bodies shaking in tandem. Exhausted and sated, we collapse into the soothing embrace of the warm bathwater, the fragrance of candles wafting in the air.

This shared bath is more than just a simple act. It's an exploration, an adventure filled with laughter, touch, and connection. We can't get enough of each other, our hunger for these moments insatiable. The intensity of our connection is palpable, a testament to the electric chemistry between us.

Skin and blisters

Chapter Twenty Three

Skin and blisters

Chapter Twenty Three

NICKY

I'm still pinching myself, not quite believing the rollercoaster that was last night. Picture this: Santi popping up at my doorstep, looking like he stepped out of a rom-com, soaked to the bone and hoisting a boombox above his head. Every time I replay the scene in my head, laughter bubbles up inside of me.

And this morning? Well, it just got even better. Rising from sleep, the irresistible scent of breakfast greets me. Santi, the sneaky devil, had slipped out of bed unnoticed and whipped up my favourite brunch: French toast topped with a rainbow of fresh fruits and a cascade of maple syrup. All the ingredients are fresh - he took a morning stroll to the corner store just to make sure of that. This man, he's a real wonder, leaving me sighing in awe and admiration.

His energy is a constant whirlwind of positivity that keeps me on my toes. I've come to learn that his passion for fitness is intertwined with his daily routine, with kickboxing sessions peppered throughout his week. His commitment to health and wellness is evident in the sculpted curves of his physique, a showcase of countless hours of intense training.

Just last night, we were wrapped up in a moment so passionate, so physically demanding, it left me breathless. The energy, the connection, was so powerful, it was almost tangible. My legs were buzzing from the exertion, a sweet reminder of our passionate encounter. I was left with a delicious fatigue that lingered for a good couple of hours, leaving me too weak to even move.

But, did I mind? Absolutely not! On the contrary, I basked in it. The thought of spending time with Santi, wrapped up with him, whether in the comfort of our bed or wherever else our passion takes us, fills me with an indescribable joy. His presence, his energy, his passion - these are things I willingly lose myself in, each and every day.

I'm snuggled up to Santi in bed, finding solace in the cozy cocoon of his arms wrapped around me. His scent is captivating, a fragrant spell that dances around my senses. We've been whispering sweet nothings, sharing stories, and giggling about the most random things, including his peculiar fascination — colognes. His collection is nothing short of a mini perfume boutique, borderline obsessive, really. But it all adds up when I realize that he always smells like a dream, a tantalizing mix of intriguing aromas.

The serene bubble of our morning is jolted out of place by the jarring sound of my front door creaking open. My heart skips a beat, praying it's not my housemate, Ben, back early from his regular weekend trip to Offaly.

In a flurry of movement, I wriggle into my jeans and slip on one of Santi's well-loved t-shirts. I pause for a moment to inhale the familiar scent that clings to it, grinning devilishly at him as I do so. His laughter rings through the room as I dart down the stairs to figure out the source of the disruption. But, much to my surprise, I collide with my sister, Molly, midway.

I blink at her in disbelief. "Molly? What on earth are you doing here?" I demand, bewildered by her unannounced visit. She shoots back a snappy retort, reminding me rather haughtily that she technically owns the house. Her unexpected intrusion, however, remains a mystery.

Despite her prickly attitude, I manage to maintain my calm. I'm acutely aware that Santi is still upstairs, and I'd rather not have him be privy to any family melodrama. The day is still young, and I'm determined to preserve the peaceful ambiance we've been enjoying.

But then, Molly drops a figurative bomb. Apparently, she's decided to give a tour of the house to a prospective renter today. Why, you ask? Because she's convinced that I'm incapable of affording the rent and doesn't want to be stuck without a tenant. My blood boils, but I swallow my anger, deciding to retreat back upstairs.

As I walk away, I throw a curt response over my shoulder, "Go ahead, do whatever you want. I'm going back to bed. Santi's here and I don't want to be disturbed." I can practically feel her rolling her eyes at my words, but I couldn't care less. I have much more delightful matters to attend to, like the inviting warmth of my bed and the enchanting man who's waiting for me upstairs.

SANTI

Nicky strides back into our shared sanctuary, a playful pout artfully painted across her visage. I straighten up immediately, a ripple of curiosity stirring within me. What could have possibly unfolded to orchestrate such a masterpiece of emotion on her face?

Her footfalls echo a melodious rhythm on the floor as she returns, each step weighed down with an intriguing story that wasn't there before. With a dancer's grace, she mounts the bed, caging me within her limbs, draped around my body, while her arms form a necklace around my neck. She exhales, the faint sound seeming to echo the symphony of the world.

"And who was that, mi amor?" I venture to ask, my fingers painting soothing circles on her back, pulling her closer into our shared warmth. The familiar heat of our bodies intertwining offers a comforting symphony. She retreats a tad, her eyes locking onto mine, "Molly," she declares, her eyes rolling with a dash of witty theatrics that fans the flames of my curiosity.

I reel her back into my embrace, my arms forming a protective cocoon around her, giving her a gentle squeeze as a silent proclamation of my unwavering support. "What's going on?" I question, my tone brimming with intrigue. She then embarks on the narrative of her recent conversation.

As she weaves the tale of her encounter, I find myself ensnared by the unexpected plot twist. Despite never having crossed paths with Molly, her elusive sister, it appears that today might just be the day!

Molly's sheer audacity leaves me in a state of suspended disbelief. She's managed to corner Nicky into a labyrinth of complicated decisions. Molly comes across as a puzzle waiting to be solved, and while the thought of meeting her doesn't exactly ignite a spark of joy, I find myself intrigued by the enigma that she is.

As our verbal volley cools off, a series of hushed noises seep up from the house's depths. Molly's potential new tenant is clearly here to inspect the property. Molly's audacity leaves me struck, but not surprised.

Getting up, I slip into my jeans and a fresh t-shirt, leaning over to place a gentle kiss on Nicky's forehead as she curls back into the bed's inviting warmth. "Stay snug, mi princesa. Coffee's up next on my agenda," I say, fastening my jeans.

At my words, her eyes dart downwards, a hint of mischief in her gaze. A foot peeks out from beneath the covers, tracing a teasing path against my crotch. I nab her foot, playfully placing a kiss on her wriggly toes, nibbling at them, making her giggle.

Dropping her foot, I lean in for an intimate embrace. As I pull back, a whispered "Thank you, Papi" escapes her lips. The word 'Papi' sending a wave of warmth and anticipation through me. "Oh, mi diabla..." I respond, her laughter filling the room. I force myself to step back from her, well aware that if I don't tear myself away now, we'll be lost in our desire.

Descending the staircase, I spot Molly in the kitchen, deeply involved in conversation with a young man. I assume he's the hopeful tenant. A few steps behind him is a woman, likely his partner, cradling a baby in her arms. I greet them in passing, not wanting to interrupt, as I make a beeline for the coffee machine, our late morning savior.

Molly is undeniably pretty, though she's no match for my darling Nicky. But then again, I'm admittedly biased. The chill emanating from Molly, however, is perplexing. It's a stark contrast to the radiating warmth Nicky never fails to exude. The stark difference between the two sisters is thought-provoking.

While I'm immersed in the process of brewing our coffee, retrieving oversized mugs from the cabinets and fetching milk from the fridge, Molly makes her exit from the room, her potential tenants trailing behind her.

The house falls silent again, save for the comforting hum of the coffee maker.

The kitchen door closes with a soft thud, separating me from the murmuring voices by the entrance.

Intrigue pulsates within me, a magnetic pull drawing me closer to the source of the conversation. I feel a sudden desire to eavesdrop - not my proudest moment, but I rationalize it as an act of safeguarding Nicky's interests.

The voices, though hushed, echo through the door, the subject of their conversation becoming clear - the rent. A disagreement about the price sparks, and I can understand why. The rent is, for lack of a better word, outrageous. Shock and distaste ripple through me as I overhear Molly offering the stranger a rental fee significantly lower than what she charges her own sister.

I'm left reeling, speechless at the audacity. What a sneaky maneuver.

As the conversation winds down, I step away from the door, refocusing on crafting our coffees to perfection.

Molly saunters back into the kitchen, reaching for her purse with a flourish. I guess she's on her way out, but I can't let her leave without giving her a piece of my mind. I take a sip of my coffee, eyeing her over the rim.

"Hi Molly, I'm Santiago," I say, keeping my voice steady. She responds with a curt smile, not bothering to say a word, and makes to leave.

I halt her retreat with my words, "We've never met before, and I can't pretend to know you. But I do know that overcharging your sister for a room she can hardly afford isn't exactly sisterly." I take another sip of my coffee, maintaining eye contact.

Caught off guard, Molly stammers for a response, her mouth opening and closing like a dumbfounded goldfish. She finally counters, "It's none of your business, Santiago," her tone dripping with disdain.

I respond calmly, yet firmly, "That's where you're mistaken, Molly. Nicky's well-being happens to be very much my business. And it's unsettling that you'd show a stranger more kindness than your own sister." I arch an eyebrow at her, throwing down the gauntlet.

Her response is laughter, a reaction that seems to tickle her more than it should.

A hint of annoyance flares within me. I'm not one to lose my cool easily, and I refuse to let this woman ruffle my feathers.

Making a firm decision, I tell her, "Molly, I suggest you let your new tenants know they can move in within the month. Nicky won't be needing the room much longer." The disgust on her face is palpable as she huffs out of the kitchen, her exit resembling a petulant child throwing a tantrum.

A sly grin spreads across my face as I find myself alone in the kitchen. The stage is set for the grand reveal - it's time to let Nicky know she's about to embark on a new adventure in Barcelona, living with yours truly.

Greener pastures

Chapter Twenty Four

By Nicky Ireland

Greener pastures

Twenty Four

NICKY

Well, well, well, what do we have here? Just a casual two weeks since Santi's unforgettable brainwave with my sis, Molly. If I could, I'd have loved to become a teensy, unseen fly on the wall, just to see the utter astonishment on Molly's face as Santi just casually dropped the bombshell. Oh, the drama of it all — it's like something straight out of a soap opera!

Now, don't get me wrong, the initial jolt of finding out I'm supposed to pack up and move to Barcelona to be with Santi was quite something. But hey, that surprise has now been replaced with a heart-thumping, adrenaline-fueled excitement. I mean, who wouldn't jump at the chance to spend more time with their beau in a pulsating, vibrant city, right? It's like a thrilling roller coaster ride, and I'm buckling up for the adventure!

Moving isn't exactly an alien concept to me. I've had my fair share of bouncing around different parts of the UK alongside my ex.

The thrill of exploring a new city, getting lost in its labyrinthine streets, immersing myself in the local culture—there's a certain joy to it, you know? But I've always had a hankering for something a bit more... Mediterranean.

And now, as if by Santi-magic, the universe has served up just the opportunity.

The cherry on top? It's all happening with Santi, and that just makes this entire thing a whole lot more exciting!

The past week has been all about wrapping up loose ends before zipping off to Barcelona. It's not too complicated, really. I don't own a house or furniture, and my possessions mainly consist of clothes, toiletries, and my trusty makeup kit.

A good chunk of it is already packed and ready to jet off to my new abode. And Santi? Oh, he's been an absolute gem, handling all the logistics and arranging for a moving company to whisk my stuff off to his mansion in Bellamar. Once I'm there, I can choose what I want to take to his swanky apartment in the Gothic Quarter. And trust me, it's as straightforward as it gets!

Of course, I've also had to have the conversation with Ben, breaking the news that I'm packing my bags and he might need to do the same. But get this, he and the delightful Sarah have been weaving a love story in the shadows! Turns out, he's been scratching his head, wondering how to spill the beans that he's also hitting the road.

Sure, he's a bit of a mess, has a unique 'aroma', and his life's as organized as a teenager's closet, but hey, the kid's barely out of his teens and he's trying his best.

We decide to keep the banter going, texting or blasting each other on social media, and that works for me!"

Now, you must be wondering, did I just take all of this lying down? Of course not! I gave Santi a good ribbing just to make a point. But let's be real, I'm secretly over the moon about the whole thing. So, here's to the new chapter, and greener pastures, where the fun, hopefully, will never end!

Standing on the precipice of this thrilling new adventure, I've decided I'm holding onto my lucrative commercial gigs for as long as I can. Why? Well, let's just say they're not only a hoot but also a financial lifeline. They've got me covered for those quick hops on a plane to and from Barcelona, and even the odd Dublin hotel stay. Plus, they're a gold mine, so why not keep them in my back pocket as long as I can juggle it, right?

Now, here's the exciting part. I'm plunging headfirst into the creative scene in Barcelona, I've been rubbing virtual shoulders with agencies that are just as artsy as they come. The initial vibes are super promising!

By Nicky Ireland

Luckily Barcelona's fashion and commercial sectors are skyrocketing, and they're practically screaming for talented makeup artists like me. So, with all these positive signals, it seems the universe is pretty much rolling out the red carpet for me.

The game plan is as follows: weekdays spent in Santi's quaint Gothic Quarter apartment and weekends unwinding in his swanky Bellamar mansion. Just picturing myself basking under the Barcelona sun, sipping on a cup of Joe at one of those charming cafes in the Gothic Quarter, waking up next to Santi's smiling face, and drifting off to sleep wrapped in his arms - it will be pure bliss! It's like a bubble of excitement is forming within me, growing bigger and bursting with joy with every tick of the clock.

In a matter of days, I'll be catching a flight to Barcelona. Santi and I have been apart for a fortnight, thanks to the whirlwind of wrapping up my life here. But, we've been tethered by constant phone and text chitter-chatter throughout the day and late into the night. The distance has only stoked the fire of longing to see him again, turning the upcoming reunion into a thrilling countdown. Video calls have been our lifeline, our bridge over the gap of miles. Honestly, I don't know how I would've kept my sanity without seeing his handsome mug!

Right now I'm sitting smack dab in the middle of my favourite cozy chair, bouncing with anticipation for Santi's video call tonight. We're putting the final touches on our moving plans – a whole new adventure awaits us! I can hardly wait to see his grin light up my screen and to hear the sound of his laughter fill my room.

Grasping a thrilling novel in one hand that sends me spiraling into a vortex of captivating stories, a delightful escape from the mundane. Each word morphs into a hidden portal, enticing me to delve deeper into its maze of narratives.

In my free hand, a fine glass of ruby red wine twirls around, whispering sweet promises through its fragrant bouquet. With each sip, an invigorating fusion of bold, velvety Flavors cascades over my palate. This cherished ritual serves as my serene oasis, an island of calm amid the exhilarating tempest of tales.

This is my sanctuary, my safe haven from the world where I blissfully while away the hours, a good book, a delicious glass of wine and the anticipation of a call from Santi. The man who has captured my heart.

SANTI

As I unfolded the tale of my tête-à-tête with her sister Molly, Nicky responded with a burst of laughter. Her eyes, twinkled with a cocktail of delight and surprise, reflected in the humor she found in my interaction with her infamously challenging sister. However, her emotions swiftly changed its course when I revealed, with an unintentional air of command, that she would be packing her bags for Barcelona to join me. She was visibly rattled by my bold decision-making.

As time ticked on, our conversation escalated in intensity, peppered with a handful of tart comments from Nicky. Her annoyance at my audacity to make such a decision without her input was palpable. I had to concede, her argument held water.

Yet, by nature, I am a person that relentlessly pursues my desires. And my heart desires her. It longs for her proximity, and I'm steadfast in this chase. I have savored the sour pangs of her absence and the heady sweetness of her company.

Right now, I pick up my phone and dial her number. A few rings later, she appears on my screen, answering my video call. "Mi amor," I greet her, my face brightening into a broad grin. My heart pounds in my chest as I soak in the sight of her, lounging on her bed, wearing the sluttiest crimson lingerie.

She is a tantalizing temptress, her smile mirroring mine, acutely aware of the effect she casts on me and delighting in it. This facet of her has me under her spell. Mi diabla!

By Nicky Ireland

Over the recent weeks, our dialogues have plunged deeper into the realm of our shared physical desires. We've been forthright about our cravings, our needs, discovering that they harmoniously coincide.

She possesses a deep submissiveness, and my innate yearning to dominate her has infused our love life, much to our shared amusement and satisfaction.

"Hi Papi," she hails cheerfully, her voice as rich and velvety as a river of melted chocolate. There's a playful lilt to her tone, a clever wit behind her words that makes my pulse quicken.

In an instant, my cock responds to her flirtatious tenor and the sight of her daringly provocative red lingerie, a scarlet ensemble that's more suggestion than actual fabric.

Intrigued and yet maintaining a composed demeanor, I waste no time in shedding the stiff, confining layers of my business attire. As the ties of formality fall away, I sink into the plush comfort of my living room chair, a soft smile playing on my lips.

"Lie back and spread your legs for me, mi amor?" I command, my voice as smooth as the single malt whiskey resting on the coffee table.

She doesn't skip a beat, complying with my request as if it were the most natural thing in the world. The sight of her, poised and ready, sends a thrill of anticipation coursing through my veins. And the evening has only just begun.

My attention is riveted to her as she leans back onto her bed, her legs spread invitingly. Her full breasts strains against the sheer fabric of her crimson bra, her flushed, hardened nipples revealing her excitement.

I reach into my trousers, freeing my already eager cock. An anticipatory drop of pre-cum gathers at the tip, and I gently distribute it over the vibrant head, my excitement mirroring hers. A wave of pleasure washes over me, and I can't help but release a deep sigh as I observe her.

"Slide your panties to the side for me," I instruct, my voice gravelly with longing. She obliges, her fingers expertly manipulating the delicate fabric, exposing her moist pussy, glistening with her desire.

I angle my phone, allowing her a glimpse of my rock hard cock. Her eyes widen at the sight of my engorged length. "Do you like what you see, mi chica ardiente?" I playfully ask, and her response, a breathless "Yes, Sir," stirs a primal growl from deep within me.

"Show me your wet pussy," I demand, my voice resonating with calm authority. Her fingers explore the

dewy moisture that pools around her cunt, a testament to her longing. Her gaze is fixed on me, imploring and passionate, a silent request for my approval.

I meet her gaze, recognizing her desire, the rawness of her need. "You're doing so well, mi amore. Show me how much you want me; my touch, my scent, my taste."

The ambiance brims with an irresistible allure. Kina's 'Can we kiss forever' croons playfully in the background, filling the room with a rhythmic cadence. A nearby lamp showers her with a soft, warm radiance, accentuating the glistening beads of anticipation that trace her eager pussy.

A smile plays on my lips as I watch her, my hard cock throbbing in response. My hand moves leisurely over my cock, a slow rhythm that mirrors her own. "Good girl, buena putita," I praise, my voice deep, a low purr that resonates in the silence of the room. "Don't stop. Show me how much you crave me."

Her response is immediate, a shiver that ripples through her body, arching her back off the bed. Her breath hitches as her fingers quicken their pace, circling her hardened clit with a newfound urgency. The sight is visually stunning, an intimate spectacle of raw passion and desire.

"Speak up, tell me what you want, Nicky. Don't hold back, let it out!", I roar with gritted determination.

Her response is a desperate plea, a cry that rings out in the silence, "You! Only you, Sir! I crave you. I crave your cock deep within me. I crave your cum inside me. I crave the flavor of your skin on my tongue, the flavor of your big, hard cock in my mouth, the flavor of your cum in my throat. I need your scent lingering on me, inside me, dripping out of me. Every part, every piece of you, I need it."

Her tormented declaration sends a rush of adrenaline through me, stirring a primal instinct that leads my hand to move with increasing speed over my hardened cock. I can feel the tension building, a wave of pleasure about to crest. My balls tighten in anticipation. The impending release is within grasp, and I know she is teetering on the same precipice.

"Cum with me, puta sucia, cum with me!", I roar as I surrender to the impending climax. Streams of my cum shoot all over my stomach and over the fabric of my expensive suit trousers.

In sync with my release, she also succumbs to the overwhelming pleasure, her voice rising in a scream that carries my name, her body convulsing on the soft sheets of her bed in the throes of ecstasy.

As the thrill subsides and our heartbeats find their normal pace, we dive headfirst into a night-time chat-a-thon.

We leapfrog across a universe of topics, plumbing the depths of our minds, exchanging brainwaves, dreams, and chuckles. Bathed in the gentle luminescence of the evening, I begin to paint a picture for Nicky, sketching out my vision for our playroom.

I lay bare my ambitions and wishes for our space, an arena I hope will become a second home to her once she has acclimated to her new surroundings. My dream is that this room will morph into a haven for us, a maze where we can map the contours of our connection, uncovering fresh layers of our relationship. I relay my fantasies of countless hours we will clock in that room, on a voyage of discovery that extends beyond the tangible.

Nicky's reaction is a mirror of my enthusiasm, her eyes twinkling like stars with expectation. The sheer joy of it is a genie I struggle to keep in its bottle. In my mind, the playroom is more than just four walls; it's a portal, a gateway that will guide our relationship into uncharted waters. It's a realm brimming with the potential for us to deepen our bond, to understand each other on a more intrinsic level, to experience a closeness that's new to both of us.

I am confident that our joint adventures in that room will act as a springboard, launching us into a new facet of our relationship. A facet characterized by shared discovery, comprehension, and evolution.

The room, once solely mine, will now be ours - a communal space, a monument to our shared journey. It is within these walls that we will author our narrative, a narrative as unique as we are.

Faith, hope, love & luck

Chapter Twenty Five

Faith, hope, love and luck

Chapter Twenty Five

NICKY

Stepping foot into Dublin airport with nothing more than my trusty overnight bag and oh-so-precious professional makeup kit is where this tale begins.

By the way, let's get one thing straight — this makeup kit is my life, it's practically attached to me!

The excitement? It's bubbling up like a freshly poured soda, fizzing and dancing around so much that I'm literally scared I might need a change of knickers. Good thing I've got a spare pair tucked away in my carry-on — always be prepared, right?

With a few hours to spare before my flight, I reckon a cup of rich, aromatic java is in order.

Cruising through the duty-free shops, piping hot takeaway coffee in hand, I'm like a hawk, carefully sidestepping any potential wallet traps. But then, something catches my eye. It's perfect, it's him — well, not literally him. I mean, it's a little something for my handsome man back at what will be my new home.

I can already see his smile and possible confusion, as he unwraps it.

Next stop? The Aer Lingus Lounge, the exclusive haven for us, the business class travelers. Can you spell VIP? Thanks to my travel angel Santiago, I get to indulge in these luxuries.

The lounge is decked out with comfy seats that beckon me to sink into their plush depths. I connect to the complimentary high-speed Wi-Fi and help myself to the spread of snacks and beverages — and yes, that includes alcoholic drinks!

By Nicky Ireland

But hey, let's take it slow on the alcopops for now. It's not everyday you get to enjoy free newspapers and magazines, right?

Now, while I'm not planning on using the complimentary shower facilities — I know, madness! — I do seize this opportunity to give my makeup a little touch-up. All while savoring the light snacks spread out in front of me. Delicious!

An hour or so later, my belly full of snacks and maybe an alcopop (or two), I'm ready. Ready to board my flight to the vibrant city of Barcelona. The excitement is real!

Cozied up in my business class seat (thanks again, Santi), I can't help but smile. The hum of the plane fades away as I slip on my headphones, exchanging it for the dulcet tones of 'In the City' by Charli XCX and Sam Smith.

A glass of bubbly champagne in hand, I'm a picture of contentment and anticipation. Ah, this is bliss, total bliss. With a heart full of excitement and adventure, I'm ready to take on Barcelona and Santiago Maspinco. Bring it on!

Just about two and a half hours zip by and here I am, spotting Santi, waiting for me outside the arrivals hall. He's flashing a grin that rivals the Cheshire cat and is holding a massive bouquet of flowers for yours truly. Talk about unexpected!

As soon as I'm within arm's reach, I practically toss everything to the ground and launch myself into his arms, almost bowling him over. Good thing he's sturdy as a rock; to him, I probably feel as light as a feather.

He catches me with ease, showering my face with kisses before handing me the gigantic bouquet. It's an exquisite mix of blue, white and pink Dainty Maid and Excelsior Spanish bluebells. Their long, graceful stems and bell-shaped blooms simply take my breath away.

In true Santi fashion, he starts to explain the significance of the Spanish bluebells, apparently they symbolize humility and gratitude. He tells me they were the perfect way to express gratitude in Victorian times because the flowers look like they're bowing. "Bowing for mi princesa," he charms me. Seriously, this man is so irresistible, I could devour him!

And of course, he couldn't resist adding a bit of historical trivia. He tells me that back in medieval times, people were terrified of Spanish bluebells. They believed bluebell meadows were the hideouts for witches who were once fairies. According to the lore, these creatures would cast a terrible spell if you dared to touch or ring a bell. Alright, Santi, calm down there, buddy.

Zipping through the streets with Santi, who's got a need for speed, we're at the apartment in the Gothic

Quarter in a half-hour flat. I ditch my shoes at the front door — instant house rule — and get hit by the most amazing sight. The apartment is a riot of colour, adorned with an array of vases in every shape, size, and hue. Each one is brimming with stunning Spanish bluebells in shades of blue, white, and pink. Holy cow! It's like stepping into the most enchanting fairy garden.

The sight is so overwhelming it takes my breath away. I turn to Santi and drop some flower knowledge, explaining that bluebells symbolize love in Ireland. He gives me a look that screams "duh," and I realize he probably already knew that. Clever so and so.

As the sun sets on our first day together, Santi, the master chef, whips up an absolute feast. Sitting at the dining table, enveloped by the intoxicating scent of bluebells, we dig into succulent Vieiras al Ajillo — Spanish garlic scallops — accompanied by perfectly roasted potatoes and a fresh salad. And naturally, he has the perfect wine to go with it, a crisp Verdejo.

Before we start cleaning up, I take a moment to reach into my bag and pull out a small bottle green velvet pouch, the surprise I picked up at Dublin Airport earlier today.

As I hand it over, he insists, "You didn't need to buy me anything, mi amor. You are gift enough." I laugh and plant a kiss on his cheek, knowing this little trinket is just a fun reminder of our incredible day.

He opens the pouch and a sterling silver keyring with a four-leaf clover charm falls into his hand. His eyes widen as he reads the words: Faith, Hope, Love, and Luck. "I love it, thank you, mi amor, thank you," he exclaims, planting a kiss on my eagerly awaiting lips.

Now, it's my turn to drop some knowledge.

I explain the meaning behind each leaf of a four-leaf clover: faith, hope, love, and if you're lucky enough to find a fourth leaf, luck.

"Four-leaf clovers have this perfect symmetry that most leaves don't, which is why they're considered a symbol of balance — the key to a happy life," I tell him. His face lights up in response, "Thank you, mi princesa, thank you, truly."

I can't help but grin from ear to ear. This is already shaping up to be an unforgettable day.

SANTI

Deciding on the perfect conclusion to the evening, I opt for a visit to our cherished sanctuary - our playroom. A glass of my preferred whiskey, complete with a few ice cubes and my favored cigar accompanies us on our exciting journey. A sense of anticipation effervesces between us.

As we cross the threshold into the room, Nicky swivels towards me, her eyes sparkling with a mix of mischief and obedience. She's waiting, like the clever submissive she is, for my lead. I raise an eyebrow and in an instant, she recalls the ground rules. With a graceful drop to all fours, she sends a grin dancing across my face. She is, in a word, flawless.

While she finds comfort on her sturdy knees, I ceremoniously place my whiskey glass and beloved cigar on a petite table adjacent to my throne of choice. I then approach the wall panel, engaging the room's ambient sounds and setting the pulsating red lighting. I am, without a doubt, in my own slice of paradise.

I stride towards the locked cabinet and retrieve a little something, returning to find Nicky still poised patiently on all fours. As I tower over her, feet spread wide in a commanding stance, she looks up, her eyes filled with anticipation, ready for my direction.

Matching her gaze, I lean down and secure her collar and leash. "Tu eres mi puta," I remind her, and I'm rewarded with a twinkle in her eye. An unexpected wave of desire washes over me.

She's already divested of any clothing, a new rule I've put in place for our playroom adventures. While she's bared to my gaze, I'm in my usual attire, low-hung jeans. My cock already hardening against the constraining zipper.

Standing poised and composed, leash in hand, with a playful yet commanding twinkle in my eyes.

"Crawl," I dictate, the word crisp and clear, as I guide her towards the grandeur of my throne.

"Sit," I command, my voice echoing in the room. In an instant, she complies, sitting on my throne, a curious sparkle in her eyes. "Such a good girl," I reward her, my words laced with approval and intrigue.

Leaning forward, I gently stroke her cheek with my knuckles and thumb, a tender contrast to my dominant presence. She settles herself comfortably on the firm black leather seat, her beautiful porcelain skin enhanced in its stark contrast.

"Knees up!" My order cuts through the air and she obeys instantly. Her knees draw up close to her chest, her feet firmly planted on the chair beneath her. She waits in anticipation, her hands resting on the armrests, palms up in submission.

As I circle around her, each stride exuding my dominance, she remains still. She is in my territory, under my command, and the thrill of it electrifies the air around us.

I reach into my back pocket, retrieving a length of hemp rope. I let it slide through my fingers, relishing its rough texture before stretching it across her legs. I catch her eyes on me, on the rope, and I see her swallow, an eager glint in her eyes that brings a satisfied smirk to my face.

With a firm grip, I take hold of her ankles, spreading her legs to their limit, revealing every inch of her pussy to me. The sight is exquisite - a tantalizing display of intimacy that leaves me breathless.

With the rope in hand, I proceed to skillfully intertwine it around her body. My proficiency in the art of shibari becomes evident as I bind her to my throne using complex knots, each twist a symbol of my authority.

I meticulously bind her ankles, positioning her legs in a wide split, knees bent towards her chest, while I trail the rope around the back of the chair. The rope, taut and rough beneath my hands, is then stretched around the curve of her thighs and secured to the back of the chair. I guide the rope, feeling the tug as it tightens, across her chest, looping it around each of her beautiful full breasts. She inhales sharply as her skin turns a deep shade of pink, and I confirm that she's securely tethered, her back rigid against the chair.

Lastly, I secure her forearms to the chair's arms. As I tie a tight knot, my fingers work expertly, shaping a Shibari-style frictions knot and a half-hitch knot. The rope is secure, its tension unyielding, ensuring she is immobilized.

There is an undeniable allure in her submission, bound and at my disposal. This powerful realization sends a wave of intense desire through me, leaving me intensely turned on. Fuck me, she looks beautiful tied up and at my mercy. And the realization hits me with a potent rush, leaving my cock as hard as stone.

The sight of the rope biting into her skin, the anticipation of the marks it will leave behind, sends a thrilling shudder down my spine. This is our game, a dance of dominance and submission, and I fuckin' love it.

With a twinkle in my eye, I pause for a moment, taking in the sight of her. Her chest rising and falling like the rhythmic waves of an ocean under my ever-watchful gaze. Every blink of her eye is a silent conversation, her gaze unwavering, meeting mine directly.

Her limbs are secured to the majestic throne, making any movement an impossible task - not that I have any intentions to let her move.

Nonchalantly, I saunter over to the quaint table, my fingers curling around the glass of rich, amber whiskey. As I meander back, her eyes are trained on me, the anticipation palpable.

Gently, I lift her chin with my free hand and tilt her head upward. "Open wide, mi puta sucia," I tease, and just like that, her mouth parts in obedience. "And now, the tongue," I say, and her tongue obediently unfurls from her mouth.

I bring the whiskey glass to my lips, savoring the initial burn of the first sip. It's a delightful sting that sets my senses ablaze. I indulge in another sip, letting it linger in my mouth this time.

With a foot on the step of my throne, I lean in, my face inches away from hers. The whiskey trickles from my mouth onto her waiting tongue, and she eagerly drinks in every drop, messy and undeniably captivating. Fuck me! This woman!

I crouch down on the first step, finding myself at eye level with her eager and already soaked pussy. I study it with a blend of curiosity and command.

Lifting my gaze to meet hers, she observes as I delicately extract a sizeable piece of ice from my whiskey glass with my thumb and forefinger. Holding it in my hand, I guide it towards her pussy and she inhales sharply in anticipation. Gently, I trace the folds of her pussy with the icy cube and she trembles at the extreme chill. I flash her a confident grin and she returns a breathless smile.

Guiding the ice into the entrance of her warm pussy, I watch as she writhes beneath my touch. "Hush, my little one," I advise in a tone of control, and she quickly stifles her gasps. Precious.

I leave the ice inside her, freely melting within her warmth. Rising to my feet, I gaze down at her once more.

Teasingly, I maneuver the whiskey glass towards her lips, promising another taste directly from the source this time. With a wicked smirk, I pull the glass just out of reach, tipping it slightly towards her. The amber liquid cascades down her neck, trickling tantalizingly across her breasts and pooling gently on her stomach and in her lap.

I'm finding my playful instincts impossible to suppress this evening.

Setting aside the empty glass on the nearby table, I make my way unhurriedly towards the other significant seat in the room — a commanding high-backed chair. Another throne, if you will. The symbol of my undisputed reign within these four walls.

I settle into the sturdy seat, a satisfied smirk playing on my lips as I cross one leg over the other at the knee and reach for my choice cigar, a Cohiba.

The flame sparks to life, illuminating the room as I light up the cigar, tilting my head back against the chair and shutting my eyes for a moment to savor the taste. As I open my eyes, the curl of smoke appears to dance in front of me, creating the perfect smoky veil through which to observe my delightful prey. It's a sight for the Gods!

My gaze lingers on Nicky, her cheeks flushed, a picture of vulnerability. Picture-perfect!

I watch her, taking every inch of her in, all the while enjoying my delicious cigar.

After a few minutes I rise from my throne and approach her with deliberate, unhurried steps, stopping right in front of her.

I rest my foot on the step of the throne she's secured to, and gently grasp her chin, opening her mouth. After a deep inhale from the cigar, I lean in to press my lips against hers, sharing the smoky kiss. The moans escape us simultaneously as our tongues explore, the taste of the cigar still present.

Pulling away, I place the cigar on the ashtray of the nearby table.

Standing before her, I calmly unzip my jeans. "What is it you need, mi chica ardiente?" I ask, and she knows the answer. "You, Sir, I need your cock inside me. All of you. Please. Every single inch."

The words elicit a low growl from me as I free my throbbing cock from the confines of my jeans. My hard cock now eye level with her slick wet cunt, the melted ice cube dripping from her, pooling beneath her ass. Her legs and chest tied tightly, her feet planted on the seat of the chair, her ankles tightly bound, her arms tied to the armrests.

Her breaths are ragged, anticipating the pleasure to come.

My hands find the bars on either side of the throne, providing me with the necessary leverage. I push forward, placing my rock-solid cock at the entrance to her beautiful cunt and she cries out, the sensation overwhelming as I enter her in one swift, powerful motion, roaring out loudly as I do so. Hitting her so fiercely that she is forced backwards in the seat with a thud.

Yes! I am the fuckin' king of this castle, a commander in his element, the Lord of this fuckin' throne and she is my slut to use, to devour.

I drive my cock harder and harder into her slick cunt, using the rigid bars as a fulcrum, propelling my rigid cock into her with an assertive finesse. Her movements so restrained it only feeds my primal urge and excitement.

I begin to lose myself in the rhythm of my thrusts and watch as her head rolls back against the back of the seat, eyes sealed shut, lost in the intoxicating fullness of my big cock inside her tight pussy. "Open your fuckin' eyes, mi putita" I shout loudly, my rhythm intensifying as I take no prisoners. My wild abandon mirrored in her expressions of pure ecstasy. She opens her eyes and locks them with mine, a shared grin passing between us.

Amidst these throes of passion, words tumble out of me, an affirmation of my feelings that I'm certain won't surprise her. "Nicky, I fuckin' love you so much, mi Princesa" I confess. Her voice a mix of pleasure and pain, "I love you too, Santi, so frickin' much it hurts as much as your big cock right now." And our sudden shared laughter punctuates the moment.

But the mirth is fleeting, soon replaced by a regained composure. I adjust my rhythm now to a steady pace, our gaze locked on eachother, a silent testament of mutual love and adoration.

I draw myself closer to her, captivated by the raw emotion displayed in her eyes. A single tear, a silent scream from her soul, breaks free and trickles down her cheek. I'm pulled towards it, a beacon of her vulnerability. With a careful movement, I use the tip of my tongue to catch the tear, tasting the bittersweet mix of her sorrow and strength.

The moment hangs heavy between us, charged with an intensity that sends shivers down my spine. I lean in further, our lips meeting in a kiss that's as electrifying as it is comforting. The moans we share, muffled against each other's mouths, serve as a testament to the intimacy we're entwined in.

She implores me with her sapphire eyes, a silent plea I answer by shifting one hand from the bars to circle her warm, pink clit with my thumb. She shudders, panting, "Yes Sir, yes! Let me cum. Please Sir, please let me cum for you?" And I'm undone, carried away in the waves of her orgasm, a symphony of pleasure that brings us both to peak in unison

This amazing moment of pure bliss, a King and his Princess, reveling in their own slice of heaven, together.

Siren

Chapter Twenty Six

Siren

Twenty Six

NICKY

Living the Barcelona dream, that's me! Right here, right now, I'm soaking up the vibrant energy of this city. The past few hours, days, weeks? They've all blurred into a colorful whirl of work and play. I'm networking like a pro, meeting fascinating people left and right, and diving headfirst into my work. You could say I'm hustling, but it's the kind of hustle that brings a smile to my face. And the best part? I get to share all this excitement with Santi. The city lights are brighter, the nights livelier, and the sangrias sweeter with him by my side. Barcelona, you've got me! I'm not just living here; I'm thriving!

And now I'm grooving to Luma's 'Devil Saint' that's blasting through our bedroom, catching my own reflection in a towering mirror. A devilish grin is playing on my lips, making me wonder what his reaction will be. The adrenaline of surprising him is zipping through my bloodstream, lighting up my eyes. The joy of catching him off guard never fades, and today promises to be another unforgettable episode.

I'm pulling on my cherished cashmere overcoat when the signature honk of the cab cuts through the quiet outside the apartment. That's my cue. I grab my purse and begin my journey down the winding staircase of our plush Bellamar apartment.

Making sure every button on my overcoat is done up just right, I slide into the inviting comfort of the cab's backseat. "A Fuego Lento, del Parlamento, please," I tell the driver, who nods and smoothly pulls away from the curb.

City lights whiz past the window as I settle deeper into the soft seat, my heart thumping with excitement over the daring plan I've hatched. My current attire is nowhere near comfortable, but it's all about the striking visual effect it's going to create. Because let's face it, sometimes you have to put up with a little discomfort for the ultimate reward.

My phone pings in my pocket. A text from my BFF Liam.

Liam: You won't believe it Nic, but a big juicy, slice of pizza just took a leap of faith right into my mouth!

Me: Nice!

Liam: I know right. It was such a shock that I accidentally gulped it down.

Me: No way! The universe must be playing tricks on us today. A rich, creamy cheesecake mysteriously vanished into my mouth in a similar fashion recently.

Liam: Wow. It appears our stomachs have sync'd up their comedy routines!

Me: I know right! Our appetites definitely share a sense of humor.

Liam: Soon our waistlines will too.

Me: Shurrup you!

Putting away my phone, I'm well aware that Santi is hunkered down in his office today, carving out a world of his own where solitude is his only companion. It's a rule he's made, and I can't help but grin, knowing I'm his favourite rule-breaker.

The cab screeches to a halt outside the restaurant, interrupting my musings. I toss the fare to the driver and step out, gulping in lungful's of the sharp fresh air. A jittery thrill races through me, keeping pace with the beat of my heart all through the ride. I try to calm it, to slow my pulse.

By Nicky Ireland

I choose the side door, the one leading upstairs to his office. As I climb, I start undoing the buttons of my coat, eager to savor every moment once I'm inside.

Standing at his office door, my heart is literally pounding with anticipation. I knock gently, my heartbeats dancing to the rhythm.

"Come in," he calls.

Let the fun begin!

SANTI

Tucked away in my office, I'm hunched over my desk, expertly weaving through a labyrinth of paperwork. The dull serenity is abruptly interrupted as the office door eases open, and in strides Nicky, an invigorating gust of life. My humdrum day instantly spins into an exciting whirlwind.

"Mi amor," I welcome her, a warmth pouring from my voice, my lips pulling into a smile reflecting my joy. I sit back in my chair, relaxed yet captivated, my eyes indulging in her striking figure. Even cloaked in a bulky overcoat, her allure is irrefutable, glowing. Golden locks of hair spill over her shoulders, stoking the fire of my longing, sparking wild daydreams of pulling them in impassioned moments right here on my desk. A wave of desire sweeps over me, forcing me to subtly handle my mounting unease.

I scrutinize her, noticing her slender hands crossing over her chest, holding her coat defensively. Intrigued, I ask, "Chilly, mi amor?" Her hurried denial, paired with an anxious grin, hooks my curiosity even more. "Busy?" she asks, and I can't help but smile, my attention caught by her unvoiced intentions. "Not when it comes to you, Princesa. What's up?"

Her sapphire eyes are a bewitching spectacle, her skin flushing with an ardor that begins at her chest and gradually creeps up her neck, a sight I find too enticing to resist. A raised eyebrow is my only response to her unvoiced question, and I watch as her shaky hands reach for her coat collar, allowing it to slide off her shoulders. It falls in a graceful puddle around her feet, unveiling the alluring attire beneath.

I suck in a breath. Fuck, this woman!

She stands before me, her outfit a black leather harness that's more of a suggestion than a cover. I'm frozen in place for a moment, simply appreciating the view. Leaning forward, I prop my elbows on the desk, hands clasped under my chin, a picture of calm contemplation. My forefinger taps lightly against my lips, a gesture that doesn't go unnoticed. She catches her breath, the sound sharp in the quiet room.

Our eyes meet, a silent conversation passing between us. Her anticipation is palpable, but she's clearly enjoying herself, delighting in the game of keeping me guessing. Little does she know, the effect she has on me is hardly one-sided. She could be my downfall, and I'd welcome it, knowing I'd met my match in a dance of passion and desire. She is irrevocably the heaven in my hell.

She stands with her hands behind her back, her eyes never leaving mine. Her legs tremble slightly, a touch of nerves betraying her bold exterior. My fingers drift unconsciously to my beard, stroking it thoughtfully. A quick swipe of my tongue over my lower lip gives me a moment to take her all in. This is a sight I want to immortalize in my memory, a moment to savor.

Her outfit is a single-piece leather harness, a network of slender black straps that leave little to the imagination. Her curves are on full display, the harness leaving tantalizing imprints on her skin. It's a sight that takes my breath away.

My gaze lingers on the leather bands that drape over her shoulders, the metallic studs that hold everything together. The straps circle her breasts, accentuating their fullness and the rosy pink of her nipples against her fair skin. A wave of desire washes over me, and I can almost taste her, imagining the sounds she'd make as I bring her to the brink.

By Nicky Ireland

But for now, I keep my composure, intrigued by this beautiful woman of mine who's managed to capture my attention so completely. The game is afoot, and I can't wait to see what happens next.

My eyes can't help but embark on an adventure, following the contours of her revealed silhouette. An unexpected thrill pulses within me at the sight of the leather-framed aperture that unveils her enticingly snug pussy. Thin leather straps frame those impeccable, rosy, for now untouched lip. Her petite, pink clit remains hidden, beckoning for my touch.

She is bewitching, a delightful puzzle that I can't help but want to solve. She is my kryptonite. It's clear she's been crafted for a man of unrestrained passions like myself.

"Are you pleased, Sir?" she teases, her wide eyes glancing at me from beneath her long lashes, feigning a charming insecurity. She plays coy, completely aware of how irresistibly appealing she is.

Suppressing a grin, I stand, pushing my chair back, and bridge the gap between us, rolling up the sleeves of my sweater to reveal the tattoos I know she finds fascinating. Our eyes remain locked in a playful challenge, and true to her feisty spirit, she doesn't break the eye contact.

Her hands are still playfully placed behind her back as she watches me, her cheeks glowing with anticipation. She nibbles on her lower lip, a sight that draws a low chuckle from me, sparking a nervous giggle from her.

Stopping in front of her, I circle a finger in the air, prompting her to spin around. She twirls gracefully on her heels as my eyes wander along her legs. Her toned, porcelain legs, ending in daring, black leather stilettos that emphasize her calf muscles, triggering vivid memories of the times I've held those ankles above her head or over my shoulders during our passionate encounters, our bodies melting into one.

As my gaze travels along her legs, I admire the leather straps that gently outline the curves of her generous, tempting, and delightfully ripe ass. The sight sparks a profound, commanding hunger in me, my interest obvious, testing the limits of my trousers. It's then that I notice the cuffs, a teasing detail, gently swaying at the base of her spine, attached securely to the body harness.

"Well, well," I muse aloud, barely containing a chuckle. She throws a sly look over her shoulder, her grin mischievous and teasing. Oh, she's fully aware of her effect on me, Siren! The pull her charm and grace hold on my senses is irresistible.

I move closer to stand directly behind her, my hands lightly resting on her shoulders. I lean in, my lips a breath away from her ear, as my fingers dance a playful rhythm down her arms. I need her to know how much she means to me. I am committed to guarding and treasuring her, always.

"Mi putita, you see, everything in this world revolves around sex, except for sex itself, which is all about power. I'm in command, and you're the chess piece in my grand game. But remember, after the game, I'll be the one to bring you comfort with a tender kiss and a comforting embrace, mi amor. Got it?" My words hang in the air as I lock eyes with her, a playful smirk on my face. She quickly fires back, "Crystal clear, thank you, Sir."

I place a light peck on her graceful neck, my hands meandering down to her wrists. I grasp them firmly in one hand, while the other fetches the cuffs. A sharp gasp escapes her, and I can't help but chuckle, a victorious grin tugging at my lips. I know she shares the same intense anticipation.

I take my time fastening the cuffs around her slender wrists, making sure they're secure but not overly tight. I step back to admire my handiwork, my hand trailing her ass before delivering a swift, sharp slap, eliciting a surprised and delighted squeal from her.

I leave her briefly to lock my office door. This space is my haven, a quiet corner where I am seldom interrupted, but I must ensure our privacy. Not just to safeguard my claim on her enticing figure, but also to guarantee her comfort and security. The passion between us is a roaring fire, and I plan to let it burn, without interruption.

Returning to her, the knuckles of my right hand lightly trace a path up her back. She obligingly arches in response. Once my hand reaches the back of her neck, it forms a gentle, yet firm circle around it. With a forceful pressure, I push her towards the wall, and the sound of her gasp fills the room as she makes contact. Her cheek finds the cold, hard surface, and she turns her head, breathing heavily. Her face, flushed and expressive, is a picture of playful surrender. I'm all set to enjoy every beat of this intimate tango.

Leaning in, my lips lightly touch the back of her neck, my breath leaving a faint whisper as I take in her captivating fragrance. Vanilla and musk mingle together in a heady mix, enough to make my senses spin. With my eyes shut, I get lost in her, in the unique connection we share.

My tongue ventures on a little tour of her neck and I can't suppress a groan as I gently bite down, leaving my mark. Her head tilts back onto my shoulder, a soft sound of pleasure escaping her. "You know how I love to leave my mark on what's mine," I say, continuing my path of playful nips around her neck, jaw and shoulders. The feeling of my teeth sinking into her soft skin is my undoing. My cock is throbbing now. Desperate for it's release.

I embark on a slow exploration down her spine with my tongue, from her neck to the tiny indentation housing my favourite dimple. I playfully tease it, kissing and lightly sucking her skin, relishing the taste of her unique essence, a mix of her salty skin and my own saliva. The unmistakable flavor of two lovers intertwined.

Her reactions make my cock twitch, her body squirming under my lips, the scent of her excitement filling the room, igniting my own primal instincts. My arousal is evident and I'm rock hard.

Fuck!

Owned – A BDSM Erotic Romance

I grip her hips, pulling her ass into my crotch. She responds with a teasing grind against my growing hardness, but I stop her with a hard slap on her gorgeous ass, issuing a caution, "Hold still, mi chica ardiente." "Santi," she manages to say, her eyes locking with mine. I match her gaze with a raised eyebrow, and she complies.

"Rest your face against the wall, mi princesa," I command. She obliges, releasing an enticing sigh. I need her to be steady for what's about to follow.

Taking a small step back, I unzip my pants and free my throbbing cock. I'm aching, desperate to be enveloped by the welcoming warmth of her tight cunt. Desperate to lose myself in her.

Positioning my foot strategically between hers, I forcefully nudge her legs apart. "Spread!" I demand, my voice resonating a calm authority. I grip my cock, performing a few slow pumps to ease the tension, my eyes focused on the task at hand. Using my hand, I part one of her ass cheeks, eager to witness the regularly explored terrain I intend to navigate once more. Invoking the classic spit-shine method, I ensure my cock is sufficiently lubricated.

"Ready for the grand unveiling?" I ask, now using my hands to part her pussy lips, revealing the enticing entry point hidden between her round ass cheeks. The sight quickens my pulse, and I anoint her pussy with my saliva, spitting down onto her. A soft sigh escapes her, my name rolling off her tongue like a whispered secret, and the sound sends a jolt of desire coursing through me.

With precision, I align my cock against her, the warmth emanating from her pussy is breath-taking. I explore her further, spreading her pussy lips wide for me, revealing more of the intimate territory that now holds my undivided attention. Every gasp, every shiver of anticipation, serves as further fuel to my desire. Guiding her with a firm grip on her hips, I slide my solid cock, forcefully into her pussy, the sensation spreading a tingling anticipation along my length.

"Open your eyes and look at me, Nicky" I demand, maintaining a composed demeanor. Her eyes flutter open, meeting mine in a shared moment of raw anticipation. My gaze locked on hers, I thrust deeply into her a number of times before I wrap my right hand around my cock, observing her reactions as I remove it from her pussy and begin to journey from her warmth to the tight pucker of her asshole.

Her moan punctuates the thick silence, her legs trembling in sweet anticipation. "Keep your eyes on me while I fuck your tight ass, mi pequeña zorra," I instruct, a playful edge to my voice as I tease her with a hint of what's to come.

I firmly grasp the round curves of her ass and with a calculated, yet eager plunge, I merge with her, submerging the entirety of my cock within her ass. The sudden unity sends her lurching forward, her soft contours pressing into the stony resistance of the wall. A surprised gasp slips from her lips, but a wicked grin dances at the corners of her mouth. She's the siren to my attentive sailor, a delightful conundrum of impropriety and purity.

"Draw your legs together," I demand, my voice echoing through the room. She follows my command instantly, her compliance stoking the embers of my calm dominance. Pausing, I'm enveloped by the warmth of her ass, her inner muscles contracting around my cock in a heated, rhythmic embrace that's so intoxicating, I find myself momentarily spellbound.

Leaning into her, my weight a reassuring presence on her back, I tighten my hold onto her hips, my fingertips pressing into her smooth skin. With a free hand, I weave my fingers through her hair, gently tilting her head back to reveal her poised neck. "Remember," I whisper into her ear, "I'm the one leading the dance. I guide you, I own you, and I cherish the freedom to enjoy this dance with you as I please, mi amor."

"Oohhh... Yes Sir," she breathlessly agrees, her voice reverberating beautifully in the room, adding to the harmony of our intense encounter.

With each rhythmic thrust, my body meets hers with a forceful collision, stirring a deep, resonant groan from my chest, "Fuck!." My eyes are captivated by the hypnotic sway of her body as I join her in this dance, my hands exploring the inviting curves of her ass, parting her ass cheeks to see our intimate connection. Her hands are playfully bound behind her back in the cuffs, she's willingly surrendered to my lead. A vibrant display of dominance and submission, just the way we both enjoy it.

Drawing my hand away from the warmth of her ass, it dances a trail around to the front of her body, gliding between her thighs and venturing towards her now hardened clit. The evidence of her arousal is a slick trail on her thighs. As my fingers follow the moist path up to her pussy, they slip with ease through her slick folds. She is glistening, primed for me. "You're always so damn ready for me, aren't you, Princesa?" I tease.

My fingers plunge into her sweet depths and she responds with a resonating moan, my name a soft plea on her lips, "Santi, please". she replies with a slow rhythm, a tantalizing tease, my fingers dancing in and out of her warm, soaking wet cunt. I spread her wetness, diving deeper into her warmth, until I hit her sensitive clit. Her response is a loud moan, "Mmmmmm, Santi...".

"What do you need, mi puta obediente? Speak up!" I demand, my voice a commanding melody.

"I need your cum. All of it. I need to feel it inside me. Give me your cum, please, please, Sir" she pants between breaths.

The desperation in her voice is like sweet music to my ears. Slowly, I withdraw my fingers from her pussy, shifting focus to her swollen, sensitive clit. Her response is immediate, a loud moan reverberates as her ass rocks against my cock. We move in sync, our bodies melding together in a dance of raw passion and primal need. I'm already so deep within her, but the urge to go deeper, to claim her further, is insatiable.

Her reactions, her gasps, her moans – I've decoded them like a cryptic puzzle. I know just how close she is to the precipice, teetering on the edge of pure ecstasy. And fuck me, she is on the brink.

By Nicky Ireland

Keeping a steady rhythm, my fingers twirl around her sensitive, pink clit, pushing her towards that sweet release, while my thick cock continues to move slowly, deeply within her tight asshole.

"You're my paradise in this pandemonium, mi diabla" I murmur, our breaths ragged, matching the rhythm of our bodies, each thrust a testament of my claim. The depth of my possession serves as a reminder that she is mine, and mine alone. I will never let her go.

Balancing on the precipice of her climax, she's panting, her moans amplifying, and my impending release races towards me like a speeding train. "Ohhhhhhhh, fuuccckkkk," we exclaim in sync, my body tensing as I sense my imminent climax, my cock buried so deep within her, it could challenge the base of the Mariana Trench.

With a deep, throaty groan, I yield to the overpowering pleasure and we cum together, as I releasing my sticky, hot cum within her ass. I hand over all I've got – warm, relentless, and unstoppable, she welcomes it all, every final, sticky, messy bit.

As we come down from our climactic high, I pull her nimble silhouette into the shelter of my arms, locking her close to me. We yield to the force of gravity, gliding effortlessly onto the floor; our bodies are devoid of energy, utterly spent, yet basking in the afterglow of a personal connection that satisfies us completely.

I pull her back onto my lap, her shape nestling comfortably against mine, my yearning staying unquenched as it continues to mark her as its own, my gradually softening cock still resting inside her ass. The proof of our mutual climax clings to her silky thighs and mine, slowly seeping out of her, a mute witness to the fiery passion we've just savored.

She lets her head roll back against the nook of my shoulder, a soft giggle slipping from her lips, followed by a beaming smile that she sends my way. The sight of her delight has me reflecting her joy with a smile of my own.

"Feeling good, mi amor?" I ask, my voice overflowing with care and adoration. I seek confirmation of her comfort, eager to ensure her well-being. "I'm more than good, thank you Papi" she retorts, her words filled with satisfaction.

I lean in to plant a gentle kiss on the tip of her nose, a habitual sign of affection. My stare fixes on my favourite freckle, a tiny speck that decorates her cheek, high and noticeable. I pause to relish our combined scents, intoxicating and unique - a blend that is distinctly ours. As I inhale the essence of our shared intimacy, I close my eyes and snuggle further into her, savoring the comfort and warmth that her presence brings.

This day, this moment, is completely and irrevocably amazing. The love that we share, the bond that we've reinforced, has my heart performing a jubilant dance. Day, well and truly made!

Worship at my alter of sin

Chapter Twenty Seven

Worship at my alter of sin

Chapter Twenty Seven

SANTI

Today, we're embarking on a whirlwind adventure through Barcelona's Gothic Quarter, a treasure trove of memories that I hold dear. My one hope is that Nicky will continue to fall head over heels for the city's enchantment that I've become smitten with. The sun is out in full force, its golden rays bathing Nicky in a warm glow. Draped in a brilliant yellow dress, she is a sight to behold. Her hair, bound in a lofty ponytail, swishes in sync with our steps, stirring up memories of intimate moments where I've forcefully held her ponytail as we've fucked mercilessly.

Nicky is not just surviving in Barcelona, she's flourishing, and I couldn't be prouder. She's welcomed this life change with open arms and elegance. Her work is taking off and her jaunts to Dublin for those high-paying commercial gigs are becoming sparse. No complaints here, I'm always happier when she's by my side.

As we meander past a grand cathedral, one among many in Barcelona, Nicky's curiosity is piqued. This architectural wonder, constructed between the 13th and 15th centuries, is crowned with an intricate roof teeming with gargoyles, reflecting both household and mythical beasts. The cathedral's pseudo-basilica design unfolds before us, its vaults spanning across five aisles, the exterior ones partitioned into chapels.

The truncated transept and the chevet, formed of nine interconnected chapels by an ambulatory, add to its grandeur.

Upon entering, we find ourselves alone, the cathedral void of any gathering. The resonating sounds of 'Ascension' surround us, as Nicky's eyes widen in awe at the sight of the raised high altar, offering a clear path into the crypt. Seeing her in such a solemn and majestic setting stirs something in me. I find myself yearning for her, my desire amplified in the empty cathedral. She is a sparkling wit, a burst of energy in the serene surroundings, while I remain composed, yet captivated by her.

In the heart of the timeless cathedral, a chorus of laughter dances among the archaic walls, our playful repartee breathing a sense of youth and vibrancy into the hallowed space. Yet, beneath the jovial surface, my longing for her to revel in my presence swells with each passing moment. The cathedral's majesty mirrored in her wide-eyed wonder only amplifies my yearning. I want her, and I want her now!

Approaching the somber confessional, a solemn island amid the cathedral's majestic tapestry, I pause on its threshold, her hand comfortably cradled in mine. She stops, her breath a silent murmur in the sacred expanse, and I send her a playful wink. A delicate smile unfurls across her face, a quiet love poem that articulates our mutual anticipation. My fingers trace the aged wood of the door, a silent chronicle of countless confidential whispers. With a gentle push, I shepherd her into the dim-lit interior.

Bathed in a soft, otherworldly light filtering through the stained-glass windows, the confessional - a sacred chamber of atonement - comes alive with a radiant spectrum of colors playing on the stone-cold floor. I ease onto the simple wooden bench, its surface polished smooth by years of contrite visitors.

"On your knees," I command, my voice just above a whisper yet reverberating with a gentle authority. Without a beat missed, she lowers herself onto the stone floor, its frosty touch permeating the thin fabric of her dress. "Keep your eyes on me, understood?" I demand, my words hanging thick in the air, heavy with incense. Her response is a soft murmur, a playful defiance dancing in her eyes, "Yes, Sir."

I watch her posture, her hands gently resting on her thighs, palms open to the heavens in a silent admission of acquiescence. The intoxicating scent of incense saturates the confessional, a robust blend of sandalwood and myrrh, a divine fragrance that mingles with the electricity of our anticipation. I unzip my pants, revealing my hardened cock. Her gaze, wide yet mischievous, remains unwaveringly on me.

Perched on the edge of the bench, I extend my legs and spread them wide, a playful chuckle escaping my lips. "A game of worship, mi diabla. A prayer for your shenanigans," I say, holding my engorged cock in clear view, the anticipation palpable.

With a witty sparkle in her eyes, she artfully cradles my cock in her hands, her fingers held in a revered display, pointing skyward as if in prayer. Her gaze locks with mine, a silent promise of shared secrets. I can't help but draw a sharp breath, a quiet surrender to the wave of desire that she so effortlessly stirs within me.

As her fingers trace an enticing path over my cock, a low groan of pleasure resonates against the stone walls. It's as though we're engaged in a playful match of hide and seek amid the winding shelves of an ancient library. Composed, yet undeniably intrigued, I find myself willingly lost in this game.

In a mirror movement, my larger hands join hers, guiding our shared touch, our hands moving up and down slowly along my cock, the friction a delightful challenge that elicits shivers of pleasure. Her mouth forms a silent 'Ooh', her breath a gentle breeze against my skin. In this moment, teetering between the solemn and the scandalous, I can't tell if I've ascended to the gates of heaven or tumbled into the fires of hell.

I coax her to the edge of indulgence, whispering, "Revel in these hallowed halls of mischief, mi chica ardiente." I yearn for her unabashed commitment to the tantalizing realm of impropriety, a captivating curiosity for joy and self-satisfaction. "Together, we will raise our enticing, sinful endeavors above everything else, as you venerate at my shrine of sin. You are my deity and my cock is your God to worship."

By Nicky Ireland

The twinkle in her eyes makes it abundantly clear, she's surrendered, but not to sin. Rather, she's in for the ride, following the man leading her into its captivating hold. She revels in the power this gives me, and I can't help but be intrigued by her audacity.

I place my hand lightly on the top of her head, and her movements on my rigid, throbbing cock pick up tempo. Our breathing synchronizes, creating a rhythm that resonates in the charged air between us. She is the force that propels me headfirst into a sea of pleasure that I never knew existed. Our eyes remain locked, reflecting the pure, unadulterated desire that consumes us.

As the heat builds up within me, her eyes widen in response to my gruff calling of her name, which echoes through the room like a secret incantation. I let myself go, caught up in the whirlwind of passion, leaving traces of my cum on her face. The sight of my release, like silken ribbons across her face, signifies our shared intimacy.

Her skin, smooth and unblemished as porcelain, becomes a canvas, decorated with our shared passion. We are enveloped in a wave of deep connection, a silent affirmation of our bond. The sight of my sticky cum trickling down her flawless skin leaves me breathless. I'm a mess, overpowered by the intensity of the moment. Reaching out to her, I softly whisper, "Open wide, mi diabla." She obeys, not a hint of hesitation in her actions.

My fingers trace the path of my cum on her skin, gathering it gently in a soft scoop. The act, evidence of our combined arousal, peaks as I guide it towards her eager mouth. Her lips part, accepting my offering with a trust that warms my heart.

Locking my gaze with hers, I tell her, "You will swallow every drop. It is our communion." The words hang in the air, a solemn promise, a shared secret. "You will savor its taste." My command is not a demand, but an invitation to a shared sacrilegious ritual that showcases our mutual desire.

At this very instant, our unique bond manifests itself in a raw and delightful interaction that is just between us. It's a moment that leaves a potent imprint, intensely personal in its nature. With her mouth agape, I trace a circle around her lips with my cum, spreading it across her lips, before gently nudging it inside her parted mouth, ensuring she savors each drop.

She playfully wraps her lips around my fingers, savoring them with a moan of pleasure. I find myself unable to tear my gaze away as she swallows each drop, teasingly protruding her tongue to confirm that there's nothing left. She's taken it all in, like the perfect temptress she is.

She looks up at me and playfully declares, "Our Lord and Savior didn't exactly hand out a step-by-step guide on how to take communion. Rather, he provided a meaningful example to his disciples: Notice how this bread and drink are essential for sustaining your life? Similarly, here I am bringing some liveliness into your world, my supreme deity ." We can't resist the gales of giggles erupting from us, as we scramble to reclaim our breath.

Stepping out of the hushed confessional, I take her hand, her fingers fitting perfectly within mine. The majestic, ancient door creaks open and we find ourselves smack in the middle of a prayer circle of devout elderly women. The women, lips silently moving in prayer, hands shaking as they light their candles, radiate a profound sense of devotion. The unexpected sight sends another fit of giggles from deep within us, a sound that seems to play a jarring note in the sacred cathedral.

Our laughter, youthful and irreverent, bounces off the stone arches, drawing a collection of scandalized glances from the women. Their faces, maps of age and faith, crease further into frowns as their grip on their rosaries tighten. But there's no stopping our mirth as we leave behind the old-world guilt, grinning at each other, reveling in the surprise lightness in such a heavy place.

With a renewed sense of energy, I quicken my stride, gently pulling Nicky along by the hand. We burst out of the cathedral, climbing the exterior stone steps. Turning, I stop a few steps below her, her figure silhouetted against the cathedral's grand outline.

Our laughter still hangs in the air, a joyful melody contrasting the quiet afternoon. Looking up at her, I gently cradle her face, her skin warm and soft against my hands. I lose myself in her eyes, sapphire pools that hold an entire universe of emotions. I lean in to kiss her softly, her lips a sweet intoxicant. Pressing my forehead against hers, I let out a whisper, barely audible, "Te quiero". The words hang in the air, a sacred vow of my feelings for her.

Her response is immediate. She pulls back slightly, her face aglow with a radiant smile, her eyes sparkling with a mix of love, desire, and a spectrum of emotions that defy description. She returns my gaze, her eyes intense, filled with passion and adoration. In a voice that's warm and husky, she whispers back, "I love you too, my handsome man, my everything, my King, my God." Her declaration of love, deeply heartfelt, freezes this moment in time, creating a memory of our shared love. A memory that will remain unforgettable.

Vitamin D

Chapter Twenty Eight

By Nicky Ireland

Vitamin D

Chapter Twenty Eight

NICKY

It's a delicious October day, but you could mistake it for a glorious Dublin summer. Can you believe it? I almost can't. So, naturally, Santi and I are beach-bound this afternoon, and I'm buzzing with anticipation. Yes, there will be a bikini involved, and perhaps even a suntan, in spite of my traditionally pasty Irish skin's inclination to burn and peel like a stubborn orange. But hey... a healthy dose of vitamin D today will make it all worthwhile.

Weekend vibes are in full swing and we've been lounging at the mansion in Bellamar. That means our destination is the beckoning shores of Platja de Bellamar. We're zipping there in Santi's prized Audi A7, with a sneaky little picnic packed, a captivating book in tow, and yes, my mobile phone is coming along too. But that's only because I plan to send a barrage of pictures to my best mate, Liam, just to stoke the flames of his envy.

With the car windows rolled down, the breeze is having a field day with my hair, transforming it into a bird's nest. But who cares? I'm belting out Kate McGill's version of The Beach Boys' 'Wouldn't it be nice' through the stereo, my voice echoing at full volume. Poor Santi's ears might be protesting, but he's grown used to my antics. Plus, he's head over heels in love with me, so he wouldn't have it any other way.

As we roll up to the beach, we claim a picturesque spot right next to the rhythmically crashing waves. Life simply couldn't get any sweeter. I spread a cozy blue and white picnic blanket on the sand. Standing up, I slip out of my t-shirt and shorts to reveal my sizzling, scarlet-red bikini. Santi's appreciative whistle rings in my ears, and I can't help but feel a rush of glee. He joins in, stripping down to his swim shorts. His muscular physique, decorated with tattoos and complemented by his golden skin, leaves me absolutely drooling. I mean, this man is the definition of hot!

Resting comfortably on the blanket, I leverage our tossed-aside garments as my makeshift recliner, diving headfirst into an enticing novel. Santi, my partner in this seaside escapade, finds his spot nestled between my legs, his head a comforting weight against my belly. As my fingers idly comb through his soft, dark hair, I can't help but relish in the tranquil rhythm of our shared moment.

Despite the protective armor of SPF 50 sunscreen, I know I'm probably destined to roast to a lobster-like shade of red. But right now, peering over the edge of my racy book at my handsome man, I'm overcome with a wave of sheer happiness. This is bliss. Pure, unadulterated bliss.

As the afternoon matures, Santi suggests a plunge into the beckoning waters, and I'm quick to concur. The sea presents an inviting spectacle, its surface sparkling under the sun's relentless gaze. It's high time for some aquatic frolicking.

Our bodies submerge into the cool water, initiating a playful bout of paddling. My swimming prowess is limited to the humble doggy paddle, a stark contrast to Santi's expert swimming skills. Of course, he's practically a professional! But for now, his agenda is dominated by the mission to get me as drenched as possible, seemingly eager to have my bikini adhere to me even more snugly than it already is. What a deviant!

The post-swim hunger pangs strike us quickly, and we decide it's time to feast upon the picnic I've lovingly put together. I can't help but tease Santi about the gastronomic treats I've whipped up for our beachside banquet. As I unpack our meal, his anticipation is as palpable as the sea breeze.

His eyes follow my every move as I reveal a variety of fruits, including grapes, oranges, and my favourite - pears. To accompany our fruity feast, there's also some sparkling water. But the pièce de résistance of our picnic is undoubtedly the whimsical sandwiches I've crafted with every ounce of my culinary prowess.

By Nicky Ireland

Presenting him with a plate of these unique creations, his gratitude is quickly replaced with an expression of bemused curiosity. His appreciation erupts into an infectious belly laugh as he takes in the sight of the miniature sandwiches, cut into the shape of little phalluses and filled with nothing but jam or banana. It's a testament to my unorthodox culinary skills, but hey, I like to keep things creative.

"I hope we're clear that this is the only time I'll ever put anything shaped like a penis in my mouth, mi amor," he teases. "Crystal clear, Sir," I retort, joining in his laughter.

So here we are, lounging on the beach, mid-November, with the sun kissing our skin and I watch as Santiago, my handsome man, takes a bite of the miniature appendages I've lovingly prepared. He promptly spits it out, and I can't help but tease him. "What's the matter? Can't handle a sandwich containing banana? Too penis shaped for you eh."

He grins back at me, "No, mi Princesa, it seems your sandwich has a bit of extra crunch. Sand, perhaps?"

I gasp in mock horror. "Oh no! The beach must have conspired against our picnic when I opened the basket." I pause, a giggle bubbling up as I say, "But isn't that why they're called 'sand'-wiches?" I'm practically snorting with laughter at my own joke, and I can tell it's a winner when Santiago can't help but join in the giggles.

Just as our laughter starts to die down, my phone rings. A video call from none other than Liam. With a mischievous grin, I answer, making sure my bikini-clad self and beautiful beach backdrop are in full view.

"Liamo!" I exclaim into the phone.

His response is immediate. "You're evil, showing off like that!" The envy is palpable even through the phone.

I can't help but chuckle. "Oh, you haven't seen the best part yet." I quickly pan the phone around, giving him a breath-taking view of the ocean, the beach, and of course, Santiago, who's looking every bit the beach god.

Liam, ever the charmer, greets Santiago with a cheeky, "Hello there, Sexy Santiago." Santiago, cool

as ever, waves back, his smile dazzling even under the shades.

As we catch up, Liam regales me with his hilarious misadventures back in Dublin. I can't help but suggest he joins us in Barcelona, and I know him well enough to bet he's booking his flight even as we speak. I miss our yoga classes and our usual banter. But right now, I wouldn't trade this sunny beach day with Santiago for anything. Life here is just too sweet.

Lounging on the picnic blanket with my delectably handsome man after a lengthy chat with Liam, where we exchanged all the latest gossip. I nestle into Santi's side, while he wraps his arm around me, his fingers tracing tiny circles on my back. My mind begins to wander, as it often does, and I find myself yearning for him in a way that's impossible to ignore.

Propping myself onto my elbows, I take a quick glance around. We're tucked away on this beach, hidden from prying eyes. A mischievous grin tugs at the corners of my mouth as my hand begins its descent down his torso. As I lean in and start to pepper kisses on his tattooed neck, he's lying there, eyes closed, lost in the moment. His moan of approval sends a rush of excitement through me. I've got him.

"Be careful, mi chica ardiente," he warns, a playful note in his voice. "You might end up with a lot more vitamin D than you anticipated today if you keep that up." I can't help but giggle into his neck. Oh, bring it on, Mr. Maspinco. Bring it on.

Ignoring his warning, I continue my playful assault on his neck, gradually moving towards his earlobe. I tug at it gently with my teeth, causing him to gasp slightly. Next, I move to his full, inviting lips and plant a soft kiss, our lips locking in a desperate, passionate embrace. As my hand ventures further down, I'm pleasantly unsurprised to find he's already rock solid. This man is a machine, and I can't get enough of him.

His deep, rumbling moan echoes in my ears as my hand slips inside his swim shorts, stroking along his firm length. The feel of him, smooth and warm beneath my touch, sends a thrill through me. I yearn to taste him, to take him in.

His gaze falls on me as I gradually slide down his belly and towards his crotch. As I free him from his shorts, his large cock springs free, and I find myself licking my lips in anticipation. This is one of my favourite things to do for him. It's a sight to behold - Santi, the ever-controlled, dominant man, turning into putty in my hands the moment my mouth encompasses him.

Nestled between his legs, I keenly watch him as he creates a makeshift recliner from our discarded clothing. He arranges himself just right, ensuring a perfect view of the spectacle that's about to unfold — my adoration for his magnificent cock.

A sense of heightened anticipation fills the air as I lean in, my eyes locked on his. Looking up from beneath my lashes, I initiate a tantalizing game of tease and denial with the engorged head of his cock. My tongue dances around him, slow and deliberate, paying special homage to the sensually sensitive spot beneath the head. Each lick, each tease, sends a delicious shiver through his body.

I alternate between gentle nibbles and soft suckling on the head of his large cock, releasing him every so often with a wet pop. Cradling the base of his manhood in my hand, I gaze up at him. His eyes remain fixed on me, captivated by the scene.

A low moan escapes my lips, its vibrations reverberating around him, as I spit delicately onto his already glistening head. The sight of my saliva, trickling down from my mouth onto him, intensifies the moment. I lean forward, sending a shiver of ecstasy through him that prompts him to tilt his head back in pure bliss.

My hand starts to glide along his length, establishing a steady rhythm. I continue to tease, lick, and suck his sweet spot and the entirety of his head, driving him towards the edge. His breaths become ragged, signaling his unravelling. The sound of my amplified moans, muffled around him, ignites a primal response within him.

His hand finds its way to the crown of my head, urging me deeper as he arches his hips upward to meet my lips. The onslaught is deep and intoxicating. His pace quickens, my responses becoming more unruly and messy, an erotic symphony that triggers his ultimate surrender.

With a few more thrusts, he holds my head steady, his cock reaching its deepest within my throat. The restriction of my airway heightens the intensity as he releases himself, a resonating groan marking his climax. I accept his warm, sticky cum, continuing my struggle with his size even as I swallow, relishing every bit of this erotic dance as much as he does.

As his breath gradually steadies, I slide up along his torso, my head finding a perfect resting spot in the crook of his neck. Nestled against his warm chest, I feel a playful smack on my ass. He whispers, "I love you, mi Princesa", to which I retort, "I love you too, my King. So, so much". This intimate exchange cements the end of our carnal dance, leaving a lingering sense of seductive satisfaction in its wake.

As the sun begins to dip in the sky, we can't help but drag our feet in the sand, bemoaning our departure from the beach. But let's be real here, we're not exactly heading back to a dusty shack. No, our destination is a Bellamar mansion! Sprawling grounds, grand architecture, and luxury that makes you pinch yourself. So, are we really slumming it? Absolutely not! Let's face it, our post-beach retreat is a haven of opulence, a far cry from simple living. Get yourself together Nicky!

My gilded princesa

Chapter Twenty Nine

My gilded princesa

Chapter Twenty Nine

SANTI

Today is one of those extra bustling days, and I think, what better way to steam off than an invigorating kickboxing session at the club with my trainer? He's an ex-pro in the sport and pushes me to my limits. To say I give it my all against him would be putting it lightly.

His boxing club is an oasis of stress relief, a sanctuary when Nicky can't be by my side in our playroom. She's off working with a local photographer today, adding some new shots to her portfolio. I'm sure she's in her element.

I retreat to the changing rooms, slipping into my shorts and securing my protective gear - mouth-guard, hand wraps, boxing gloves, shin guards, groin guard - protecting mi princesa's favored goods is vital. The gear is loose enough to allow free movement for my kicks and punches, but not so loose that it hinders my workout. Shoes aren't obligatory in the ring, but I opt for them anyway, for the cushioning sole's protection during side-to-side movements.

I stride towards the ring, the pulsating rhythm of Sage's 'Tik Tik Boom' fills the gym, injecting the extra dose of energy we crave. My trainer, Miguel, is an expert in this full-contact martial art, demanding intensive full-body training. He's crafted my training regimen to bolster my strength, speed, agility, and endurance.

The cardio aspect of kickboxing gives me a rigorous workout, enhancing my heart health and stamina, handy for keeping pace with my ever-demanding Princesa. Our routine often includes running, skipping, or cycling.

Strength training demands considerable upper body power. We frequently use resistance bands, dumbbells, or kettlebells to develop upper body might.

By Nicky Ireland

Plyometric exercises are designed to boost my explosive prowess and speed. We rely on box jumps, squat jumps, and burpees for this.

Bag work is a critical part of the training. It refines my technique, speed, and power. We use heavy bags, speed bags, and double-end bags for practicing punches and kicks.

Finally, it's time for sparring. It's a vital part of the training, honing my timing, footwork, and defensive skills.

As I engage in this intense workout with Miguel, beads of sweat trickle down my tattooed muscles, serving as a testament to the strenuous training. The tattoos, an intricate tapestry etched into my skin, glisten under the gym lights, their vibrancy accentuated by the perspiration. Each punch, jab, and kick showcases the powerful flex and movement of my muscles, a testament to the strength I've cultivated. Each session, a symphony of agility, power, and resilience, played out in the canvas of the boxing ring.

An hour and a half later and I'm left with my muscles singing a sweet song of ache, a melody that sends sparks of excitement across my skin. It's time to bounce back to my home turf, to the loving arms of mi amor. The anticipation I feel is electric.

Strolling into the locker room with a rhythm in my steps, I am welcomed by a smorgasbord of masculine anatomy, a kaleidoscope of forms and dimensions. Sweet mother of pearl! It's a peculiar phenomenon, this brazen display of male prowess in the sanctity of a locker room. A chill of amusement scurries down my spine.

With an air of composed nonchalance, I navigate this sea of unabashed nudity. My movements are swift yet deliberate - an elegant ballet of changing clothes. Not a trace of my own manhood is put on parade for the curious gazers. In this grand theatre of the locker room, I prefer to keep my performance understated, leaving the spotlight to the more audacious performers.

As I'm on the verge of hopping into my car, my phone starts doing the cha-cha with a text from Nicky. All it says is 'Ven a jugar conmigo señor'. Oh, game on, mi chica sucia. It's absolutely happening.

I step into the apartment and I make a beeline for our cherished playroom, fully aware that my delightful mischief-maker is already there, eagerly awaiting my arrival. Just the way I like her.

Fresh from my workout, I'm still soaked in sweat, and I know she wouldn't have it any other way at this moment. I'm clueless about what she has planned for us, but I'm certain she won't topping from the bottom for too long.

I push open the door to our sanctuary, a room that has transformed into our sacred space. She's there, situated next to the door, seated docilely on her haunches atop a large waterproof sheet. In her outstretched hands, she cradles a collection of sizable paintbrushes. A vibrant assortment of paints encircles her, presumably body paints, given her customary nudity in this room. Her head is bowed low.

I pause momentarily to take in the sight of her. Already undressed, I notice her sneaking glances at me from under her lashes. "Eyes down," I instruct firmly. Before she can even comply, I stride over to the wall panel that controls the music. I can't help but suppress a laugh as I notice that she's pre-set the song to Breakdlaw's 'Paint me like a French girl'. As I swing around, I see her shoulders shaking in silent laughter at her own jest.

I return to her side and tower over her. Gently, I take the paintbrushes from her hands. "Lie back," I order in a calm, controlled tone, and she obligingly reclines onto the sheet with elegance. She's a sight to behold.

Choosing a bright red paint, I swirl a large brush in it, ensuring every bristle is coated. I then dip the brush into a jar of water conveniently placed next to the paints. I lower myself to my knees, my body parallel to her torso. I catch her eye, drawn irresistibly to my already erect cock. Insatiable vixen!

By Nicky Ireland

With a swift motion, I raise the brush high above my head and bring it down sharply. The paint splatters all over her breasts, and she gasps as the cold liquid hits her skin. Her porcelain white skin is now dappled with vibrant red splatters. A masterpiece!

As she tips her head back, her chin pointing up towards the high ceiling, I carefully guide the brush to her neck. A slow, deliberate stroke from her chin down her neck, around the contours of her collar bones and encircling each breast, the brush teases each of her pink nipples, leaving trails of vibrant red paint. A low moan escapes her lips, sending a thrilling jolt to my throbbing cock.

I pick up a clean brush, dipping it in the pot of gold paint. "Mi princesa deserves a golden touch," I declare with a hint of amusement. The sound of her giggles fills the room as I bring the brush to her hardened nipples, painting each bud gold against the contrasting red. Delicious!

I descend further, positioning myself at her ankles. With a light tap of the brush against her ankle, I command, "Spread, mi puta obediente." And she does, spreading her legs wide, revealing her glistening pussy to me. I stifle a groan, my gaze drawn upwards to a sight that solely belongs to me.

"This golden treasure is mine, and mine alone. Do you understand?" I assert, watching her breathlessly nod in agreement. With a gentle stroke, I paint the length of her pussy lips, my hand parting them wide to expose her tight entrance and her beautifully pink clit. The brush continues its dance, gilding her intimately. As it grazes her clit, she arches beneath me, a loud moan filling the air.

This game, this dance of power and desire, is nothing short of an erotic masterpiece. The brush, the paint, they are just tools. It's the art of dominance, the thrill of the moment that makes it truly breath-taking.

With a playful shimmer in my eyes, I command, "Assume the position, mi amor." She's on her hands and knees before I even finish my sentence, her shapely ass aimed at me like an invitation. I retrieve a pristine brush and a pot filled with the deepest, darkest paint.

"Spread wide for me, mi puta asquerosa." She complies effortlessly. "Lower your face," I instruct, and she bends down onto her elbows, her cheek resting on the sheet. I take a moment to bask in the sight before me - her golden pussy glistening in the soft light. It's a tantalizing canvas, one that I ache to surround with my burning desire.

In my hand, the brush drips with black paint and I start my work, painting words across her luscious curvaceous ass. The letters W, H, O, R, E stand bold and clear, the 'O' artfully crafted around her puckered asshole. It's a picture of flawless beauty. Absolute perfection!

I cast aside the brush and paint, my control unravelling. The sight of her, marked by my words, arouses an insatiable desire within me. I trace my fingers along my throbbing cock, all the while catching her eye. Flashing her a devilish wink, I deliver a sharp spank onto her painted skin, causing her to gasp and jolt forward.

Alternating slaps between her plump cheeks, I add a fiery red hue to my dark artwork. Her soft moans and the sight of her flushed skin send a wave of pleasure coursing through my throbbing cock.

Grasping my cock firmly, I guide myself to her 'O', my other hand holding her ass open for me. The moment I thrust into her, she cries out in ecstasy. The intensity of her pleasure sends me spiraling further into desire.

As I penetrate her deeper, my hand reaches around to caress her golden clit, causing her to shudder beneath me. There's a desperate urgency to be as close to her as possible, to feel the heat of her skin against mine. I adjust my position, my knees on either side of her ass, and with a firm grip on her ponytail for balance, I drive into her with fiery abandon. Our shared moans echo loudly through the room as we surrender to the pleasure.

"Cum for me, mi princesa," I coax, and soon enough, we're both riding the wave of a powerful orgasm. As I withdraw, I watch in awe as my sticky, hot wet cum trickles from her ass, down her thighs and pools onto the sheet below. "Turn around and taste my royal gift," I instruct, and she obediently laps up every drop. It's a sight to behold, one that I wouldn't trade for anything.

Happy birthday rey mío

Chapter Thirty

Happy birthday rey mio

Chapter Thirty

NICKY

Currently I'm juggling a million things on my plate as my beloved, ceaselessly occupied other half is off gallivanting on a business trip. It's been days, but who's counting? Oh, wait a minute, I am! You see, I've been sneakily orchestrating a birthday surprise for him. Mr. Maspinco, my forever love, is about to hit the glorious 33-year milestone on November 8th. Just like the most exquisite bottle of wine, he only gets more enticing with time.

The day he jetted off on his trip, my surprise gift set off on its own journey. Since then, it's been an intricate ballet of skirting around lengthy phone conversations and, much to his dismay, completely dodging video calls. Apparently, he's not thrilled about the no video call rule. Who would've thought? I've been spinning this yarn about it being a move to heighten the anticipation for when he comes back home. You know, absence makes the heart grow fonder and all that jazz.

The phone call dodging? I've convinced him that I've got a slight cold, and the sympathy has been pouring in. There is indeed a throbbing somewhere, but it's definitely not a cold, and it's definitely not because of the November chill. If I say I've missed Santi, it would be the understatement of the century. It's like I'm a puzzle missing a crucial piece.

In between all this, I'm swamped with work and an absurd number of daily phone calls with my confidante, Liam.

"Hey, Liamo!" I find myself hollering into the phone, my laughter bubbling up. My best friend seems to find my newly acquired lisp downright hysterical. "I taut I taw a puddy tat" he mimics in a giggle, to mirror my current speech impediment. "You're such a bifth," I retort, wallowing in self-pity.

Liam, the darling that he is, decides to lift my spirits with tales of his recent romantic escapades. And boy, they are not singular! It's not just one handsome man that's been sharing his bed but also a man and his wife. My jaw nearly hits the floor. It appears that Dublin's more adventurous married couples are embracing the pineapple life, spreading their sweet and tart flavor all over town. Can you believe it? Oh, the things you learn!

The clock is ticking down to the moment Santi steps foot in the house again, and I'm practically vibrating with anticipation. In just a handful of days, we'll be gathered around a table, sharing laughter and stories over a birthday feast with his family. His radiant mother, Sofia, is the mastermind behind that plan, and I couldn't agree more.

Santi's family is his rock, his anchor. They're like celestial beings descended from the heavens just for him, and I'm head over heels for them. His mother, Sofia, is like my personal cheerleader. She has this spark in her eyes whenever she looks at me, the potential future mother of her grandbabies. It's as if I've been elevated to Goddess status in her books, and let's be honest, who wouldn't relish that?

But tonight? Tonight is all about Santi. Tonight, the spotlight is solely on him.

Now, I briefly toyed with the idea of surprising him with a homemade birthday cake. But the thought of gifting him with a bout of food poisoning quickly put that idea to rest. Instead, I've decided to enlist the skills of the culinary geniuses at Santi's restaurant, A Fuego Lento. I've tasked them with crafting a magnificent Tarta de Santiago, a cake as fitting as his name.

This Spanish delight is a harmonious blend of ground almonds, sugar, eggs, and a zing of lemon zest. Traditionally, it's adorned with a stencil of the cross of Santiago in powdered sugar. While the religious symbolism holds no particular significance for either of us, the epic journey that this cake represents does. It's a journey we've embarked on together, full of ups and beautiful moments. As a nod to our personal interpretation, I've requested the cake without the cross.

As I prepare for his arrival, the dining table is a riot of colour and festivity. The Tarta de Santiago takes center stage, surrounded by a sea of balloons, streamers, and all things birthday-related. Yes, he's a grown man, but that doesn't mean he can't appreciate a good surprise party! And trust me, I may be a grown woman, but I know how to throw a party that will be remembered for years to come. Tonight is going to be one for the books!

SANTI

As the workweek fades into the rear-view mirror, I can't help but yearn for the comforts of home and the delightful company of my cherished Nicky.

Excitement bubbles up within me as I step into the elevator, eagerly keying in the topmost floor - our shared sanctuary.

The elevator doors glide open with a soft ping, revealing an unexpected sight that nearly topples me off balance. There, right outside the elevator, is my compliant Nicky, perched on all fours with an envelope held delicately in her mouth. Her collar and leash are a playful touch, and she's wagging her backside with the enthusiasm of a puppy eagerly awaiting its master.

I step out of the elevator, my eyes meeting hers as a grin threatens to split my face. Affection wells up within me as I pat her head playfully, praising her with a soft 'good girl' before taking the envelope from her.

Settling back seductively on her haunches, her paws held up enticingly before her, she pants in the manner of a puppy dutifully playing its part. Her voice, heavy with promise, breaks through, "I am your Tarta de Santiago," she growls softly, punctuated by a playful 'woof' and a flirtatious wag of her hips.

The words catch me off guard, nearly causing me to choke. I take her in, my gaze drinking in the sight of her, my beautiful pet, adorned with the most seductive micro lingerie.

Suddenly, the atmosphere morphs, becoming charged with anticipation. She transforms before my eyes, becoming a Femme Fatale whispering tantalizing promises of dark fantasies. The straps of the lingerie cradle her body in a seductive embrace. In this moment, I am under her spell. She is the seductress, the cloak and dagger to my intrigue.

Her outfit, an alluring ensemble in black, features an open cup bra that screams sultry sophistication. The sexy leather look is both playful and seductive, accentuated with gold hardware and multi-fastened straps. The thong, with its strategically placed peek-a-boo holes, playfully teases, while the suspender belts lend a final touch of allure.

I lean in, gently lifting her chin for a kiss. She responds with playful panting, her tongue sticking out in jest, and I can't help but chuckle at our little game. As her lips part however, I spot something unexpected - a small, shiny silver bar piercing in her tongue, which I immediately recognize as a vibrating tongue piercing. My composed facade falters, replaced by a look of surprised delight. She beams at my reaction, and I can only think one thing - Holy fuck! This is going to be a night to remember.

With her puppy-dog eyes gleaming up at me, she teases, "What's the perfect gift for the man who has everything? Something that money can't touch, of course!"

In one hand, I have her leash, and in the other, the crisp white envelope. I guide her towards our bedroom, and she obediently follows, crawling on all fours, my faithful little cachorra.

We traverse the spacious hallway, and I lead her into our sanctuary. I stop at the foot of the bed, comfortably settling into my seat. I firmly command, "Sit," and she obediently complies. She sits back on her hind legs, paws raised playfully, tongue lolling out in a pant. Grasping her leash firmly, I take a moment to savor the anticipation before opening the envelope.

I pull out a birthday card. The cover features a jubilant puppy donning a party hat, and inside, a cheeky message reads, 'I heard you like to pawty'. I can't help

By Nicky Ireland

but chuckle at her antics. This woman, she never fails to surprise me!

Lifting her chin gently, I plant a fervent kiss on her lips before settling back to read her heartfelt message.

To Santiago,

The love of my life, on the day that's all about you.

No string of words could ever encapsulate the monumental

influence you've had on my life.

Your arrival into my world has sparked a transformation more extraordinary.

than my wildest dreams, infusing each second with pure joy.

On your day of celebration, my wish for you is to experience all the magnificent

treasures the world holds, and then some, because no one deserves it more than you.

You are my everything, my lover, my most trusted confidant, and my majestic king.

Happy Birthday, my love.

I am forever yours,

Your Princesa, your puta obediente,

Nicky XOXO

The card finds a resting place on the bed as I sit, elbows on my knees, chin cradled in my hands. My eyes meet those of my spirited puppy, her unwavering gaze fixed on me. "What am I to do with you, mi cachorra juguetón," I muse aloud. She knows it's not a question. She doesn't answer. Instead, she pants playfully, wiggles her tail, then lets out a spirited howl before scampering away, every bit the mischievous puppy.

A grin plays on my lips, 'Oh two can play that game pup,' I muse to myself.

With a surge of energy, I leap to my feet, giving chase. Our collision sends her tumbling into the wooden floor below. I pin her down with a force that makes her writhe beneath me, face flushed, panting heavily. Not to be outdone, I match her breath for breath - not from the exertion, but from the primal surge of power coursing through me. This is me, unrestrained, at my peak, and she knows it. She craves for me to ravage her, and I am more than ready to oblige.

Keeping her under control with one hand, I use the free one to unzip my pants, reaching for my hard cock. I push my cock into her pussy forcefully, with a guttural groan, drawing out a cry from her. My chest presses against her back as I thrust into her with a fervor that surprises even me. I can't get deep enough inside her. Pushing her body forward with each thrust.

My hand fists her hair, pulling it back, while the other covers her mouth and nose. My lips find her neck, biting down forcefully. A muffled cry escapes from beneath my hand, only serving to turn me on even more. I grunt with each thrust, ensuring she feels every inch of me, pressing her hard into the floor. She writhes beneath me.

I lean in close, my voice a husky whisper laced with desire, "It's my birthday, and I'm taking exactly what I want, my puta obediente." The intensity of my dominance fills the air, as primal and powerful as the desire that binds us.

I ram into her relentlessly. Releasing my ironclad grip on her mouth and nose, I command, "Open." She complies instantly, her mouth opening wide. Leaning in, I spit into her mouth and swiftly push my fingers inside, inducing a gag reflex. The sound of her choking and spluttering around my fingers sends my head spinning. I whisper softly into her ear, "Are you doing ok, mi amor?" She nods, a fiery spark igniting in her eyes.

My fingers continue their assault on her mouth, in sync with my cock that's wreaking havoc on her cunt. The rhythm of my hand and hips align perfectly. A fire blazes within me, intense and consuming like an inferno.

Getting off her, I bark, "On your knees now, mi puta." She obeys, rising instantly, then collapsing onto all fours, panting in anticipation. Grasping her head with my hand, I yank her hair, pressing her beautiful face onto my raging cock. Then I'm reminded of the tongue ring as I feel the vibrations against my cock. Fuuccckkkk!

"Show me what a cachorra obediente you are," I order, intentionally slowing the movement of my hips, wanting to savor the vibrations against my cock. I gyrate my hips to ensure she takes in every inch of me, her sapphire puppy eyes gazing up at me.

"Good girl," I praise, her pleased response manifesting in a wag. A deep, guttural groan of pleasure escapes my lips as my cock throbs and buzzes in her mouth. I cease movement, allowing her to attend to me like the obedient puppy she is. Her warm, wet tongue slowly, seductively traces the underside of my cock. The vibrating tongue ring sends a surge of pleasure racing through me, my grip on her hair reflexively tightening.

Her ministrations persist, the vibrating tongue ring stimulating that sweet spot on the underside of my cock's head, sending waves of pleasure pulsating through me. My balls respond by tightening, a silent testament to the pleasure she's inflicting.

As she takes me further into her mouth, she teases my cock with her vibrating tongue, her lips setting a fierce rhythm. I'm guided to the back of her throat, the vibrations maintaining their tantalizing dance on my sweet spot. Holy fuck!

"I'm going to cum, mi cachorra obediente," I warn, my hips involuntarily bucking into her intoxicating mouth, every inch of my big, thick cock disappearing within her as she splutters and dribbles along my length. Her eyes now streaming with mascara. Tears flowing from them. "You look so fuckin' beautiful mi puta asquerosa" I tell her.

Quickly her name rips from my throat as I climax, warm, sticky ribbons of cum for her alone. She swallows every drop, her deep moan coaxing more from me.

Catching our breaths, she settles back on her legs, paws resting atop her knees. She breaks the silence with a quiet, "Happy Birthday Rey Mío."

Best birthday, ever!

Mi trébol de 4 hojas

Chapter Thirty One

Mi trébol de 4 hojas

Chapter Thirty One

SANTI

You know that feeling when you just can't get enough of something? Yeah, that's me, totally head over heels, no, scratch that, obsessively in love with anything and everything that smells divine. It's like I'm some kind of fragrance aficionado or scent savant. I can't help it, it's the primal in me, I guess. A whiff of a certain scent can be a deal maker or breaker for me.

It's kind of hilarious that most people underestimate the potency of fragrances. They are like invisible wizards, conjuring up all sorts of emotions and reactions in the blink of an eye. They can conjure vivid memories, act as a warning system, signaling safety or danger, friend or enemy. They can sway your behavior without you even realizing it. And this, my friends, is the reason why I am on a mission to create a unique perfume for my dear Nicky. Not just to have a piece of her with me when she's not around, but to craft something as special and wonderful as she is.

So instead of heading to the usual grind at the restaurant, I've taken a detour to the enchanting Diseñadoras De Perfumes nestled in the heart of the Gothic Quarter. This ain't my first rodeo, as you might have guessed. I'm a frequent flyer here, always on the hunt for new tantalizing scents. Lately, I've been here more often, brainstorming with the brilliant shop owner, Esmeralda. We've been discussing all the exciting options for my masterpiece and let me tell you, I'm not holding back. Everything about this perfume has to be nothing short of perfection.

This morning, as I step inside of Diseñadoras De Perfumes, where the magic of fragrance unfolds, dances, and comes alive, I'm buzzing with excitement! Today I'll be putting the finishing touches to my creation for Nicky. This is me, in my

By Nicky Ireland

element.

The place oozes elegance and sophistication, it's like stepping into a whimsical wonderland of scents. Soft, inviting lights cast a warm glow in every corner, making the place feel like a cozy sanctuary.

Everywhere I look, a multitude of exquisite bottles catch my eye. Some are simple and classic, others intricately designed, but each one beautiful in its own right. I see bottles crafted from gleaming glass, sparkling crystal, and even delicate porcelain. It's like a museum of aromatic art!

Rows and rows of fragrant creations line the shelves, each display meticulously arranged by colour or size. It's like a rainbow of perfumes! And oh, the new arrivals! They're showcased in all their glory, beckoning me to come closer, to discover their secrets.

And then there are the testing stations, my favourite part! Here, I can dive into an ocean of different scents. Miniature perfume bottles are waiting for me to spritz their contents onto my skin, inviting me to embark on a sensory voyage. One moment I'm in a field of roses, the next, I'm wandering through a forest of sandalwood.

As I wander deeper into this fragrant labyrinth, the air around me is a symphony of scents. From the sweet whispers of jasmine to the spicy undertones of cloves, each breath is an adventure. With every step, a new fragrance greets me, like an unseen guide leading me on this olfactory journey.

Being here feels like being a kid in a candy store, except instead of sweets, it's an endless array of enchanting fragrances! It's hard to contain my excitement as I explore this scent-filled playground, a place where every fragrance tells a story, and every story is waiting to be discovered!

I'm buzzing with anticipation, cooking up an intoxicating concoction specially tailored for my muse, the enigmatic Nicky. Together with my trusted Perfumer, we're stirring up something audacious and alluring. This isn't just a fragrance;

it's an embodiment of character, as intoxicatingly unique as the woman it's inspired by.

We're not just mixing scents; we're composing an olfactory symphony. Picture this: the overture is a medley of top notes, followed by the heart notes playing the grand waltz, and finally, the base notes concluding with a triumphant finale. As the fragrance dances with her skin's natural oils, it's like a melody unravelling over time, creating a sensory experience that's hard to resist. Just like her.

The scent we're creating is as intriguing and diverse as a global expedition. It features citrusy and herbaceous notes of bergamot, the intoxicating allure of narcissus, and the earthy charm of patchouli. The top notes are a world tour in themselves, featuring Italian bergamote, ylang ylang from Mohéli, and Chinese magnolia flowers. The heart notes strike a floral chord with violet absolute, jasminum sambac absolute from India, French narcissus absolute, and the timeless lily of the valley. The grand finale, our base notes, include exotic Benzoin from Laos, Indonesian patchouli, and the clean aroma of white musk.

The final masterpiece won't be housed in just any vessel. It will reside in a custom-made, one-of-a-kind, glass bottle, as unique and radiant as Nicky herself. Every intricate detail, every beautifully inscribed word on the bottle, mirrors her special charm.

Later today, I'll be making a beeline home, cradling this precious gift, and I can't wait to see her eyes light up. I can already imagine her excitement mirroring mine, and it fills me with a joy that's as thrilling as creating this unique fragrance for her.

NICKY

I'm lounging gleefully in the living room of our cozy apartment, when I catch the familiar sound of his arrival. A thrill of excitement always courses through me, even though we practically share every second of our lives together. Can you blame me? I'm totally smitten, and I can't help but hum along to the tune that's stuck in my head: "I'm addicted, wanna drown inside your love, I wouldn't wanna have it any other way, I'm addicted and I just can't get enough..." Oh, how fitting! Thank you earworms!

There he is, strolling in, strikingly handsome as always and — wait for it — holding a grand bouquet of dark red carnations! My jaw drops in surprise as I leap to my feet, barely containing the urge to sprint, hop, and skip towards him.

"Santi, what's all this?" I question, gazing at his ear-to-ear grin. I can't help but wonder what he's got up his sexy sleeves.

"For you, mi amor," he replies, presenting the carnations to me. I draw in a deep breath, their scent captivating me. "In Spain, dark red carnations symbolize deep, sincere love and affection. They're a token of profound love and devotion, mi princesa." I'm speechless.

"But... why? Is there an occasion?" I ask, genuinely perplexed.

"No occasion, Nicky. I just want you to understand how much you mean to me. Come, sit back down," he gently guides me back to our comfy chairs. I'm clueless about what's happening, but I'm all for surprises and grand romantic gestures. And Santi is an expert when it comes to it.

"I have something special for you, mi Princesa," he reveals, joining me on the soft lounger. From behind his back, he produces a pristine white box adorned with a golden satin ribbon. "Open it," he instructs, his eyes sparkling with anticipation.

As I carefully place the surprisingly heavy box on my lap and begin to untie the ribbon, I keep shooting him curious glances. Inside the box, I find a bottle. But, it's not just any bottle, it's the most exquisite perfume bottle I've ever laid eyes on. Inside the large glass vessel is an amber liquid, and raised on the front is a stunning green four-leaf clover. The bottle's gold lid is beautifully etched with a matching clover. Then, I see the words. As I read them, my eyes dart to Santi.

"Mi trébol de 4 hojas," he announces. "My 4-leaf clover," I echo, and he nods in approval. Overwhelmed, I fling myself at him, wrapping my arms around him and peppering him with kisses. We topple backwards onto the lounger, a fit of giggles escaping from him.

"I take it you like it, mi amor?" he teases, chuckling. "Like it? I love it, Santi. Wow, just wow..." I reply, continuing to smother him with kisses.

This wonderful man believes I'm his lucky charm, his four-leaf clover. Little does he know, he's the one who has brought me protection, prosperity, and balance in this world. Santiago Maspinco is my lucky charm, my everything.

As the evening blends into night, we find ourselves sinking into the plush cushions of our comfortable sofa, transfixed by the flickering images on the television screen.

Despite my best efforts, I've failed to entice Santi into the fascinating world of reality TV. My preferences lean towards shows like Married at First Sight, The Bachelor, The Bachelorette, 90 Day Fiancé, and The Ultimatum. It seems I have a penchant for love in all its dramatic and unpredictable forms.

However, Santi has taken a surprising liking to Open House - The Great Sex Experiment. The show follows committed couples as they retreat into a luxurious haven, testing the controversial hypothesis that engaging in open relationships and intimate encounters with others could, in fact, fortify their bond.

Inevitably, the subject of multiple partners becomes the evening's main topic of discussion. Santi is quick to establish his stance, stating with absolute certainty that the idea of sharing our bedroom with another man is off the table. No room for negotiation or discussion. I respond with a playful smirk, "Fine by me. I've got more than I can handle with you, my sexy beast." His reaction is noticeably absent, however.

Prodding further, I question him, "And what if we were to invite another woman into the bedroom, with or without me?" My eyebrow arches inquisitively. "Never without you, mi amor," he counters swiftly. I can't help but feel a twinge of indignation at his response.

"Hold up, Mr. Fancy Pants. So, no extra man for me, but you're all for an additional woman for you?" He simply shrugs in response, and I'm left stunned. Sharing this delicious man of mine? It's a difficult concept to wrap my head around.

The conversation continues to evolve, a dance of curiosity and uncertainty. His assurances that I am more than enough for him do little to quell my swirling thoughts. Yet, he admits that the idea of seeing me with another woman is intriguing to him. His confession sparks a flurry of emotions inside me - surprise, amusement, and a hint of flattery. His comment about the appeal of another woman in the equation hangs in the air, but I see a twinkle in his eye that I can't help but challenge.

"Oh, really? Another woman?" I retort, my voice laced with feigned shock and disapproval. "And here I thought I was all the woman you could handle."

His laughter rings out, a rich, warm sound that seems to fill the room. "Mi amor," he counters, "I was just curious to see how you'd react."

His confession takes me by surprise, and I can't help but let out a snort of laughter. "You're a piece of work, you know that?" I say, leaping from the sofa and launching myself at him. He catches me with a grunt of surprise, and we tumble into a heap of laughter and tangled limbs, our playful wrestling match filling the room with echoes of our joy.

Our playful wrestling turns into a mashup of laughter and surprise tickles that send us falling to the floor and a wave of unstoppable laughter. The flirty subtext of our banter adds more spark to the fun energy bouncing between us. As we playfully roll around, the echoes of our laughter slowly morph into meaningful looks and gentle touches.

In the silent, special bubble we've created, our hands naturally find each other, fingers locking in a quiet nod to the playful battle that's just ended. Drained but satisfied, we crash on the floor, our bodies tangled. The last traces of laughter fade into the soothing calm that wraps us up. His gaze, alive with a multitude of emotions, hooks me, leaving me mesmerized by its intensity. "I wouldn't trade this, us, for anything," he murmurs, pulling me closer.

A sigh of pure contentment slips from me as I nestle into his arms. "Same here," I mumble, my voice barely above a whisper, "Just us, that's all I need." Our eyes remain locked as we melt into each other's arms. Our foreheads gently touch, while our tongues begin to trace each other's lips with a tantalizing slowness, our breaths mixing in a rhythmic dance.

Driven by the beat of our hearts, I start tracing a path across his body with my hands, gradually discovering him with each touch. The sensation of his fingers lightly gliding over my skin sparks a fire within me, sending ripples of pleasure coursing through my body.

He begins to gently nibble and delicately suck on my neck, jaw, and shoulders and I reciprocate, doing the same to him. It's an enticing exploration that peaks in a moment of passion that feels otherworldly.

Our slow-paced exploration continues. Suddenly, Santi rolls on top of me, his eyes brimming with desire, lock onto mine as he starts to lower his sweatpants. His cock, a symbol of his raw masculinity, stands firm and proud, gripping the base with his hand he slowly slides inside me. A low moan slips from my lips.

As we melt into one another, the room seems to contract around us, every detail fading into insignificance, until only we remain. His tongue gently traces the line of my collarbone, his teeth lightly brushing against my skin, causing my breath to catch in anticipation.

He starts to move his cock deeper within me, our eyes remain locked, our pace quickens, our breaths become choppy and urgent, each one a beautiful tribute to our shared pleasure. I feel him harden, his grip on me intensifying as we balance on the verge of climax. His name slips from my lips in a hushed plea, a silent prayer encouraging him to climax with me. His reaction is immediate, his final thrust propelling us into a powerful orgasm.

Our gasps and moans echo in the room as waves of pleasure wash over us, sharing every tremor, every shared breath, every heartbeat. This moment is ours, a tribute to the love and passion we share.

We collapse in each other's embrace, our bodies entwined in a lover's knot. Our breaths gradually slow, reverting to a peaceful rhythm that mirrors the tranquility after our passionate love making. We lie there, satisfied and exhausted, basking in the lingering bliss of our climax. Intoxicated with pleasure.

This is undeniably us, two bodies, two souls, fused in passion, bound by love, as we lay nestled in each other's arms. For now, there is only us, and the love we share. And in this moment, that is more than enough.

Owned

Chapter Thirty Two

Owned

Chapter Thirty Two

SANTI

As dawn breaks, our day kickstarts with an exhilarating round of primal play. Nicky and I have been on this wild journey for quite some time now, immersing ourselves in a realm of sensuality that doesn't stem from our conscious minds. Oh no, we're not that predictable. Instead, we let the raw, untamed facets of our primal selves take the driver's seat.

This energy - it's what most crave from their partners. It's an energy that flows naturally, especially when those intoxicating neurochemicals of passion are in full swing. Now, let me tell you, if it doesn't make us vulnerable or seem a bit risky, we're probably not tapping into our primal sexual selves. And where's the fun in that?

The kind of intimacy that radiates from the body is far more intense than the one responding to mere thoughts. We're learning the art of expressing our body's desires and being in sync with it - total embodiment. It's like learning a new language, but this one's all about senses and sensations.

With practice and diligence being our watchwords, we've embarked on regular sessions of meditation and yoga. I must admit, Nicky seems to have quite a knack for both. Our thoughts can be so loud and persuasive that, without conscious effort, we tend to lend them our ears most of the time. Hence, tuning into our bodies becomes quintessential.

Our playtime continues to be a blend of intensity and fun. It's filled with laughter, deep sexual presence, and the joy of embracing each other's raw passion. We never, ever dilute it in any way. Why would we want to tamper with such intensity?

Now, here comes the thrilling part: I am the Hunter and, needless to say, Nicky is my prey. Our fantasies run wild and free as we engage in uninhibited sexual activities, guided solely by raw desire and instinct. It's like a dance, but with no choreography, just pure, spontaneous movement.

On a very regular basis we dive deep into sensory exploration, using all of our senses, like smell and taste. And my favourite part, indeed, is the physical dominance. Wrestling, overpowering, or physically challenging Nicky to establish dominance or submission within the scene. It's a game we both love playing.

Our deep emotional bond has turned into an incredible journey of self-discovery. It's a celebration of the raw, powerful connection that can exist between human beings. It's not just about sex; it's about experiencing humanity in the most profound and liberating way.

We're blessed to have found this and so much more in each other. It's like finding a treasure chest in a vast sea, and every day, we discover a new gem. It's a journey, and there's still so much to explore.

After an equally vigorous morning spent exploring the architectural marvels of Barcelona, we decide to saunter into the heart of the Gothic Quarter, seeking the solace of a leisurely brunch. I have a carefree air about me, but there's a tiny secret tucked away in my pocket — a special appointment later in the day, a surprise for Nicky that I'm certain will paint a smile on her face.

We weave our way through the labyrinthine streets, finally arriving at our cherished café, a quaint little spot that's fast becoming our go-to for indulgent brunches. The aroma of fresh coffee and baking bread greets us as we step in, and we slide into our favourite corner booth, the cushioned seats comfortably worn from countless patrons before us.

"French toast and crispy bacon drowned in a deluge of maple syrup, gracias" Nicky orders, her eyes sparkling with anticipation. Our waitress, who recognizes us by now, scribbles down the order with a knowing smile. "Make that a double order," I add, sharing a conspiratorial grin with Nicky.

Nicky leans back in her seat, her gaze taking in the bustling café, the vibrant street outside, and then finally settling on me. "Isn't it just lovely, Santi?" she says, her voice imbued with warmth. "Days like these... they're just the best, wouldn't you agree?"

"Absolutely, mi amor," I reply, reaching across the table to gently squeeze her hand. "I've never been happier."

Her eyes dance with mischief as she makes her next proposition, an offer that's become an enticing ritual between us. "Later this evening," she begins, a devilish twinkle in her eye, "I can offer you a little foot and hand massage, Sir." The subtle emphasis on 'Sir' and the cheeky grin that accompanies it sends a wave of heat surging through me. "Mi diabla," I retort, causing her to erupt into a fit of giggles.

Nicky's massages are far from ordinary, and they're usually anything but 'little'. They tend to evolve into an erotic dance all of their own, with her rhythmically gyrating her eager pussy against either my foot or my hand. The tantalizing friction, the breathless anticipation, until I can't stand it anymore, and I have to get inside her right then and there. She's a vixen, a seductress, and I wouldn't have her any other way.

Our orders arrive, and we dive into the meal with fervor, our conversation sprinkled with playful banter about the exquisite food — the perfect crunch of the bacon, the sweetness of the syrup, our shared love for these simple moments. The café around us fades into the background as we lose ourselves in the shared laughter, the shared love, and the shared promise of an exciting evening. It's these days — the ones filled with exploration, indulgence, laughter, and love — that make life truly worth living.

Later that afternoon, I've steered us into a delightfully quirky tattoo parlor, 'Tatuajes de diablos rojos', nestled in the heart of the city's winding maze of narrow streets. The place is alive with stories of love, whispered promises, and the unspoken bonds of its patrons, all told through the vibrant artistry inked on their skin.

The walls, a colorful gallery of intricate designs and bold hues, proudly showcase the artist's talent and imagination. The air is faintly tinged with antiseptic, its clinical scent blending with the earthy tones of ink and leather, wrapping us in an unexpected cocoon of comfort and security within this tucked-away haven.

With a grin, I guide Nicky into this secret sanctuary, my fingers lightly clasping hers, offering a wordless promise of trust. Sia's 'Dressed in black' throbs through the speakers and I lead her, her faith in me unwavering, her trust complete. Our relationship is so deep, so profound, that words are superfluous; our actions, the sparkle in our eyes, they say everything about our connection.

I've meticulously planned for this surprise, engaging in lengthy discussions with the artist about the designs, ensuring they perfectly encapsulate our shared love and dedication.

From the instant our paths crossed at Trinity College in Dublin, a gut instinct told me that Nicky was the one, my twin flame, the person I'd been unconsciously seeking my whole life. This intense connection we share has utterly transformed me; she is my mirror soul, a reflection of myself in another. It's a breathtakingly beautiful idea: a single soul, split into two, yet irresistibly drawn to each other like magnets.

There's an overwhelming, energy that pulses between us, as if we were cosmically meant to find each other in this vast universe. The resonance of her soul with mine is undeniable, a sweet harmony I've longed for, sought out, but didn't find until she graced my life. It's as if I've finally found the missing piece of a puzzle I didn't even know was incomplete.

In the same vein, she mirrors my feelings, reciprocating my intense emotions with equal passion. She, too, is entranced by the magic of our bond, the irresistible draw that makes us twin flames.

She loves me just as deeply as I love her, entrusting every part of herself, every

By Nicky Ireland

facet of her soul, to me.

And now, I'm standing by Nicky's side as she settles into the tattoo chair. My touch is her anchor, a comforting presence as the needle starts its dance on her skin. She's clueless about the design I've created, but it doesn't matter. Each stroke, each shadow, is a chapter in our tale, an homage to her love and commitment to me.

Hours tick by and finally, it's done! Nicky slowly jumps to her feet, catching her first glimpse of it in the mirror.

Her eyes catch the reflection in the mirror, the elaborate, yet delicate design that's taking shape, blooming on her skin. The tattoo design elegantly graces her neck, a testament to the unique bond shared between her and I. It's not just a tattoo, but a declaration of a profound connection, a symbol of our enduring love and commitment.

Delicately etched on her skin is a necklace style collar tattoo, where the ink takes on a metallic sheen, mimicking the appearance of a delicate chain. The design swirls around her neck in an enchanting dance that is both feminine and meaningful. Nestled within this design are two powerful symbols — a four-leaf clover and an infinity sign — each serving as a potent reminder of luck, eternity, and the infinite possibilities that our love offers.

At the back, the chain subtly transitions into a soft leather effect collar, adding depth and texture to the intricate design. The design culminates in a heart-shaped lock that seems to pulsate with life. This lock, embedded in her skin, is a declaration of my claim over her, my ownership, an emblem of our unique connection.

The initials 'S' and 'N' wrap around each side of the lock, a permanent fusion of our identities etched in ink. This emblem, a testament to our shared love and commitment, is more than just a piece of body art. It's a vow of her undying devotion to me, a symbol of ownership and submission, forever etched on her skin.

This tattoo, with its beautiful and delicate design, is a vivid portrayal of our relationship. It's a testament to our love, an acknowledgment of our shared journey, and a promise of our shared future.

At the same time, on my ring finger, a simple yet poignant tattoo is being born - a key. This is not just any key, it's simplicity belies its profound significance. It is a depiction wrought from ink and skin, a promise inscribed in the permanent canvas of my body. It serves as an emblem of eternal love and unwavering fidelity, a vow that transcends the realms of spoken words.

This key, though small in stature, holds a weighty promise. It is a pledge that I will always be there, ever-ready to unlock the heart-shaped lock that guards her deepest affections, her most vulnerable self. It is a commitment that, in times of joy and sorrow, in moments of clarity and confusion, my love for her will remain the constant key to her heart.

These tattoos are more than mere pigment on our skin; they are a testament to our dedication. It's a silent proclamation of the depth of our love, a love that is as enduring as the ink that now marks our flesh.

"You are the essence of my life, mi amor. You are my twin flame, the fire that lights up my world, and I am irrevocably yours. I will claim you and I will own you for all eternity, in every life time." I declare, each word pulsating with genuine sincerity.

With a sparkle of tears in her eyes, she looks at me and whispers, "I am completely yours. Forever. Through joy and through pain. In our heaven and in our hell, I will forever be your puta obediente."

We're laughing, tears streaming down our faces, as the words of our vows echo around us. They're the ultimate proof of this unbreakable bond we share. Finally sealed with a kiss, a thrilling manifestation of the intense love we're so lost in, right here, right now, always and forever.

By Nicky Ireland

The end.

or is it?...

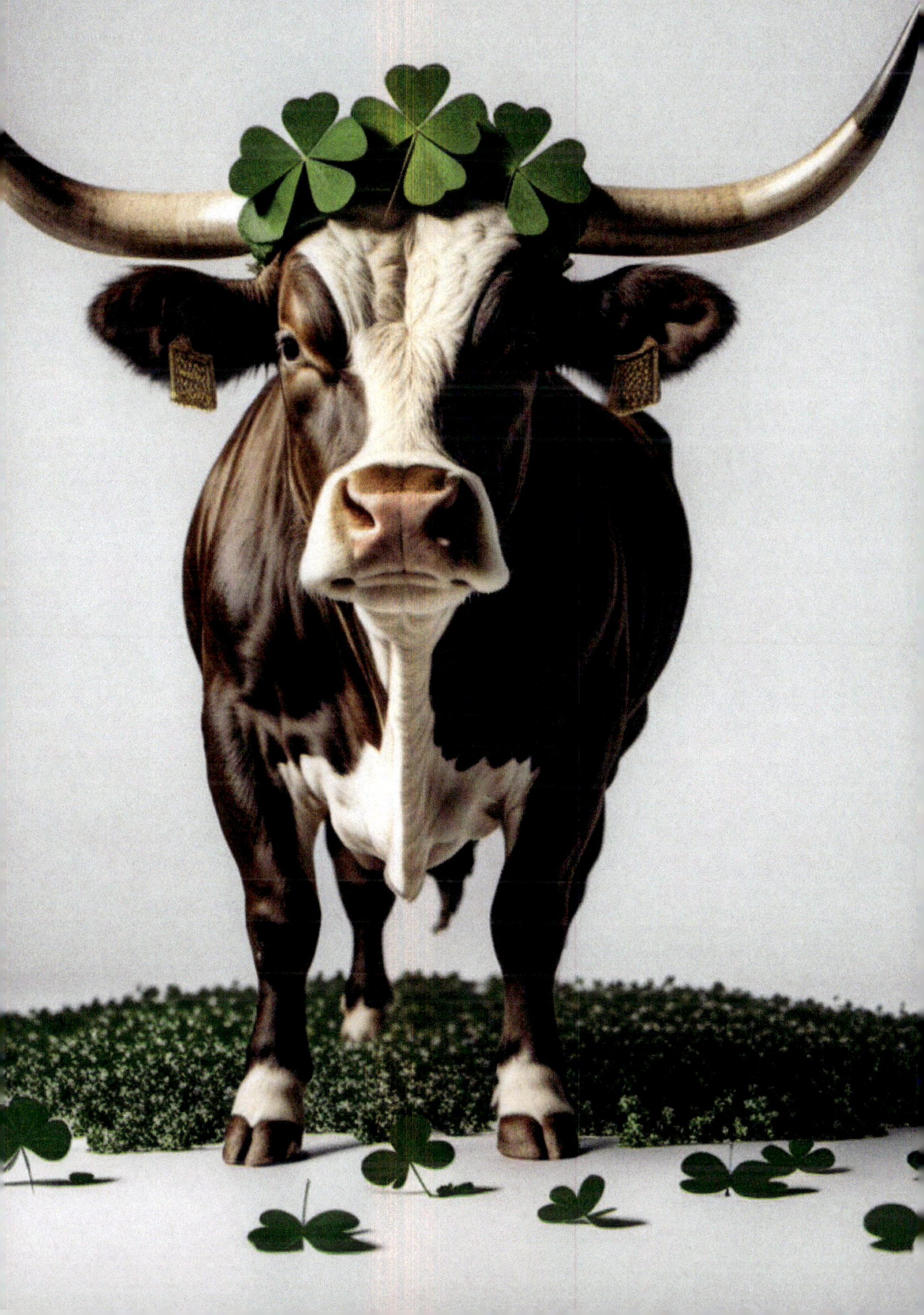

NI
NICKY IRELAND

Turn the page for a sneak peek at Nicky Ireland's next novel

'Triad'

©Nicky Ireland 2023

Triad

A BDSM Erotic Romance

The Owned Series: A BDSM Exploration
by **NICKY IRELAND**

Triad

Andrea Valentini, a man as enigmatic as the city he calls home, is a compelling blend of dominance and mystery. He's an alpha-hole — a man who exudes authority and control, his allure as captivating as it is infuriating. His sharp wit and charisma are as renowned as his notorious reputation. Andrea is a paradox, a man who commands respect and yet remains aloof, his rough edges and brash confidence a testament to his complex nature.

As the owner of the infamous BDSM club, "The Velvet Chain", Andrea is a master of dominance, his presence commanding the room. He's a man who knows what he wants and isn't afraid to claim it. Yet underneath his rugged exterior and alpha tendencies, there's an unexpected tenderness. His genuine care for Ava and Zoe, his ability to balance his affections and attention, and his commitment to their shared journey adds a depth to his character that few get to see.

His dominance in the world of BDSM and his role as the head of their unconventional triad is a sight to behold. Andrea is not just an alpha-hole, he's a man who embodies power, passion, and contradiction, making their journey as thrilling as it is unpredictable.

And so, in the pulsating heart of Manhattan, New York, Andrea's story unfolds, as complex and captivating as the man himself. Are you ready to delve into the enthralling dynamics of this unconventional triad, their journey of discovery, and the captivating life they live under Andrea's rule? Your invitation to the next novel in the "Owned Series" awaits. Be prepared to be enticed, enthralled, and utterly captivated.

©Nicky Ireland 2023

Resources

Venturing into the world of BDSM may seem daunting at first, especially if it's a completely new world to you. Like starting any journey into the unknown, it can be a little confusing to know where to begin. But don't worry, you're not alone!

I'm no grandmaster in this domain, but I am an enthusiastic adventurer who has discovered a treasure trove of resources and content creators that have guided and enriched my journey through this fascinating world.

My first piece of advice? Embrace your curiosity and dive into research. Knowledge is the key that will unlock many doors in the BDSM world. There are countless books, websites, podcasts, and YouTube channels dedicated to educating and guiding newcomers.

Next, don't be afraid to ask questions. The BDSM community is an incredibly open and supportive one. Remember, there's no such thing as a silly question. We've all been newbies once, and we're all here to learn and grow together.

Take part in conversations, both online and offline. Join forums, participate in chat rooms, attend workshops, or even sign up for webinars. The more you engage, the more you'll learn and the more comfortable you'll become in this lifestyle.

Events are also an amazing way to immerse yourself in the BDSM culture. They provide a safe and inclusive environment where you can meet like-minded individuals, learn from experts, and even try out new experiences in a controlled setting.

Above all, remember to have fun! This journey is unique to you, and there's no one-size-fits-all approach to it. Whether you're a curious onlooker, a brave newbie, or a seasoned expert, each person's journey in this lifestyle is distinctive, and that's what makes it so exciting.

Below, you'll find a list of invaluable resources and content creators that I've found incredibly helpful on my own journey. These individuals and communities are treasure troves of knowledge, experiences, and advice that have enriched my understanding of the world of BDSM. I hope they will do the same for you.

Now, here's a quick note: While I've found these resources to be insightful, it's important to remember that everyone's perspectives and journeys are unique. The opinions, posts, and advice shared by these resources are their own and may not reflect my viewpoints or experiences. So, while I'm sharing these resources with you, I'm not responsible for their content.

Feel free to explore, learn, and form your own opinions. After all, the beauty of this world lies in its diversity and the freedom to shape our own unique experiences. So buckle up and enjoy your journey!

Experts / Authors / Websites / Content Creators:
Dr Lori Beth Bisbey - www.drloribethbisbey.com
The Funny Dom - www.beacons.ai/thefunnydom
Aoife Murray - www.instagram.com/aoife.murray.life
Sub Guide - linktr.ee/subguide
Shibari Study - www.instagram.com/shibari.study
Dom Sub Relationship - www.domsubrelationship.com

Events:
Seed Talks - www.seedtalks.co.uk

Accessories:
Daddy's Leather Shop - www.instagram.com/daddysleathershop

Furniture:
Room Sacred - www.roomsacred.com

Nicky Ireland

Enter Nicky Ireland's Sensory Universe of Sizzling Stories!

Prepare for a literary experience like no other with Nicky Ireland, the Irish author who knows how to tickle your funny bone and set your heart racing. Known for her wicked wit and love for the provocative, Nicky is your guide to an intoxicating world where love, laughter, and lust intersect.

Straight from the heart of the emerald isle, Nicky weaves tales that are as rich in imagery as they are in intrigue. Every page is a journey through vivid landscapes and captivating scenarios, making you feel like you're right there amidst the characters, experiencing their wild, passionate world.

But Nicky's immersive storytelling doesn't stop at stunning visuals. With each of her spicy stories, she pairs a carefully curated Spotify playlist, designed to tantalize your senses and set the perfect mood. The result? A multi-sensory experience that engages your imagination, stirs your emotions, and leaves you craving for more.

Falling in love with her unforgettable characters, laughing at her their playful humour, losing yourself in the intricate world of BDSM — this is what awaits you when you delve into Nicky's world. Her stories are not just books; they're an exploration of desire, a celebration of love, and a thrilling rollercoaster ride that you won't want to end.

Nicky Ireland: She's not just writing stories; she's crafting unforgettable experiences!

#OWNEDBOOK
#OWNEDSERIES
#NICKYIRELANDAUTHOR

WWW.LINKTR.EE/NICKYIRELAND

AMAZON.COM/AUTHOR/NICKYIRELAND

@NICKYIRELAND23

@NICKYIRELANDAUTHOR

@NICKYIRELANDBOOKS

Printed in Great Britain
by Amazon